by nancy thayer

Summer Light on Nantucket
The Summer We Started Over
All the Days of Summer
Summer Love
Family Reunion
Girls of Summer
Let It Snow
Surfside Sisters
A Nantucket Wedding
Secrets in Summer
The Island House
A Very Nantucket Christmas
The Guest Cottage
An Island Christmas
Nantucket Sisters
A Nantucket Christmas
Island Girls
Summer Breeze
Heat Wave
Beachcombers
Summer House
Moon Shell Beach
The Hot Flash Club Chills Out
Hot Flash Holidays
The Hot Flash Club Strikes Again
The Hot Flash Club
Custody
Between Husbands and Friends
An Act of Love
Belonging
Family Secrets
Everlasting
My Dearest Friend
Spirit Lost
Morning
Nell
Bodies and Souls
Three Women at the Water's Edge
Stepping

summer light on nantucket

nancy thayer

summer light on nantucket

a novel

ballantine books
new york

Ballantine Books
An imprint of Random House
A division of Penguin Random House LLC
1745 Broadway, New York, NY 10019
randomhousebooks.com
penguinrandomhouse.com

Hardback ISBN 978-0-593-72404-0
Ebook ISBN 978-0-593-72407-1

Printed in the United States of America on acid-free paper

2 4 6 8 9 7 5 3 1

First Edition

BOOK TEAM:
Production editor: Jennifer Rodriguez • Managing editor: Pamela Alders • Production manager: Angela McNally • Copy editor: Madeleine Hopkins • Proofreaders: Andrea Gordon, Claire Maby, Amy Harned

Book design by Sara Bereta

Title-page art: veneratio © Adobe Stock Photos

The authorized representative in the EU for product safety and compliance is Penguin Random House Ireland, Morrison Chambers, 32 Nassau Street, Dublin D02 YH68, Ireland. https://eu-contact.penguin.ie

To

Tommy Claire
Josh Thayer
David Gillum
Ellias Forbes
Emmett Forbes
Charley Walters

Acknowledgments

You know how Robert Frost wrote about choosing between two roads? Writing a novel is like driving down the Los Angeles Freeway in a minivan full of manic passengers yelling out which exit they want me to take. If I didn't have the clear, expert guiding voice of my kind and brilliant editor Shauna Summers, I'd end up in Arizona when I meant to go to Maine. (Although I do like Arizona.)

Shauna, thank you so much for all you do to make my novels better.

I'm grateful for the help of the elegant Kim Hovey, and Kara Welsh, Karen Fink, Emma Thomasch, Mae Martinez, and the patient and heroic Jennifer Rodriguez. Publishing a book, even writing a book, has gotten so complicated now, with odd programs showing up on my computer without my invitation, so it's good to know that professionals are in charge.

Meg Ruley has been my friend and agent at the Jane Rotrosen Agency for so many years, and I love her for her advice, her wisdom, and her laughter. And thanks to wonderful Jessica Errera, Logan Harper, and Christina Hogrebe.

Independent bookstores have a special place in my heart and, I hope, in yours. Off island, I love Titcombs Bookstore in Sandwich, Maine; Bank Square Books in Mystic, Connecticut; Bethany Beach Books and Browseabout Books, both in Delaware; Litchfield Books on Pawley's Island, South Carolina; and Rainy Day Books in Kansas City, Kansas.

For forty years I've been able to walk down to Mitchell's Book Corner and find just the book I need. The brilliant Wendy Hudson stocks the books she knows we want, the gorgeous Christina Macchiavelli keeps the shop humming, and they hold amazing book signings! Two blocks away, Bookworks, managed by Suzanne Bennett, has delicious chocolates in exquisite containers, toys for children, and just the right birthday gift for anyone—and books, too.

Tim Ehrenberg is the marketing and event director for Nantucket Book Partners, the author of *Tim Talks Books,* and the co-host of *Books, Beach, and Beyond* with the spectacular Elin Hildebrand. Tim is a comet blazing through the literary sky, and the universe is his.

Have you ever come to the Nantucket Book Festival in June? It's an amazing event, hosting authors like Sara DiVello, Stephen Rowley, Jodi Picoult, Kwame Alexander, Erik Larson, and Margaret Atwood. Check it out!

I probably started going to the library when I was three, and I've never stopped. I'm sending special love to libraries everywhere. The Nantucket Atheneum is lucky to have Ann Scott as director. Everything's happening at the library. I always find the best books and it's a pleasure to chat at the circulation desk with Suzanne Keating, Annye Camara, and Clara Kempf.

I've been so fortunate to have the creative and adorable Christina Higgins as my personal assistant, and Chris Mason as my intrepid website builder. Thank you, guys. And Martha Sargent at Computer Solutions: without you, as they say, I can't even.

I've dedicated this book to the men in my life who take care of those I love, and make me laugh, and tell me stuff I need to know, and give me lots of chocolate. I want to thank them again, and I want to thank my daughter, Sam Wilde, and her girl band of Superstars: Adeline, Annie, Winnie, and Avery.

Writing is a solitary job—all that listening to people who don't exist—and I'm thankful for the real people in my life. Thank you, Jill Hunter Burrill, Deborah and Mark Beale, Tricia and Jimmy Patterson, Gussy Manville, Sofia and Stoyan Popova, Melissa and Nat Philbrick, Nantucket Police Chief Jody Kasper and Melissa Lake, Gerilyn Brewer and Henry Mueller, and Mary and John West. Curlette Anglin, you know all my secrets, and I love you.

Finally, but first, really, thank *you,* whoever you are, wherever you are, for reading my books. It's a huge pleasure to connect with you on social media, and I do read every comment, and I'd love to meet you each and every one someday. But until then, I'll feel like we're all already together, curling up by a fire with a cup of cocoa, talking about books we love.

summer light on nantucket

it all begins with a kiss

Blythe and her best friend Jill were having lunch together at Legal Sea Foods in Boston's elegant Copley Place mall and they were laughing so hard Blythe worried that the manager would ask them to leave.

Blythe's oldest child, Miranda, was almost seventeen, and would be a junior at Arlington High. Jill's oldest son, Zander, was also a rising junior. When their children were babies and toddlers, Blythe and Jill pretend-planned their wedding, but as they grew, Miranda and Zander liked each other fine but showed no romantic interest at all.

"The end of a dream," Jill said with a sigh.

"It's a good thing," Blythe told Jill as they finished their healthy salmon salads. "If our children really were going to marry, I wouldn't be able to complain about Miranda's insolence to you and you wouldn't want to tell me about stuff like that boy gym smell Zander had ever since he turned fourteen."

"He doesn't anymore," Jill said quickly, defensively. "Smell like a boys' gym."

"I know, I know. He's perfect, Jill, I mean it. An Adonis. Plus, his girlfriend is a real sweetheart."

Jill tipped back her glass to drink the last of her iced tea. "I love Carrie. But they're still kids. They need to date other people, break a few hearts, get their hearts broken, before they marry. *If* they marry. This is just high school love."

"Hey, Taylor Swift is all about high school love," Blythe reminded her friend, and then she sat there silently, her mind and her heart full of memories.

"Oh, no, there you go, thinking about Aaden again," Jill said.

"No, I'm not." Blythe changed the subject. "Listen, Krebs offered me full-time seventh-grade English next year."

"Well, that's great, isn't it? You taught eighth grade when you were first married, and you've been subbing in middle school for years, right?"

"True. But full-time teaching is much more work. And seventh grade is more difficult to teach. Eighth graders have learned how to deal with themselves. Seventh graders are hormonal, insecure bullies."

"Not all of them, surely. Teddy sailed through seventh grade."

"True. But that's another concern. What would happen to *my* kids if I teach in their school?"

"The question is, what will happen to *you* if you teach full-time?"

"The answer is," Blythe said, "since Bob and I divorced, he and Teri have been great about their days with the kids. I'll have free time to do lesson plans."

Jill thought about this for a moment, then said, "You like Teri."

Blythe speared one last piece of lettuce and waved it like a pointer. "I do. I don't *love* her. The kids say she clings to Bob like a barnacle, and she always gives them way too much sugar, which makes them like her. And I'm really glad the kids like her, even though I admit she makes me jealous. She's in such good shape, she can wear crop tops and low riders and show off her belly button ring like Miranda."

"Not a good mother image."

"True. But she doesn't have to be a mother. *I'm* the mother. She's like the cool babysitter. Plus, Bob spends much more time with the kids than he did when we were married. They do things. Go to plays, ballets, the aquarium. Skiing."

The waitress appeared. "Would you like dessert?"

"No, thanks. Just the bill." Blythe reached into her purse for her wallet.

Jill brought out her credit card. They always split the bill half and half.

"Blythe, it sounds like you want to teach full-time."

"Krebs gave me a few weeks to think about it. It will be a good time for me to reevaluate everything. We leave for Nantucket in two days."

Jill said, "We'll be up at our cottage in Maine. I'll float you a message in a bottle."

"Ha!" Blythe stirred her iced coffee. "Another thing. Jill, you're right. I *was* thinking about Aaden. I've been thinking about him a lot. You know he was one of the reasons Bob and I divorced, and the funny thing is that I haven't seen him in years. Decades. I was simply mooning over old photographs."

The waitress took the little leather folder holding the bill and their credit cards.

Jill leaned forward, speaking softly. "I think Aaden was the love of your life."

"My *children* are the love of my life," Blythe countered.

"I know, but I think you still have a soft spot for Aaden. Actually, Blythe, I think you even still have a soft spot for Bob."

"Maybe." Blythe thought about this. "Okay, so maybe a person gets more than one love of her life."

Jill held up her hand like a stop sign. "But only a limited number. Because otherwise it doesn't make sense."

"Maybe a limited number *romantically,*" Blythe qualified.

The waitress returned with their credit cards. Blythe and Jill signed their tabs.

"I do still have a soft spot for Bob," Blythe confessed. "I often wonder if the divorce was a mistake. Impulsive. Our split was so . . . pleasant. But maybe that means we were right to get divorced." She shook her head. "Stop me now. No more overanalyzing. Let's go look at the sales at Nordstrom."

The two women gathered their purses and shopping bags and slid from the booth. They stepped out into the mall.

"Which way shall we go?" Jill asked.

Blythe stopped so hard Jill almost slammed into her.

Blythe whispered, "*Look.*"

Jill asked, "Where?"

"There."

A plate-glass window separated them from a posh shoe shop. They could see through that window across to the other window where a man stood kissing a woman. He was kissing her passionately, pulling her body against his with one hand, cupping the back of her head with the other as he bent toward her. The woman was short and slender, with thick red hair flowing past her shoulders. Her arms were wrapped tightly around his broad back.

"That looks like Teri," Jill whispered.

"I know," Blythe whispered back, and she did know, because her ex-husband, Bob, was now living with Teri Casey, who had that fit body and that long wavy red hair. Blythe's children spent every other weekend with their father and Teri Casey, and they all had come to feel comfortable with the young woman who called herself the "Bonus Mom." Blythe was glad Bob had Teri in his life and she trusted Teri with her children.

But here, now, right in front of them, where everyone could see, Teri was kissing, *really* kissing, another man.

"That's not Bob," Jill whispered.

"I can see that," Blythe whispered back.

"What are you going to do?" Jill asked.

Blythe shook her head. "I have no idea."

the drive

As if the drive on crowded Route 3 from Boston to the Cape wasn't enough of a challenge, most of the way down Miranda, almost seventeen and dramatically in love, begged, pleaded, and wept real tears because Blythe, forty-five and feeling every minute of it, refused to agree that Miranda's boyfriend, Brooks, seventeen and too handsome for his own good, could sleep with her in her bed in their Nantucket summer house.

"Mom." As the oldest child, Miranda got to sit in the front passenger seat of the Honda Odyssey, the best spot for irritating the driver. The other three children were playing games on their phones or reading.

"We've already talked about this, Miranda."

Miranda argued, "Mom, if we want to have sex, we can do it anywhere, on the beach, in the bushes, *anywhere*!"

Blythe stayed firm. "I'm thinking of your brother and sisters. I don't want them—"

"My brother and sisters know more about what Brooks and I do than you ever will!" When Blythe didn't respond, Miranda said, "*Dad* would let Brooks sleep in the guest room! No! Wait! *Dad* would let Brooks sleep with *me*! *In my bed!* With the door open! *Everyone* does that now."

They'd had arguments before about what their dad would let them do, and Blythe had always restrained herself from pointing out that Bob, forty-six with male-pattern baldness, and his girlfriend, Teri, thirty and pretty and sweet, lived in a condo with only two bedrooms, and one was set up as an office. When the four children spent the night with their father, two of them slept on the pullout sofa in the living room. The other two were given sleeping bags to use on the floor. Bob told the kids that someday he'd buy another house with rooms for all the children.

Now Blythe said calmly, "It doesn't matter to me what other parents do. I have my own standards."

Miranda took a deep breath. "Mom, please. You don't understand. We're really, truly in love with each other. We're *bonded* to each other. It's not just sex. It's a profound *connection*. Brooks will be my partner for all my life. I'll be his. I love him, Mommy. I trust him with my heart."

Oh, how easy it would be to give in! Blythe reminded herself that Miranda looked like an adult, but she was still a teenager, driven by immense emotions. Blythe vividly remembered those emotions and their power. But Miranda, her beautiful, bright child, had often in her life overreacted to situations. This was this hardest part of parenting—saying no, because Blythe really was older and wiser and the one who made the rules, and rules kept children safe.

Drawing on whatever inner resources she had left in her battered mental parental suitcase of values, Blythe said quietly, "If this arrangement doesn't work for you, we can send Brooks right back to Boston the moment he arrives."

"You wouldn't," Miranda said.

Blythe said, "I won't change my mind. Now let me focus on the traffic."

Miranda huffed, but finally put on her earphones and sank back into her seat.

Blythe gripped the steering wheel harder and concentrated on the six lanes of traffic speeding down Route 3. The truck behind her was tailgating her, its grille looming in her rearview window. The guy was apparently trying to make her drive faster, but if she did, she'd smash right into the Volvo in front of her.

Not for the first time, she wondered why automobiles didn't come with buttons on the dashboard that would activate flashing neon signs on the back of cars.

STOP TAILGATING OR I'LL GO EVEN SLOWER.

If she had the time, Blythe thought she'd invent that device. Only it wouldn't be so polite.

BACK OFF, ASSHOLE.

The Volvo in front of her sped onto an exit ramp and Blythe pressed her foot on the accelerator.

The high metal arch of the Sagamore Bridge over the canal came into view. They rattled over it, went around the rotary to Route 6, and were on Cape Cod. As always, everyone in the minivan cheered. They were closer and closer to their summer vacation. Three months of sunshine and fun time.

But Blythe's thoughts kept flipping back to the moment two days ago when she saw Teri kissing the man who wasn't Bob. Blythe kept wondering who the man was and if there was an innocent explanation for the kiss. She knew Teri had a brother, but not even the most adoring brother would kiss his sister the way that man had kissed Teri. Maybe, Blythe thought, it had been an old boyfriend. Blythe could absolutely imagine an old boyfriend kissing Teri that passionately. She and Jill had frozen in place, whispering about what to do. Should they walk right up to the couple? Blythe could say, coolly, "Hello, Teri." But that could have shattering consequences. Blythe didn't want Bob and Teri to break up, not now when her children were more or less settled in their new family structure. She didn't want Teri, who was gorgeous and giddy but also kind, to leave Bob and the children.

And what about Bob? He was suave and confident, brilliant even, at law. But the more successful he became, the more he needed a woman at home to lean on, to adore him, to support him. Teri seemed to be perfect for Bob—but was he perfect for her? That kiss with another man had Blythe worried.

But what could she do about it? What *should* she do?

While Blythe and Jill had whispered, Teri and the man had pulled apart and walked away together, out of Blythe's sight.

She wrenched her thoughts back to the present when she glimpsed the exit to Hyannis. She turned onto the congested two-lane road. They crept along Route 132, past hotels and malls and cafés, while the kids yelled out familiar names.

"*Dunkin'!*" Holly, eleven and still sweet, shouted.

"*Tiki Port!*" Teddy, thirteen and growing hair on his legs, hollered. One of the highlights of his life had happened when he was five and the family stopped to eat at the Chinese/Polynesian restaurant. He'd ordered a sugary non-alcoholic drink that was served in a mug shaped like a carving of a frightening god that he got to take home. He still had it on a shelf in his bedroom.

Daphne, fifteen and so over her family, said nothing, but glancing in the rearview mirror, Blythe noticed that her second daughter had stopped reading and was now staring out the window as they approached the Hyannis harbor.

Blythe's pulse quickened. They turned right, left, right, and entered the Steamship Authority's parking lot. Blythe showed her boarding pass and was waved into the line of vehicles headed up the metal ramp and into the giant hold of the steamship's car ferry. Following behind a large UPS truck, Blythe obeyed the deckhand's signals to park in the far-right lane. As soon as she turned off her engine, the four children jumped out and raced up to the passenger deck, ready to watch the steamship's engines froth the blue water into white foam as the ship slowly moved away from shore.

For a moment, Blythe remained in the car, relaxing against the car seat. She was troubled by a sense that she'd forgotten something, because it sometimes happened that she *had* forgotten something. But today, for the two hours and fifteen minutes it took to pass over Nantucket Sound to the island, she would give herself a break.

Blythe left the car, climbed the stairs to the passenger deck, did a quick tour to check on her children, bought herself a cup of coffee, and went out to lean against the railing and watch the sun flashing silver coins on the water. Teddy and Holly were already there, watching ducks and gulls bob and soar. Daphne was in the stern cabin, reading a book. Miranda was in the bow cabin, tapping on her phone.

Once they were well underway, Blythe went inside the cabin on the top passenger deck and settled in a booth. The morning had been exhausting, even though everyone had packed their luggage last night. The kids had been excited and crazy, squabbling and making terrible jokes. Of course, once they were all buckled in with the house locked up, Holly decided she had to go to the bathroom *right now* even though ten minutes before, when Blythe asked them if they had to pee, they all had said no. Blythe had to undo her seatbelt, unlock the front door, and stand patiently for her youngest daughter. But still, they'd made it in time.

It was always an emotional journey, traveling to Nantucket to live for almost three months. It felt symbolic, significant. It had been hardest three years ago, when Blythe and Bob were first divorced. Blythe had had to make the trip without the children's father and they all sensed a hollowness around them. The children were accustomed to it now. They had moved on. The school year had passed without problems and now they were on their way to Nantucket. Their beloved grandmother, Bob's mother, Celeste, lived there and still, thank God, loved Blythe. If anything, since the divorce, Celeste seemed to love Blythe more.

Blythe closed her eyes. Memories of her own youth, when she loved a man as much as Miranda loved Brooks, flooded her senses. The slight rocking motion of the ferry and the knowledge that someone else was in charge of their safety allowed Blythe to dream . . . and remember.

aaden

Aaden was her age, in her level at high school. Short, stocky, dark-eyed, dark-haired, he had the easy, magnetic charm of a bartender who could lean on the counter listening to your problems or break up a fight and toss you out the door. In Irish, Aaden meant "fire and flame, warmth of the home," and the moment Blythe saw him, she flushed with heat.

He had only that year moved to Arlington, but he was handsome, athletic, and smart. He quickly became part of the gang of popular guys. He was in only one class that Blythe took—history—and he sat behind her and to the right, so she couldn't see him except when he entered and left the classroom. But she was aware of him whenever they passed each other in the halls.

He had a great smile and broad, muscular shoulders. He wore cotton rugby shirts no matter how cold it got. He was almost always the first to answer in class, and the prettiest girls in her grade clustered around him, chattering away, trying to keep his interest. Aaden radiated a quiet masculine strength. Blythe wasn't surprised to learn that he was a wrestler, the best in his league. That was their junior year. She'd giggled with her girlfriends about him. She'd given him a lingering smile whenever their eyes met.

One day, at the end of history class, she accidentally on purpose dropped her notebook, and Aaden had picked it up for her.

"Thanks," she said casually. "I'm Blythe."

"I know," Aaden had said, smiling.

She'd blushed, become flustered, and babbled, "Oh, right, of course you know, we're in the same class, Mr. Ruoff calls on me all the time."

"True." Aaden's gaze was like sunlight on a cold day. "But I've been asking around. About you."

"You have?" Her breath caught. She was mesmerized, and she was *never* mesmerized. She was pretty and smart and popular. Lots of guys were interested in her. "I'm not always like this," she told him.

"Let me take you out Saturday night and you can show me what you're like." Aaden suddenly blushed, and it was a gorgeous, sexy sight, the way the pink flooded up from the base of his neck to his cheeks. "That sounded wrong somehow."

Blythe had shamelessly batted her eyelashes. "It sounded right to me."

Students were pouring into the room for the next class. Aaden and Blythe cut through the crowd and went out into the hall.

"I've got to go this way," she told Aaden.

"I've got to go that way. Look. I've got a car. Meet me in the parking lot when classes are over."

"I will!" she promised and hurried down the hall with the few stragglers late for class.

She sank down into her seat, her heart pounding, and for all she knew, she wasn't even in the right classroom, and it didn't matter where she was, because she had Aaden waiting for her at the end of the school day.

It happened so quickly between them. It wasn't just physical, although that was fierce and compelling. Aaden was smart, too, super smart, and he didn't hide the fact that he loved words, he loved poetry. Wait! Blythe had thought. A guy liked poetry and was also on the wrestling team?

It was his Irish heritage, he explained. Both his parents were Irish immigrants and his grandparents lived there still.

"I'll take you to meet my grandparents sometime," Aaden promised. "They'll love you and you'll see where I learned to love words."

As their junior year progressed, they became *that* couple. They went everywhere together. They spoke on the phone before going to sleep. Blythe attended all his wrestling matches even though she'd never paid much attention to any kind of wrestling before.

And the wrestling! As they became more and more intimate, Aaden showed her different wrestling moves. The screw lock throw, the fireman's carry, the takedown. First, he demonstrated the Irish collar-and-elbow grip when they were in Blythe's bedroom—with the door open, always—and when he gently thumped Blythe onto her bedroom floor with its wall-to-wall carpet, her father came up the stairs demanding to know what was going on. After that, he showed his wrestling moves in the family room, where Blythe's parents could watch. He was always gentle with Blythe, but she learned how strong he was, how powerful he could be, and how their bodies felt together, even in the strangest of holds.

Blythe's parents liked Aaden. Her mother, a high school teacher, had insisted Blythe take birth control pills the moment she turned sixteen and her main concern was that she did *not* get pregnant or decide not to go to college because of Aaden. Blythe's father liked Aaden but reminded Blythe that she was only a teenager, and that while teenage romances were passionate, they never lasted.

Aaden's family also liked Blythe. He had an older brother, Donal, who was bigger and stronger than he was. He treated Aaden like a family pet and Blythe quickly realized that when Aaden's brother punched him in the shoulder or slapped his head, it was his way of showing affection. Brendan Sullivan, Aaden's father, owned Awen, an import company specializing in Irish clothing and gifts. He'd opened a branch in Boston with his own brother still living in Ireland, and for a few decades it was successful. By the 1990s, synthetic fleece was being made into blankets, sweaters, and sweatshirts, and people were stuffing their itchy Irish wool sweaters into the back of their closets. Aaden's father and his wife, Sheila, tried to modernize the business with scarves and capes and jewelry. They went to Ireland several times a year to meet with their family and business partners there and managed to keep the company successful, but not like it had been.

Donal refused to join the business and instead went into construction. He married young and often came to Sunday dinner at the Sullivan house with his wife, Maeve. By the time they were seniors in high school, Blythe had every Sunday dinner at the Sullivan's. She and Aaden were with each other every moment they could be. They could argue fiercely, at school or a coffee shop or their own homes, but they would always make up. If Blythe had a cold, Aaden caught it. If Aaden went to a school football game, Blythe went with him. She learned a lot about families by watching Aaden and his brother and parents argue and insult one another and then sit down to dinner and talk and laugh. When Blythe argued with her parents, or when they argued with each other, it always ended with each person going into another room to sulk or think or nap, returning after an hour or so wearing their hurt feelings wrapped around them like an invisible cape, refusing to speak and going to bed mad. Because of his family, Blythe felt safe in arguing with Aaden, knowing that they would always make up.

Aaden learned to fit in with Blythe's parents, who were always more formal. Their discussions tended to touch on current weather in the area or the newest movies and television shows. Watching them together, Blythe realized how different her small family was. They never argued at the table, but gently changed the subject. They used cloth napkins, gravy boats, and good glasses, not, like Aaden's family, paper napkins, or in a pinch, paper towels, and beer or cola cans right on the table. But the families were more or less equal financially, and that made things easier.

Blythe and Aaden applied to the same colleges and agreed to go to whichever one accepted them both. Aaden wanted to major in business administration so he could take over his father's business. Blythe chose education. An only child, she enjoyed being around kids of any age.

Thanksgiving Day, which they each spent mostly in their respective parents' homes, Blythe and Aaden met by the salt-and-pepper bridge over the Charles River. The day was clouded and chilly, and they walked along Memorial Drive with their coats buttoned up and gloves on their hands.

"So," Blythe prompted. "What did you want to tell me?"

Aaden cleared his throat. "The family is going to Ireland at Christmas. They only just decided. My grandmother is ill, her son Sean, my father's brother, you've heard us talk about him, he's an alcoholic and useless, but their daughter, Sarah, wants to keep the business going and begged us to come help her sort it out. And Liam, my father's other brother, has seven children and works hard but he's getting old."

"How long will you be gone?" Blythe asked.

"A month. Maybe a bit longer."

"You can't miss your final semester." She was shrinking into herself from the cold wind and her fear.

"I know. I'll be back by then." He took her hand in his. "I'm sorry. I have to do this. I know it ruins our Christmas, but we have years of Christmases ahead of us."

"I could go with you," she suggested softly, afraid to say it, knowing what his answer would be. "You've told me I should see Ireland."

"I did think of that, but no. Not now. Not like this. It will be a mad crush, because we're a large family and we've got to sort things out. First, we'll have to have a good drunken brawling reunion with all the worst memories spread out and then some of us will have to spend days looking at the company's records and helping Sarah."

Blythe was shivering. "I'm so cold. I need to go inside."

"Come on."

Aaden took her hand and led her across the street and into the heart of Cambridge. They found a coffee shop, a warm, dark room smelling pleasantly of wet mittens and mufflers. Aaden took her to a booth and helped her slide in.

"I'll be back with drinks."

The room was cozy, but Blythe was still cold. She folded her arms across her chest to keep the warmth against her. Her parents had told her, her friends had warned her, high school romances never last. They're like fireworks, instant, explosive, gorgeous, and doomed to fade and disappear.

Aaden returned. He scooted into the same side of the booth as Blythe, his warm body touching hers, shoulder to shoulder, thigh to thigh. He'd brought her a coffee, thick with chocolate, sugar, and cream. He was wearing a Red Sox cap and his high school letter jacket which made a crackling sound as he moved next to her.

She sipped the coffee and let it warm her.

Aaden put his arm around her and pulled her close. "Say something."

All she could think about was how he had said, "The family is going to Ireland." As if he did not exist apart from his family. As if being with his family was more important than being with her.

"This seems huge," Blythe finally said very quietly. She couldn't face him. She stared at the wall opposite. She didn't want him to touch her. She would shatter like crystal. "A kind of turning point. Or maybe I mean a fork in the road."

Beside her, Aaden nodded. "I know. But things are always going to change, aren't they? We're graduating from high school in a few months. We have to be adults and face the future. I suppose I mean we need to face the present."

She couldn't speak. She didn't want to face the present, not with Aaden half a world away.

"Just tell me you'll come back," she whispered.

"I'll come back," Aaden promised.

He had kept his promise. He had come back. He'd finished his final semester at the high school.

But he was going to return to Ireland. She had known that the moment she set eyes on him when he returned from Christmas vacation.

That January evening, when Aaden picked her up to go out to dinner, he'd entered the house to say hello to her parents and to chat politely like he always did.

Blythe and Aaden didn't speak as they walked to the car, but already Blythe sensed how Aaden had changed. During his few phone calls over vacation, he'd been ebullient, unable to talk fast enough to tell her all the reasons Dublin was amazing. She had wanted him to return home so badly that she'd almost told him she'd had a car accident and was in the hospital, but of course she couldn't lie to him, she could only tell him how happy she was that he was having a great time, even though that was really a lie. When she saw him, his first evening home, he'd seemed taller, larger, more confident, and he had always been confident.

They settled in the car. It was very cold, and Aaden switched on the ignition in order to turn on the heater.

Before they pulled on their seatbelts, Blythe turned to Aaden.

"You're going back to Ireland."

He didn't lie. "I am. I wish I could explain how it is over there. For me. It's *home*. The people, the food, the weather, the architecture—I've applied to Trinity in Dublin for next year. It's where I want to be."

Her heart stopped. She couldn't think. "Aaden, could we drive somewhere? I mean, if my parents glance out the window, they'll wonder why we're still parked here."

"Sure." They both hitched on their seatbelts and he drove the car away from her house and onto Mass Ave, a wider, busier street leading into Cambridge and toward the Charles River.

Aaden said, "Are you hungry?"

"No." Blythe couldn't look at him.

Aaden kept his eyes on the road. "Blythe. Listen. I want you to come with me."

Softly, Blythe said, "I can't."

"Yes, you can!" Aaden suddenly pulled into a parking spot in front of a deli. Turning to her, he said, "Blythe, you'd love it there! You love books, you love poetry, Ireland is all about poetry. You know that."

"I'm not brave like you." Blythe leaned away, against the door, not wanting him to touch her, to pull her toward him. "I like it here. I don't want to live in a strange world."

"Ireland is not strange!" Aaden objected.

Embarrassed, hurt, and all at once angry, Blythe finally faced him. "It is to me."

"But I'll be with you," Aaden argued.

"You'll be with your friends, your family. I won't know anyone but you."

"You'll meet people," Aaden said. "You'll make friends."

"I have friends. Perfectly wonderful friends."

"You'll make new friends."

She looked away from him. "Aaden, stop. I'm not like you. I want to stay here. Go to Ireland, but don't expect me to go, too."

Aaden spoke softly, gently. "I don't want to be away from you."

She shook her head. "Go to Ireland."

"Blythe, I'm sorry. I want to hold you."

She wanted that, too. She was so confused. She pressed the button, making the seatbelt slide away from her. She leaned toward Aaden and sank into the security of his strong embrace. She laid her head on his shoulder, feeling the strength of his arms, the bristles on his jaw, the swell of muscles beneath his coat. Feeling the rise and fall of his chest as he breathed. Aaden kissed her hair and then kissed her mouth, but it wasn't a lover's kiss. It was a soothing kiss.

"Let's go eat," he said. "Let's talk things over."

"Okay." Blythe pulled away from him.

As he drove, Aaden suggested, "Tell me about your vacation. Did you go skiing?"

She tried to be as calm as he was even though she felt like a raging Irishwoman in one of their tragic plays, gesticulating and weeping and gnashing her teeth and wanting to die. She blew her nose heartily and sniffed back her tears. "Not skiing. Jenna and I went skating at Frog Pond on Boston Common. It was the most beautiful cold day with bright sun and snow covered everything like a fairy tale. Oh, and we went to an amazing Moroccan restaurant. We went shopping . . ."

She couldn't keep up the pretense.

"Oh, Aaden, is this going to be the end of us?"

The road was congested, vehicles swerving in and out, changing lanes, their lights flashing across Aaden's eyes. He didn't look away from the traffic; he couldn't. But he said, "Blythe, there will never be an end to us."

summer houses

Blythe was roused from her memories by the shudder and thud of the Steamship Authority vehicle ferry arriving at its Nantucket dock. The Benedict family squeezed down the metal stairway to the great hollow hull of the car deck where their minivan stood bumper-to-bumper with other vehicles. People chatted, doors slammed, dogs barked, and deckhands shouted directions.

She watched for the taillights in front of her to blink on and started the engine. She steered her trusty minivan down the clanking metal ramp connecting the ferry to the island. Carefully, she inched behind the line of other vehicles onto the parking lot.

"We're here!" she announced, her heart flooding with happiness.

"Open the lock!" Teddy's, Daphne's, and Miranda's doors opened and they jumped out.

Calling, "Wait for me!" Holly, from the middle seat, scooted out, too. The four raced away on the brick sidewalks, hoping to get to the summer house before Blythe did. It had become a tradition for the kids to try to beat the minivan, packed with luggage, backpacks, and bikes, to their summer house on a narrow street that had to be accessed by weaving back and forth through other one-way Nantucket streets.

Blythe smiled, letting out a sigh of happiness as she watched her small tribe hurtling together up the sidewalk, dodging around people, dogs, and luggage.

Her children, together.

Another Nantucket summer.

Slowly, she drove away from the crowded ferry terminal. As she navigated through the maze of lanes, she took the time to notice the bursts of color from the flowers in the window boxes and yards of all the handsome historic houses. Kids zipped past on their electric scooters, a girl sturdily pedaled along on her bike, landscapers trimmed privet hedges, and suddenly, there was their three-story shingled house set back from the street, with a long porch and a glossy blue door with its shining brass door knocker shaped like a mermaid. The house didn't have a view of the ocean, but it did have porches and decks and lots of bedrooms and bathrooms and a fireplace and a lawn in the backyard for badminton and croquet and railings for hanging beach towels to dry.

The children had gotten there first. Blythe remained in the car, watching them run into the house. They would scatter to their separate bedrooms, shouting with delight.

Blythe continued to wait, knowing that at any moment, Miranda would leave the house and run into town to meet her summer girlfriends and Teddy would run down to the yacht club to see if anyone was there to play tennis and Daphne would hurry over to the Maria Mitchell museum to see if they had any jobs for her. Holly would rush off to see her best island friend, Carolyn.

Or Holly might remain inside. Blythe worried about Holly, who would probably sit on her bed with her drawing pad and continue to create her graphic novels about sea gerbils, which lived in the shoals of Nantucket shores. Blythe loved to read. She'd taught her children to love to read. She told herself she shouldn't fret so much about Holly wanting to write a book about sea gerbils, who weren't even real. A graphic novel counted as a book, didn't it?

And what else could Blythe do? She'd accepted the fact that she would worry about her children all the time, all her life. She knew she couldn't protect them forever, but she would try her best to give her children happy, healthy lives.

She thought she'd done fairly well so far. This was her third summer coming to the island without Bob. It helped that her grandmother had left her the Nantucket house in her will. It was a bonus that Bob's parents lived on Nantucket, and he and Teri could stay with them in the large, rambling house on Fair Street where he grew up.

In Boston, Bob had taken an apartment near his office in Back Bay where he worked as a lawyer. He liked the hustle and action and drinking in bars with his colleagues after work. Teri was a paralegal, and lovely, and soon after the final decree, Bob started dating her. Two years ago, Teri moved in with him, and Blythe was fine with that.

Blythe liked Teri well enough. The only problem was that Teri and Bob were the fun parents. They gave all the children the newest electronic screens and toys. They didn't correct, scold, or chastise. Now, whenever Blythe disciplined her children, these children she'd patiently grown within her own body and impatiently and painfully given birth to from her own body, these children whom she'd lost sleep over and changed her entire life for, these children, when they were angry with Blythe, threatened to leave their mother and go live with their father and Teri.

Sometimes Blythe wanted to yell, "Fine! I'll drive you over now!"

She hadn't done that. Yet.

By now, her children seemed to be reconciled to the divorce, plus, they were growing older and becoming independent.

Now Blythe swung her legs out of the minivan, stepped out, and stretched. She walked up the slate walk, noticing that their caretaker, Emilio, had mowed the grass to a glossy velvet, trimmed the privet hedges, and filled the window boxes with bouquets of sweet-face violets. She went up the steps, seven exactly, and onto the porch with its pale blue ceiling, a darker blue wooden floor, and handsome, secure balusters to keep toddling children from nose-diving into the rosebushes.

She opened the front door.

And there, so soon, was the first thorn of summer.

The kids had stormed into the house because the door wasn't locked because Bob's sister, Kate, who lived year-round on the island, had a key and had come over earlier to open the windows and fill the refrigerator with milk and butter and set a vase of daisies on the dining room table.

Nice of her, absolutely, but also irritating because Blythe knew Kate snooped in every closet, drawer, and bathroom cabinet, and even rearranged their kitchen shelves. Kate was Bob's bossy older sister. Kate believed that the Nantucket house and the lives of the Benedict children belonged to her. Blythe was grateful that Bob's family never once ended their friendship and their love after the divorce and she also understood that it was necessary for someone on the island to have a key to the house in case of emergency. But still. It was an intrusion. Almost an invasion. Especially because Kate was Bob's sister, and Blythe feared Kate was funneling Blythe's secrets to her brother.

Not that Blythe had any interesting secrets.

Shaking off her thoughts, she entered the house and rested in the front hall, just breathing. After almost two hundred years of standing firm in gale force winds and thundering rain, after countless layers of paint and wallpaper and hooks for pictures, and walls wrenched apart so new plumbing could be installed, after all that patching-up and renovating, after all the noisy busy life lived in this house, it still smelled ever so slightly of some clean spice. Nutmeg, maybe. Or, simply, sunshine.

But many of the closets smelled of mildew. They *were* on an island surrounded by the sea, and in the summer, humidity curled around the town and houses like a damp ghost. Miranda said that mildew was such a constant pervasive perfume in the summer that they ought to bottle it and label it *Nantucket*. It would sell like crazy.

Blythe glanced into the living room. The sofa pillows were all plumped (by Kate), and the newest copy of the local newspaper was on the coffee table. Blythe passed through the long front hall into the kitchen, then headed up the back stairs to the bedrooms. The children had dumped their backpacks and duffel bags and hurried off to their Nantucket lives.

Blythe entered her bedroom and dropped her suitcase on the wide queen-sized bed.

Once this had been her grandparents' room when they came from Ohio to spend three months in the cool island air. Her parents had used the biggest guest room and Blythe had used the small room at the end of the hall. The other guest rooms had been saved for real guests, friends of her grandparents or her parents. It was a spacious, welcoming house.

Next to the door of the stairs to the attic, one small rectangular chamber had been made into a one-person guest room just large enough to hold a twin bed, a side table with a lamp, and an old-fashioned dresser with a mirror held by harp-shaped posts. Above the bed was a round window, like a portal in a ship, overlooking the town and the sky.

This had always been Blythe's favorite room when she was young. It had seemed less like a bedroom than a secret hideaway. She'd kept her books stacked neatly beneath her bed and her sneakers, sandals, and Mary Janes placed at the foot of the bed where she couldn't see them. Where they wouldn't break the spell.

Light came through the window like a herald from another world. The sunlight woke her in the morning, falling on the antique etched glass lamp with prisms that caught the beam and scattered it into rainbows that shivered against the wall like butterflies. In the winter, when they came for Christmas, the moonlight looked icy, striping frosty silver beams across her bed. In the summer, the moonlight was clear and strong, a slope of light leading to another world, to Blythe's dreams. When the mirror caught the light, the room glowed.

When she was a child, she knew that the house was alive, not like a zombie or a ghost, but like a wordless living creature, like trees or rabbits, capable of loving but not capable of speech. Each time she entered the room she knew she was welcomed, embraced by the light. Each summer, as a teenager, she turned the mirror to face the wall when she left, as if to keep the room dark until she returned.

Now she and each of her four children had his or her own bedroom. The hideout in the hall was empty and would be all summer. She knew that Miranda's boyfriend, Brooks, could sleep there even though it was on the same floor as Miranda's room. But Blythe couldn't tolerate the thought of Brooks, handsome athlete that he was, sleeping there. It would be like putting a tiger into a birdcage. With one swoop of his arm, the antique prism lamp would be knocked to the floor and shattered. And where would he put his clothes? His size 11 shoes?

Blythe didn't want to say all this to her daughter, so she used the excuse that she didn't want Brooks sleeping on the same floor as Miranda, and that was also true.

She left her little magic room and walked to the master bedroom at the end of the hall.

This was where Miranda was created eighteen years ago. They never told Miranda that, even though Blythe thought Miranda would like the idea of being a true Nantucket native, but Miranda had a friend named London who was horrified and grossed out when her parents told her they had named her London because that was where she was conceived. She now went by her middle name, Louise.

Back in her own spacious bedroom with the luxurious queen-sized bed, Blythe unpacked her suitcase, humming. It was summer now, really summer. She didn't have to make any significant decisions, at least not for two weeks, which was when she told Krebs she'd call him back about the seventh-grade teaching job. She changed into a light sleeveless dress and put her hair up in a sloppy bun.

Blythe and the kids were having dinner with their grandmother, Bob's mother, Celeste, tonight. It was a tradition and the beginning of their island vacation. It had begun when she and Bob were married, but the divorce had not altered the love the two women had for each other. Having a house, a history on Nantucket, and an endless love for four children had become a silken bond.

bob

Blythe and Bob had met when they were twenty-two years old and fresh out of college. They had thought they were so old, and they'd been so young.

Blythe had grown up in Arlington, Massachusetts, the only child of a physician and a high school teacher. Her parents were older than most parents, and she had no siblings or cousins. She did have books and an imagination and mornings at preschool, which she enjoyed so much that at home she practiced teaching, putting all her dolls and stuffed animals in a row and standing in front of them, lecturing them about everything she knew and much she invented. Her parents told her that was when they knew she'd grow up to be a teacher.

She was happiest when they visited her Nantucket grandparents, who let her sleep in her magic room and allowed her free range in an attic packed with trunks of old clothes. If it rained, Blythe would lie on the chintz sofa in the living room, and when she came upon a thought she wanted to consider, she'd gaze at one of the gold-framed paintings of fruit in a bowl or a ship in a stormy sea, or two little girls in white dresses and pink sashes. She knew this was an old-fashioned house in which she was living old-fashioned summers, and she cherished them for the respite they gave her, the peace of being only herself.

As a teenager, she became more social. She made friends, played tennis, learned to sail, attended movies, especially frightening ones where she screamed as loudly as the other girls in the row of seats. During her last two years of high school, she learned to sneak down the back stairs to the kitchen door where she could leave and enter without her grandparents' knowledge. When she was a junior and senior in high school, her world revolved around Aaden. When would she see him next? How could she abide living on an island so far away from him? Light was no longer magic. Only Aaden was magic.

When Aaden left for Ireland for good, everything changed.

Blythe was so heartbroken, so *destroyed,* she couldn't leave her room. She wanted to lie face down in her bed and die.

Her parents, impatient with her depression, sent her to Nantucket for the summer. She took a job working for a children's summer camp, and slowly, the campers' joy in each day woke the joy she'd thought she'd lost forever. The children swam, built sandcastles, climbed monkey bars, and went screaming down slides. They fingerpainted terrible pictures of dogs and cats and thought they'd produced masterpieces. They fought one another and made up, snubbed one another and became best friends, built entire villages out of sand and jumped up and down, destroying the villages, laughing maniacally. They thought Blythe was the most beautiful creature who had ever lived. They wanted to sit on her lap, squeeze next to her when she read a story, ask her to braid their hair. Carla, the other counselor, said, "You really have a special knack with kids."

Blythe thought about this a moment, then said, "Yes. Yes, I do."

She'd always remember Carla and how one kind word from an acquaintance had shone light on the path she hadn't even known was there, a path she wanted to follow all her life.

When she left the island to start her freshman year at college, she knew she was stronger than she'd ever been. She'd learned that love wasn't only something between two people, but like wind, invisible, uncontrollable, everywhere, and full of surprises.

She attended UMass Amherst and made good, if not spectacular grades, majoring in secondary education. She dated and flirted but didn't get involved seriously with anyone. As the months passed, she became more and more interested in the skills and arts of teaching. Her grandparents had left the Nantucket house to her, and Blythe knew that was love, too. The year she graduated from college, her parents told her they were planning to eventually move to Arizona for her mother's arthritis. Arizona was beautiful, they told her. She should come visit, and maybe she'd want to live there for a while. Blythe had told them maybe. Someday.

In late May, Blythe went to a fabulous, celebratory graduation party at the home of a classmate whose uncle had been governor of Massachusetts. The house was a massive brick mansion with an enormous backyard surrounded by tall, velvety spruce trees, making it its own little world. The tables held glittering bottles of gin, vodka, and champagne and platters of finger food. It was spring, and the night was starry. In the library, a three-piece band played dance music.

Blythe attended the party with several of her friends, all of them wearing their sexiest clothes and layers of makeup. They'd drunk champagne as they were getting ready and had taken a cab to the party because they knew they would be too tipsy from alcohol and freedom to drive home.

Blythe roamed through the enormous, sparkling house, chatting with strangers, munching caviar, and sipping champagne. The rooms were filled with laughing, hugging, yelling, kissing young people, with unruly thatches of thick hair and bright eyes and strong bodies, all emanating a luxuriant glow of health and hope. This was her tribe, she thought, and graduates in parties like this all over the country belonged to this tribe, and they were brave and good and eager. They were going to rule the world.

The world on this side of the Atlantic.

She'd heard from Aaden many times during her first year, always by email. He was studying business management at Trinity in Dublin. He spent holidays with his family at their grandparents' home in Kerry. He sent photos of waves crashing against cliffs and castles on high hills. For the first few months, Blythe didn't answer. It hurt too much to think of him, but she still sat in front of her computer, studying his pictures, missing him, loving him, hating him. By their sophomore year, his emails were less frequent, and by their junior year of college, Aaden stopped sending pictures or emails.

What a bullshit artist, Blythe decided. One night, weeping, she deleted every mention of Aaden from her files. She couldn't imagine ever finding love again.

Her thoughts had pierced the happiness she felt that night at the dazzling party.

"Stop this now!" she told herself.

A couple involved in a serious conversation turned their backs on her.

"Sorry," she told them.

She forced herself through the crowds and out onto the back patio, where she collapsed in a lawn chair with deeply soft cushions. Laying her head back, she gazed at the billions of stars and wondered where Aaden was at this very moment.

"May I join you?"

She focused her eyes and saw a handsome stranger in a tux smiling at her.

"Of course." She waved her hand carelessly at the nearest chair.

Bob was starting law school in the fall. He'd scored 170 on his LSAT, partly because his father was a lawyer who talked law constantly at the dinner table. Later, when they were on the verge of divorce, Blythe had reminded him that at their first meeting the first fact he told her about himself was his score on his LSAT.

Back then, in the beginning, Blythe had found herself charmed by this handsome, intelligent, and possibly insecure man—wasn't blurting out his score numbers a sign of insecurity?

"I can't remember any of my scores," she'd said. Then, thinking she was absolutely hilarious, she'd said, "I *can* remember my name. I'm Blythe Anderson."

Bob had slid a patio chair around to face her. "Beautiful name, Blythe. Unusual. I'm Bob Benedict."

"And our favorite band is the B-52s," Blythe joked.

They'd sat out in the sweet spring evening, talking and laughing as the moon rose and the night began, while dozens of other celebrants danced and swayed out on the patio. Two men in tuxedos dove into the swimming pool. Two women in elegant dresses were tossed, squealing and laughing, into the water, and an extremely tall, slender man stood on the diving board and orated a passage of poetry. "Hold fast to dreams / For if dreams die / Life is a broken-winged bird / That cannot fly." People cheered and clapped and other men began singing foolish drunken frat songs.

"That poem is by Langston Hughes," Blythe told Bob. She wanted to tell him that poem would be woven into her classes when she taught seventh-grade English.

"Nice," Bob had responded, clearly not impressed with the poet or his poetry.

Aaden would have known the poet's name. He could have recited those words from memory.

But Aaden was gone, and Blythe was determined to move on. Langston Hughes could not be a deal-breaker, especially with a man this charming, intelligent, and handsome. She felt no heart-stopping chemistry with him, but that was a relief, a life buoy tossed into the unsettled sea of her life.

They'd talked past midnight, discussing everything in their worlds, parents, old schools, old friends, but especially plans for the future, hopes for the future, and how it felt that they were finally grown-ups, adults, even though they'd reached the legal adult age of twenty-one a year ago. When they discovered they both had connections to Nantucket, they were elated. It was as if the world was beginning, because *they* were beginning, and Blythe sensed a bond with Bob because they were there, in that place, at the starting line together, that night.

That first evening, when most of the celebrants had left, they remained on the patio, and as the night grew dark and cool, they finally spoke about their broken hearts. Blythe told Bob about Aaden, and Bob told Blythe about Ginger, the girl who'd left him during his last semester of high school. He showed her a picture of Ginger. He still carried one in his wallet. She was very pretty, with long red hair and tilted green eyes and a cute snub nose and legs that went on forever. She wanted to be a professional dancer. Her dream was to join the Mark Morris Dance Group and eventually start a dance company of her own. Bob wanted to be a lawyer and join his father's firm. Ginger told him she was moving to New York after graduation. He researched ways he could attend a college in or near the city. During Ginger's last semester of high school, she made visits down to the city to explore professional possibilities. At the beginning of May, just before Bob would graduate and Ginger wouldn't, because she hadn't attended any classes that last semester, Ginger texted Bob that she wasn't returning to Massachusetts. She was living with another dancer, Clark, who was also her lover.

"She didn't even say she was sorry," Bob told Blythe that evening, trying to sound ironic but sounding hurt. "It was as if a robot wrote the text. Sorry," he said. "I've really got to get over her. It's been four years."

"True," Blythe said. "But high school romances are famous for breaking hearts."

"Still," Bob said, "I thought we were special."

He was such a nice man, and he looked so forlorn and Blythe was tired of herself for thinking about Aaden for four entire years.

On an impulse, she said, "*We* are special. Because people who kiss each other even before their first date are extremely special."

"What?" Bob looked confused.

Blythe rose from her chair and sat on Bob's lap and wrapped her arms around him. The surprise on his face made her laugh, and she was still laughing when he pressed his mouth against hers. He put his hands on her waist and tugged her closer, completely focused now. She gripped his hair and he cupped her head in his hand.

When they stopped kissing, Bob said, "Do you know what would be really special?"

Blythe smiled. "What?"

"Having sex in the bedroom of the house that belongs to someone we don't know."

She laughed. "I don't think so. Besides, that kiss was special all by itself, don't you think?"

"Not special enough," Bob said.

He lifted her up as he rose, holding her in the traditional crossing-the-threshold position, and carried her to the hammock hung at the back of the yard. He carefully laid her in the hammock, and very carefully climbed in next to her.

"Have you ever had sex in a hammock?" he asked.

"*Can* people have sex in a hammock?"

They were both laughing, and then they were kissing, and buttons were unbuttoned, and bare flesh was exposed, and the hammock rocked wildly as they tried to slide off their garments. Only half-undressed, Bob tried to ease his way on top of Blythe, and his movements were enough to send the hammock into a swirl that dumped them both in the grass.

They lay there chortling, ridiculously pleased with themselves.

"You know," Bob said, "for the last ten minutes, I didn't think about Ginger at all."

"Me either!" Blythe said, which didn't really make sense, and they laughed at that.

Blythe's grandmother had told her over and over, "Be sure to marry a man who makes you laugh."

After a while, Bob helped Blythe up. The party house was in darkness now. Everyone had left while they were kissing in the hammock.

"We closed down the party," Blythe said.

"Now *that's* special," Bob said.

They walked to their Ubers and agreed to meet for lunch that afternoon. Blythe knew she wasn't in love with him, and he wasn't in love with her. They knew they were both rebound cases, but she felt less heartbroken and abandoned, and he was, really, a good guy.

They dated all that summer, meeting in Bob's apartment or at restaurants or pubs to share all the events of their day. They became lovers. Bob wasn't as romantic as Aaden had been, but he was more protective. Less dramatic, more tender. Less interested in poetry, more capable of reading the small print in documents. He took her arm when they crossed the street. When they walked down a sidewalk in Boston, he made sure to be on the outside, closer to the curb, so she'd never be spattered by a car passing in the rain. He never left her alone when they went to a cocktail party where she was a stranger. When she had her period, he brought her boxes of expensive chocolates and watched any Hallmark movie she chose, even though the movies often made her cry. He understood the boundaries and laws of the real world.

When Blythe was with Bob, she felt safe. She felt loved. There was no crazy, compelling energy between them, no blazing candle that would soon burn out. This love was different from what she felt for Aaden. Aaden's love had been like lightning. Bob's love was like the sun. She flourished in his love, and he flourished in hers.

After they'd been together a year, Bob proposed. They were on Nantucket, living with his father and mother in their enormous brick house on Fair Street, and they'd taken a picnic basket with them and beach towels and walked along Surfside Beach until they found a private spot. They tossed down the blanket, holding it in place with the basket and cooler.

"Why is the cooler so heavy?" she asked.

Bob opened it and brought out a bottle of champagne. "Probably because I brought this."

"Why?" she asked. It was late morning, and the sun was high and hot, but a salty breeze rippled over them. She was wondering whether she should put on her straw sun hat.

"Because I brought this," Bob said. And he held out a velvet box.

Blythe gasped. She didn't take the box right away but studied the man holding it. Her teddy bear, she often called him in bed, because he had a hairy chest and loved to snuggle with her. He never called her pet names, not *darling* or *dear* or *honeybun,* and she knew he never would. She had asked him one day, kiddingly, if for her next birthday he would bungee jump with her in Colorado. He'd considered this and told her that he'd do many things for her, but not bungee jumping. That was too extreme an experience for a thrill. She'd known right then that she loved this man, that they could make a good life together, that he would never ignore her, like her father did, or leave her, like Aaden had.

"Go on," she'd said that morning at the beach, "you have to say it."

Bob had looked so happy. "Blythe, will you marry me?"

She laughed and cried a little when she said, "Bob, I will."

He put the exquisite oval cut diamond on her finger.

"It fits perfectly!" She was truly surprised.

Almost bashfully, Bob admitted, "I took your turquoise ring to the jewelers to be sure it was the right size."

"Of course you did," Blythe said, and threw herself against him with such emotion they both fell backward on the towel. Bob was surprised when she lunged at him, and Blythe loved him even more because he'd been surprised.

relative love

Blythe took Bob to dinner with her parents, first making him promise he would not run screaming from the table after he met them.

It was a pleasant, bland occasion. Blythe told them she and Bob were engaged to be married. Her parents replied that they were finally moving to Arizona. They had already had movers pack everything Blythe had left in her room into boxes that were taken to a storage facility. They gave Blythe the keys.

As they pulled away from the house, Blythe said to Bob, "That was very 'Thanks for coming don't let the door hit you on your way out.' "

Bob had stopped the car at the curb and reached over to take Blythe in his arms. "I'll give you a home and I'll never kick you out."

Blythe didn't know whether to laugh or cry, so she did both.

"I love that I can trust you," she said, hugging him tight.

Back when they were spending their first spring together, they had gone to Nantucket and stayed at Blythe's grandmother's house. Now it was Blythe's house.

That weekend, it had rained, a thunderous soaking daylong deluge of rain, which made sleeping late in a bed with warm blankets especially enjoyable. When they finally rose, they made strong coffee with the sugar and cream Blythe had brought over with a bag of necessary groceries. Mugs in hand, they toured the house. Blythe was slightly embarrassed because the house was so old and eccentric. Some of the bedroom and bathroom doors locked with knob locks, some with ancient hook and eyes, some with small wedges of wood that could be turned to press against the doorjambs. In several rooms and in the kitchen, drawers in dressers or cupboards had become swollen shut from the island's humidity and couldn't be opened or could only be shut partway, with some of the drawers sticking out to catch you on the leg at night. The wallpaper in the master bedroom was probably seventy years old and ugly, great swoops of blue flowers tied with extravagant pink ribbons.

The sink in the master bedroom dripped constantly, steadily, turning the white porcelain into stained rust. The beautiful antique mahogany dining table that seated twelve stood on a wide-board floor that ever so faintly slid downward. Fat old books supported the legs at the far end of the table.

"This is a wonderful vacation house," Bob told Blythe, hugging her from behind, his chin resting on the top of her head. "I'm glad we won't have to stay with my parents or my sister."

Their first trip to the island, they arrived at nine in the evening. Bob told his parents they were staying at Blythe's house and would come over after breakfast the next day. They'd brought sandwiches and chips and an expensive bottle of champagne. The house was chilly because of the rain, so Bob made a fire in the living room fireplace and they discovered that excellent champagne and potato chips went well together.

That evening, he warned her about his sister. Kate was happily married to Jack, with a son, Chip, four, and a daughter, Melissa, two. Jack was a real estate broker. Kate belonged to clubs and boards and committees. They lived in a handsome mansion on Upper Main, not far from their parents' large, picture-book Victorian.

Bob loved his sister, he stressed, but said she was bossy, nosy, and ambitious. Although they shared a history of growing up together, he found it tiring just being around her. She had to be right about everything. She could argue until you fell off your chair in exhaustion.

"She sounds a bit scary," Blythe said.

"She is a bit scary," Bob said. "But she'll love you."

Blythe wasn't so sure.

Bob's mother was completely wonderful. When Blythe first met her, she couldn't stop smiling. Celeste was striking, with her stormy dark hair webbed with silver and her dark eyes deep with secrets. She was a hugger, a kisser, a toucher, and when she embraced Blythe on their first meeting, a slight perfume-scented breeze drifted past, and it was so much like the fragrance Blythe used that Blythe immediately felt at home. Celeste was the kind of mother Blythe wanted to be.

Celeste was, as she confessed, a book addict, and in order to have a decent meal occasionally, her husband, Bob's father, bought the groceries and made the dinner, usually grilling outdoors. The weekend they were there, Celeste did cook, because it rained constantly, and it turned out that she was an excellent cook, serving roasted salmon and vegetables. When she brought the strawberry shortcake, served on gold-rimmed antique Spode china, she also set a can of Reddi-wip on the table, because, she said, everyone enjoyed putting on their own whipped cream, swirling it into towers and peaks. Blythe wondered if Spode china had ever been paired with canned whipping cream before, and she suddenly and completely adored Celeste.

Celeste liked Blythe, too, which over the years became a problem for Bob's older sister, Kate. Kate was energetic and athletic, a first-rate sailor, golfer, and tennis player. She was the head of the yacht club's entertainment committee and sat on the boards of dozens of other town committees. She was a do-gooder, full of ideas, and she seemed to run on an innate fuel of competitiveness. She was driven to be first and best, and Blythe admired her, but found her overwhelming and exhausting.

Blythe and Bob wanted to be married on Christmas Day, but Kate strongly vetoed that idea, saying that it wasn't fair for her brother to kidnap Christmas.

"And think how it will ruin the holiday if you and Blythe get divorced!" Kate had cried.

How insulting! Blythe had thought. As if Blythe and Bob would ever get divorced.

Later, when they were alone, Blythe took Bob's hand in hers.

"Are we making a mistake? They say not to marry the rebound lover."

Bob looked crushed. "Who is *they*? And I certainly don't consider you my rebound lover." Grinning, he said, "I wasn't actually celibate during college."

"I guess I wasn't, either. But I never was serious with anyone. I was a very determined student. When I wasn't in class, I volunteered at a daycare center." She flashed on memories of college men who were dangerously good-looking, and men who were brilliant and boring. She'd guarded her heart very carefully.

Bob and Blythe were married on Nantucket on New Year's Eve. They honeymooned in Costa Rica. Blythe's parents came to their wedding. They stayed with Blythe in the large old house her grandmother left her. They were amiable and generous, and they returned to Arizona where Blythe's mother recovered from the damp air.

On their honeymoon, Blythe said, "I want to have three or four children."

Bob considered this with his lawyerly expression, stroking his chin as if he had a goatee there. "I want a big family, too! But maybe three? Four is a lot."

"Bob, I was an only child. I really would like four children, but if it means that much to you, I'll settle for three."

"Three children," Bob said. They did a high five.

Bob's father was a lawyer, although, as Holly once said, not the kind people hate. Bob followed in his footsteps, joining the Boston branch of his father's firm. With the whopping big check his parents gave them for a wedding present, they were able to buy a house in one of the tree-lined suburbs of Boston, where they lived with their growing brood most of the year.

In the summer and often at Christmas, the family stayed on Nantucket in the large, light-filled house that was now Blythe's. From the house, they could bike or walk to town or bump down the cobblestone lane to South Beach Street and the Jetties tennis courts, the Sandbar restaurant, and the long, wide expanse of golden beach gently sloping to the clear waters of Nantucket Sound.

And now here Blythe was, in her beloved Nantucket house, where she would once again sleep alone in her queen-sized bed as a cool night breeze drifted through an open window.

First, though, Blythe wanted to call Celeste, to tell her they were here and would be available for dinner tonight. She stretched out on her bed and opened her phone, eager to talk with her beloved mother-in-law.

Someone answered in a haughty voice. "Benedicts' house."

Bob's sister, Kate, was obviously at their mother's house, doing all she could to remind Blythe the extent of her reach.

But Blythe could play games, too.

Blythe made her voice dense with worry. "Oh, Kate! Is Celeste all right?"

"Of course, Celeste is all right!" Kate snapped. "Why are you even asking?"

"Oh, thank heavens. I'm so glad. You nearly gave me a heart attack. You sound so worried." Blythe continued, "How are you, Kate? Thank you so much for getting the house ready for us. It's so kind of you. I'd love to take you to lunch someday to thank you."

For a moment, Kate was speechless, an extremely rare state for her to be in, and Blythe gave herself an imaginary point.

"You're welcome," Kate said. "So, I guess you're all here."

"Yes. I was hoping to speak with your mother."

"I'll tell her you've arrived."

Blythe inhaled deeply. She often wished she took fencing lessons. "Could I speak to her for just a moment? I won't bother her for long."

The unspoken topic was tonight's dinner at the opening of the yacht club. Celeste always took Blythe and her grandchildren to dinner the first night the club opened. Before their divorce, Bob had come, too. But now Bob and Teri came later in the summer. Celeste adored her grandchildren and for seventeen years had made the first night on the island *their* night together, when she could pay attention to them. Blythe knew that Kate hated being left out, even though she lived on the island with her husband, Jack, and saw Celeste all the time and was often treated to dinner by Celeste.

Kate didn't answer Blythe but called out, "Mom. Blythe's here. She wants to talk to you."

"Thank you, darling. I found the shirt you asked for. I put it on the bed. I think there's a tear in the seam." Celeste's voice was distant and then right there. "Blythe! My love! You're here? And all the children?"

Celeste's voice had become slightly gravelly with age, but her affection warmed her words.

"Hi, Celeste. Yes, we're here. The children have already disappeared. Well, Holly's still here. She's in her room drawing."

"Oh, good. Please let Holly know I'd love it if she came over with her novel, because I had an idea about how she could get the sea gerbils onto the land. Maybe there is a land turtle who is obsessed with his reflection in the water and he falls in and the sea gerbils rescue him."

From the background, Kate snapped, "Mother, you sound insane."

Celeste continued, "I did think about deer, but they're too big. Also, rabbits, but I think if one fell into the ocean, he would drown with all that fur. Although, another possibility would be that the rabbit was born without fur, so he was considered a misfit and an outcast, and when he falls in, the sea gerbils immediately love him. He might look grotesque, but then Holly enjoys the grotesque."

Finally, Celeste took a breath.

Blythe smiled. She loved the connection between her youngest child and Celeste. "I'll tell Holly that, Celeste. Would it be okay if she comes over this afternoon to talk with you?"

"Of course! I'd love that! Also, we have reservations for the yacht club at seven."

From the background, Kate called, "Mom! Is this the shirt you mean?"

Blythe rolled her eyes. "I'll let you go, Celeste. See you tonight."

"Goodbye, darling."

Blythe waited until she'd ended the call to burst out laughing. Poor Kate! Her husband, Jack, had grown pompous and pudgy. Their daughter was in college and playing tennis, and their son was traveling. Kate didn't seem to have a special best friend on the island. Blythe wasn't surprised. Kate was hard work. Blythe pitied her helplessly irritating sister-in-law but she could never show it.

Shaking off thoughts of Kate, Blythe went into Holly's room, and sure enough, there her youngest daughter was, sitting on her bed, carefully drawing on her sketchpad.

"Hey, sweetie," Blythe said, sinking down on the end of the bed. "I just spoke with Grandmother. She would love it if you came by this afternoon. She has an idea about your novel."

Holly looked up at her mother, her brown eyes worried. "Mom, Daphne said the rising seas are going to flood the island and wash out all the beaches and destroy the town."

Blythe pulled Holly into a hug. "Daphne's right. But the thing is, it will happen gradually, over hundreds of years. The sea won't reach our house, or Grandmother's house, or Aunt Kate's, for a long, long time. Some of the buildings on the coast will have to be moved. But change is natural. Human beings are resilient." She could sense her daughter's tension. "Maybe this is something the sea gerbils can help with."

Holly turned, her face glowing. "You're right. I hadn't thought of that." Gathering her sketchbook and pencils, she said, "I'm going to Grandmother's now."

"Don't stay too long. We're going out to dinner at the yacht club tonight."

Next, Blythe called her best island friend, Sandy. Sandy taught art in the elementary school in Williamstown, and her husband, Hugh, was an art history professor at the college there. They had twin daughters who didn't give a fig about art because they were competitive athletes. At thirteen, Lara and Anne played baseball, soccer, tennis, and basketball. In the winter, they skied and skated. On Nantucket, they swam and sailed and belonged to a tennis team at the yacht club.

"I don't understand where they came from," Sandy often said. Sandy got motion sick on a boat or in a car and had terrible hand-eye coordination. Hugh could sail but preferred not to.

"Sandy," Blythe said happily when her friend answered her phone. "We're here!"

"Come over! Now!" Suddenly whispering, Sandy said, "Help me. We've put up the badminton net."

"I'll be right there," Blythe promised, laughing.

Sandy's house was only a few blocks away, and the walk was blissful. Blythe strode along brick sidewalks past huge houses with widow's walks and cupolas. Many of the homes had a flowered wreath on their front door, or flags from Ireland, Canada, Japan, whatever country their guests were from. The music of a Chopin nocturne drifted out from an open window, and as Blythe strolled past, beneath the shade of a majestic old maple, she remembered that the composer died when he was thirty-nine.

Chopin was in the last year of his life when Sandy's Greek Revival house was built in 1849. Would he have traded his eternal fame for a longer, less creative life?

Blythe laughed at herself. Such foolish thoughts she had when she was on the island.

"Blythe!" Sandy exploded from her front door, running like a young girl to catch Blythe in an exuberant hug. "Come inside. We'll sit in the living room. The little darlings have given up on me and gone down to the club."

"How are they?" Blythe asked as she went up the wide steps and into the expansive house where every room was a different color and paintings and hooks waiting for more new pictures decorated the rooms. Blythe settled on a sofa.

Sandy sat next to Blythe. "Energetic. How are *you*? You look wonderful."

"I'm good. Well, tired. The drive from Boston to the Sagamore Bridge went okay, but getting over the bridge took forever."

"I always thought *Sagamore* was an unfortunate name for a bridge," Sandy remarked. "I really don't want to be on a sagging more bridge."

"The important thing is that we're here." Blythe stretched luxuriously. "Another Nantucket summer."

"So, are you going to dinner at the yacht club with Celeste tonight?"

"Absolutely. I've already spoken to her. Will you be there?"

Sandy studied her nails and casually said, "Yes, Hugh and I will be there, too. We're taking a friend to dinner, Nick Roth. I don't think you've met him yet. He's a widower. Nice guy. Handsome, too."

Blythe groaned. "Please, not another fix-up. At least let me get my bags unpacked."

"When do Bob and Teri get here?"

"Not for a few weeks, I think. Truthfully, I'd be glad if they arrived tomorrow. I'd send Miranda over to stay with them and Celeste."

"What's up with Miranda?"

"She's in love with a guy at her school. Brooks Tillingham. *Brooks.* Why does that name make my teeth hurt? He's a nice guy and a star athlete. Captain of the football team. He sails, plays tennis, and is more handsome than he should be. I mean he knows he's handsome. He uses it."

"Miranda is beautiful," Sandy says. "Don't forget that. No guy could be more handsome than Miranda is beautiful."

"Yes, but . . . Miranda is so obsessed with him. I'm afraid he'll break her heart."

"Oh, Blythe, remember. We all get our hearts broken in high school."

"I certainly did."

"The wrestler."

"Yes. Aaden Sullivan." Saying his name sent a thrill through her. "I thought we'd be together forever. When he broke up with me, I was crushed."

"But you recovered. And if Brooks dumps Miranda, she will, too." Sandy rose. "Let's get some iced tea."

Blythe followed her friend into the kitchen and then, a glass of iced tea in hand, out to the back deck. Sandy's garden was beautiful—a work of art. Blythe drifted along the flower beds with Sandy, admiring the deep purple iris, the clusters of pansies with their sweet faces, the clematis sweeping up and over the picket fence, the petunias spilling from window boxes, and roses, deep blood-red roses, everywhere. The hydrangeas were just waking up from winter and the cold spring.

"This is luscious, Sandy. An overabundance. I don't know how you do it. Do your girls help weed and water?"

"Are you kidding? Flowers bore them. Look, they've set up the badminton net at the far end of the yard, and they'll be complaining all summer that it's so far away and they have to walk through 'all those plants' to get to it."

Sandy sat in a pale blue patio chair and Blythe took the red one.

"I'm finally getting to the part of my life where I feel at home," Sandy said. "My twenties were so confusing. I thought I'd study art in Paris. Live in a garret, bike everywhere with a baguette in my backpack, drink at Deux Magots. Then I met Hugh and entered another stage of life. Then the twins. It was so hard, the hardest thing in my life, those first few years when they were babies. God, all the nights I was up with them with a flu or croup or a tummy ache. It seems like years I walked with a child attached to each leg. Now they're thirteen, and obsessed with sports, and I can take a breath."

"Just wait," Blythe warned. "Once their hormones really hit, you'll wish they were toddlers again. I've taught seventh and eighth grade, so I thought I was prepared for teenagers, but when it's personal, it can be grueling." She laughed gently.

"Are you worried?" Sandy asked.

"For my kids? Of course. Also, I've been asked to teach full-time in our local middle school next year."

"You told me you enjoyed substituting there."

"Yes, but that's a completely different job. If I teach, I'm responsible for the kids *learning* something. I'd have to upscale my skills with technology. Girls are carrying their phones in their bra straps. Guys are playing video games in class. How much are they going to learn about what a comma is or *Catcher in the Rye*?"

"I'm completely certain that if you decide to teach full-time, you'll do a fabulous job. You always have."

"Maybe." Blythe stared down into her iced tea, as if to find the answer there.

After a moment, Sandy asked, "How's Daphne?"

Blythe smiled. "She's my rock. Wrapped up in her plans to save the world. She's already gone over to Maria Mitchell. I'm glad she's obsessed with environmental causes. She *is* scrawny. She eats well, but she hasn't filled out yet."

"And the others?"

"Holly is still sweet and easy. Teddy—he's thirteen. He's got hair on his upper lip and probably elsewhere, but I give him his privacy and hope that Bob tells him how to be a man. Shaving and deodorant and all that, whatever turns boys into men."

"Is it hard, seeing Bob with another woman?"

Blythe laughed. "To be honest, it's a relief. A few years ago, I told Miranda that her bad grades were going to make Bob blow a gasket. Teddy wanted to know what a gasket was, so I googled it. I told him, 'It's a mechanical seal which fills the space between two or more mating surfaces.' Teddy had laughed like a donkey at the term 'mating surfaces.' I wondered if that meant our children were gaskets filling the space between me and Bob. It kind of hit home, made me realize how drab our marriage was."

"All marriages are drab now and then," Sandy pointed out.

"Yes, but Bob and I were so distant from each other emotionally. We didn't hate each other, but we didn't love each other, either. Plus, I didn't like it that he was never home, never attended a child's recital or baseball game or doctor's appointment. We both knew we'd married too young, too fast. Someone said sometimes you have to marry the wrong person to get the right children, and that's the way we explained it to the kids. After three years, I think the kids are okay with everything. Although I think Teri might be embarrassing with her long bouncy hair and overflowing bikinis."

"She's gorgeous, Blythe. The men don't consider her embarrassing."

"I know. I do know. And I know she loves Bob more than I could. More than I did. I'm glad for Bob. Do you think men need bolstering as they get older, and women just relax?"

"I think some men need bolstering, but many women do, too. I get what you're saying, Blythe, but you're only forty-five."

Blythe stared into her iced tea for a moment. "I get it that you think I need a man in my life. Sex and love and all that. But honestly, Sandy, I'm just fine right now. I'm relaxed. Well, as relaxed as anyone can be with a houseful of teenagers."

"Aren't you lonely? Wouldn't you like, I don't know, someone on your side, someone who is interested in *you*? Someone to *hold* you?"

Blythe shrugged. "I can always hug Holly. Oh, I know what you mean, Sandy. You want me to *be with* someone because you and Hugh are so bonded. I'm just not sure that's for me. *Of course,* I cared for Bob when I married him, and I know he loved me, in a way. But we were young. We were a pair, two lost souls finding comfort and—normality. We were together, not alone. Somewhere along the way our lives became all about the children. It's like our marriage just wore out."

"Like a tire that's worn off its tread."

Blythe laughed. "Yes, just like that. We'd become co-chairs of our family. We're both happier now."

"You have to admit it's unusual for a divorce to be so easy."

"The hard part was staying together. We shared the children, but we were completely disinterested in each other. Last year when I was talking to Bob's mother, she told me that Bob was laughing again, the way he had laughed as a boy, full-hearted, happy. She hadn't heard him laugh like that for years."

"But what about you? Bob's got Teri but you're not seeing anyone. You ought to at least have a fling this summer."

Blythe leaned over and hugged Sandy. "You're such a good friend. Thank you for worrying about me. But I'm fine. I'm going to swim and lie in the sun and read every beach read I can find. I don't have to worry about the kids. Well, I always have to worry about the kids, but they're pretty independent these days. And you know what? It's fun watching them grow up. Finding out what it is in life that captures their interest."

"Maybe this summer someone will catch your interest."

"Maybe." Blythe closed her eyes and lifted her face to the sun. She wanted to tell someone about the man kissing Teri. She couldn't tell Kate. Kate would somehow make it Blythe's fault. She couldn't tell Celeste. The older woman didn't need to deal with something so peculiar and upsetting. But what did it mean? What did it mean for the stability of her children's lives? Blythe couldn't get it out of her head.

"What are you thinking about?" Sandy asked. "Or should I say who?"

Blythe opened her eyes and stood. Her foot hit her iced tea glass and knocked it over. The liquid quickly sank into the grass, the ice cubes glittering.

"I was thinking that I should go home and unpack and organize the house," Blythe said. "Sorry I babbled on so much, but it's your fault. You asked. Next time I'll ask about you."

"I'm not nearly as interesting as you are," Sandy said.

"That's not true," Blythe objected. "You have twins."

They rose and strolled slowly together through Sandy's garden and into the shade of the house. They lingered in the doorway, discussing the weather for the week and their plans, and then Blythe kissed Sandy's cheek and went down the front steps and walked home.

yacht club dinner

At six-thirty, Blythe stood in the front hall.

She called out, "Is everyone ready?"

She often wished she had a big brass gong to bang to get her children's attention.

The yacht club tennis courts were ready in late May, but the dining room didn't open until early June. Tonight was the first dinner in the beautiful Fair Winds Room and it would be packed.

Most important, this was their traditional first night dinner with Celeste.

Blythe knew that Celeste loved her grandchildren so much she wouldn't criticize them if they wore their pajamas into the yacht club dining room, but she knew how proud Celeste was of her grandchildren, and Blythe wanted to keep her mother-in-law happy because she was a wonderful woman and a good friend.

She also knew that her children adored their grandmother and would dress appropriately because they wanted to please her.

Holly showed up first, wearing the pretty blue dress with the white collar that Blythe loved. Teddy arrived dressed in a button-down shirt and khakis because he knew the rules. Daphne, fifteen, slouched in wearing a sundress and holding a book in her hand with a finger marking her place. Finally, Miranda sauntered in, clad in a very short Zara denim dress that showed off her long legs but met Blythe's standards because it was a dress, and it covered her belly button at least. Blythe wasn't going to quarrel with her oldest child because it was their first Nantucket dinner together and maybe their only dinner together at the club.

Now Blythe announced, "It's a beautiful evening. Let's walk to the club!"

It *was* a beautiful evening, still bright at six-thirty, warm but not humid, an invitation to summer, and the summer house was only five blocks from the club.

Miranda begged, "Please, Mom, let's go in the car."

Blythe wanted the evening to be pleasant, so she held back a sarcastic remark about how impossible it would be for Miranda to walk far in that tight, short dress. She said easily, "Okay, we'll do that."

The children piled into the minivan, every single one of them doing something on their phones, as if this were their last opportunity before cellphones became illegal. Blythe drove them all to the club's parking lot, waved at Eddie O'Brian, the attendant at the gate, and searched for an open spot among all the Jeeps, Range Rovers, and convertibles. They ended up parking at the far end of the lot, and they were lucky to get that. Everyone would be here tonight.

As they entered the club, three children surged ahead to greet their old summer friends. Miranda stayed by Blythe's side, obsessed with her phone.

"No phones in the dining room," Blythe told her.

Tossing her head with exasperation, Miranda slid the phone into her clutch. The great open hall of the club was filled with clusters of people, everyone greeting everyone else with cries of delight. Some of the club members had known one another since they were children. Blythe spotted Carolyn Post in the distance. She was Holly's best summer friend, and they waved enthusiastically at each other. Joy lit her heart. Was there anything better than seeing a child happy?

Finally, Blythe stood before the podium. Horace White, the maître d' of the Fair Winds dining room, was a tall, handsome man with silver hair and a commanding presence.

"Hello, Mrs. Benedict, so happy to see you again."

"Good to see you, Horace. How's your summer so far?"

"Very good, thank you."

He showed them to a round table for six. Celeste was already seated there, at her preferred spot in the corner. She always asked for this table because she was slightly deaf and the large dining room, even with its high ceiling, was noisy. Anyway, it suited her, and she probably knew, although she'd never say so, that she enjoyed being enthroned at the large table, with its white cloth, shining silver, and candles. Both Daphne and Teddy had been blessed with the same dramatic dark eyes and hair that Celeste had passed along to her son, Bob. Miranda and Holly had Blythe's less intense coloring, light brown hair and eyes. Celeste wore a turquoise silk dress and a lime silk jacket. She wore *her* mother's silver earrings and necklace. Blythe had seen pictures of Celeste when she was young, and she had been breathtaking. Even now, she hadn't acquired too many old-age wrinkles and lines, but her skin was speckled with brown spots. They were not malignant, she had told her family, so she wasn't going to bother with them. Her entire beauty regime was washing her face and smoothing on Pond's Cold Cream.

Now Celeste rose from her chair to embrace her grandchildren, one by one. When they finally took their seats, the four children fought—in a quiet, pleasant way, to sit next to their grandmother. Miranda and Teddy, the oldest, won, but then Teddy took pity on his little sister and gave Holly his seat. He and Daphne were doomed to sit on either side of Blythe.

The waiter arrived and handed them menus. Before they could check the offerings, they were deluged by a wave of summer friends. Holly jumped up to talk with Carolyn, and Daphne left her chair to make a quick visit to Lincoln's table. The other kids teased Daphne about having a boyfriend, but Lincoln, handsome as an angel, had come out a couple of years ago. Daphne had bonded with him over the problem of rising seas, and everyone hoped they would provide the solution. Teddy talked with his grandmother, and Blythe was left with Miranda, who had mastered the blank fifty-yard stare.

Celeste and Blythe each ordered champagne, as they always did the first meal of summer.

"And for you?" The waiter smiled at Miranda. He was tall, handsome, and tanned, with a strong Southern accent.

"Maybe a glass of tonic over ice?" Miranda was implying, Blythe knew, that her usual tonic drink had gin in it.

"Of course," the waiter said, smiling.

For a few seconds, the waiter and Miranda locked eyes.

Bless you, Andrew, Blythe wanted to say, because if Miranda could flirt with Andrew, whose name and town were printed on a white club label on his jacket, then Miranda wasn't completely obsessed with Brooks.

"So, Andrew, you're from Charleston," Blythe said.

"Yes, ma'am, I attended UVA and I'm going into their business master's program."

Blythe said, "That's impressive."

"Thank you. I'll be right back with your drinks."

"Mom," Miranda whispered. "I don't need you to find guys for me. I'm with Brooks, remember?"

"Miranda, I've always talked with the summer staff. I want them to feel at home."

"Find one who'll feel at home with Daphne," Miranda muttered.

Holly and Daphne returned to the table in time to give Andrew their orders and then Daphne shared the latest news from Lincoln about the various storms that had flooded the island. Friends in Polpis, on the inner harbor, had had water up to the decks of their summer cottages. Not for the first time, boys had paddled kayaks down some of the streets in town. Blythe shared what she'd read in various island newsletters about possible solutions, and there had to be solutions because, if not, so many of the town's structures were doomed to become submerged, slowly, but absolutely. Because the yacht club was on the water—of course it was, that was the purpose of the yacht club—this was a problem of monumental importance. All four children talked at once, offering their visions of a deluged and ruined Main Street and what the town ought to do to prevent this.

"It is happening sooner than we think," Celeste told them. "I belong to a committee exploring various possibilities for saving the town. Unfortunately, there are many committees like ours, and none of us has a solution. I'm going to Boston for a few days in September to attend a conference on rising seas."

"Cool," Teddy said.

Celeste patted her mouth with her napkin, effectively hiding her smile, but her eyes danced with mischief. "I'll be going with my new friend, Roland Wilson."

All four children glanced at one another, unsure what to do with this information.

"Is his wife coming, too?" Daphne asked.

"Roland's wife died a few years ago. She was a lovely woman."

For a long moment, everyone was quiet, assessing this information.

Holly broke the silence. "Is he your *boyfriend*?"

At that moment, Andrew arrived at the table. He set drinks before them all, then stood with his notepad. "May I ask who is signing tonight?"

"I am," Celeste replied.

The table was hushed as Celeste signed the ticket. Andrew asked if they were ready to order.

"We are," Blythe said, trying to give her children a moment to recover from their grandmother's news—and needing a moment herself. *Was* Roland Wilson Celeste's boyfriend? If so, what on earth did that mean?

Ordering took some time, because Daphne considered herself a vegetarian except for bacon, and Holly didn't understand what bluefish pâté was, and Teddy ordered scallops wrapped in bacon for an appetizer and salmon for his entrée, and Daphne added the scallops in bacon to her order but told everyone she felt guilty. Miranda wanted a dish that had no meat or pasta, because, she whispered to Blythe, she felt bloated, so finally she ordered three side dishes of vegetables, and added, at the last moment, the scallops wrapped in bacon, because as she said to Blythe, scallops had no calories. She didn't mention the bacon. The dining room had three walls of long, wide windows overlooking the slope of lawn to the dock and the harbor. It was still light, so they could see the American flag and the yacht club burgee flying from the flagpole at the end of the lawn. Only a few boats were moored in the harbor because it was June, and tonight the wind was calm, so the outside looked cool and serene compared to the warm buzzing conversation in the dining room.

Celeste was in a serious discussion with Holly about sea gerbils. Miranda was pretending to listen, which was good of her. Daphne and Teddy were discussing the cast of a new sci-fi show. Blythe leaned back in her chair and took a deep breath. They were here. They were all here, and no one had left her mouthguard or bathing suit back home, and how fortunate she was, to have an evening like this. As she glanced around the room, Blythe saw several summer friends, mothers who had children the same age as Blythe's.

A handsome white-haired man wearing a navy blazer and white flannels approached the table.

Celeste sparkled. "Roland! How nice to see you." Reaching out, she took his hand.

"Everyone, this is my friend Roland."

Introductions were made with all the children, and under the table Daphne knocked her knee against Blythe's knee and wiggled her eyebrows at her mother.

"Can you join us?" Celeste asked Roland.

Daphne bugged her eyes out at Blythe. The children considered this *their* night with their grandmother.

"I wish I could, but I'm here with Henry Manning, and I'd rather not leave him alone. But some other time, I hope." Roland smiled at Blythe.

"It's lovely to meet you, Roland," Blythe said. "I hope we see you again soon."

Daphne knocked her knee against Blythe's again.

As soon as Roland had walked off, Holly said, "He's *cute,* Grandmother!"

Celeste twinkled a bit. "I certainly think so."

As her children gabbled away with each other about their grandmother's friend, Blythe reminded herself that her life was full. She was happy, and aware that now was the time for her to let her children grow up while keeping them safe. She didn't have to have a boyfriend as well. Still . . .

"Madam?"

Blythe looked up. The gorgeous Andrew was bending toward her, a dinner plate in his hand.

"Oh, thank you." Blythe leaned back so that he could place the plate in front of her.

She'd been distracted from the bright, buzzing world she was living in, and she wanted to "be here now." They were on Nantucket. Tonight was the beginning of summer.

"Mmm," Celeste hummed. "This looks delicious. Bon appétit, everyone."

The dining room, especially Blythe's table, grew quiet when the meals were served. Tender filet mignon, delicate cod, risotto with carrots, green beans, and broccoli for the vegetarians, salmon with a mint sauce. Ernest, the club's chef, was adept and obsessive and his meals made the diners moan appreciatively. Other clubs in the country had tried to steal him, but he was loyal and had been the yacht club chef for nine years. Bob and his friends used to joke that they all hoped they died before Ernest did.

Holly interrupted her meal to ask, "Grandmother, *is* Roland Wilson your boyfriend?"

Celeste smiled mischievously. "Darling, I think I'm far too old to have a *boyfriend*."

Daphne, who would probably be a lawyer like her father, asked, "Well, then is Roland Wilson your *lover*?"

Holly giggled with surprise. "Daphne!"

Miranda's head whipped toward Blythe to see if she would correct Daphne. Teddy stared at his older sister with wide eyes. Daphne held her head high. Blythe wondered if she should say something or let Celeste handle it.

Celeste smiled calmly at Daphne, but her eyes were sharp. "I'm not certain that's a question I'm obligated to answer."

Daphne was like a terrier. "I've actually spent some time trying to find synonyms for the word 'boyfriend' and the most appropriate ones are 'suitor' and 'beau,' which I think are outdated. The other suggestion is 'escort,' which I think has tasteless connotations. Is there a word you would prefer I use?"

Blythe shifted uncomfortably in her chair. She didn't think Daphne was being insolent, but she was overstepping the line, some invisible, unwritten line, with her grandmother.

"Why don't we simply call Roland my friend," Celeste said gently, and returned to her plate.

The rest of the meal passed without incident, and after dessert, the four children were allowed to leave the table and roam the club, finding friends from last year.

Blythe took her coffee and moved to sit next to her ex-mother-in-law.

"I feel like I should apologize for Daphne's rudeness."

Celeste set her cup of cappuccino back in the saucer. "I don't think she was being rude. I do think she's being influenced by Teri."

An unexpected kind of happiness flowered inside Blythe. Celeste rarely criticized her son's new partner.

"Really? In what way?"

"Oh, she doesn't mean to do it on purpose. I think it's just that Teri is younger and this is the vernacular of her age group. Once 'fuck' became a commonplace term, other words followed. And Daphne made a good point. She is sharp and she has done what you might call her due diligence."

Blythe stirred her coffee, thinking. "Daphne *is* smart. Her grades are amazing. I haven't been worried about her. She's so interested in marine biology. I didn't even think she might be aware of words like 'lover.' "

"Blythe, darling, Daphne is *fifteen*. She probably knows more about sex than we do." When Blythe looked shocked, Celeste added, "I don't mean she's *had* more sex. I mean she's read about it, seen it in movies, on the internet, on TikTok. You can google anything these days."

"Still . . ." Blythe's mind struggled to understand Celeste's statement. "What should I do? Am I hopelessly old-fashioned?"

"Not hopelessly so," Celeste replied. "But if you *are* old-fashioned, don't change. You have your standards. I've always admired you for that. Not buying sugary cereal for the children's breakfast. Not letting each child have a television in his or her room, like many other parents do. And so on."

Blythe chuckled. "Now they have laptops and phones. Who knows what they're watching while I'm driving."

For twenty years, Blythe had maintained a cordial relationship with Celeste. The older woman had been welcoming when Bob brought Blythe home that first time and as the years passed, they had entered into a true friendship. Celeste had been generous, helpful, and kind while never once interfering in Blythe's parenting decisions. That was rare, Blythe's friends told her. One friend's mother-in-law was upset because she was nursing her babies. Another one's mother-in-law was upset because she *wasn't* nursing her babies. One woman was upset because her daughter-in-law had only two children. Another was angry because her daughter-in-law had *too many* children.

Blythe knew she was lucky in the mother-in-law sweepstakes. Last year, Celeste had surgery and needed assistance as she recovered. Her husband had died the year before, so Celeste was alone. Blythe had left the children with Bob and spent a week on the island, helping Celeste gradually return to her normal strength and energy. During those days and nights, Blythe and Celeste had talked, shared secrets, laughed and cried together. During those days and nights, Blythe and Celeste weren't in-laws, they were two women, with secrets and sorrows and joy and hope.

Three years ago, when Bob and Blythe had sat together with Celeste and Robert and told them they were divorcing, Bob's parents had been surprised and confused.

Bob's father had asked his son, "Is there another woman?"

Bob smiled, sounding cocky when he answered. "Not yet."

Robert had flushed scarlet. "This is not a situation to take lightly."

Blythe had rushed in to smooth the troubled waters. "Robert, Bob and I are not unfaithful to each other. We're simply . . . aware that we have changed, and we want different things in life."

"That's selfish," Robert barked. "You're not thinking of your children."

"Actually, we are, Dad."

Blythe came to her husband's defense. "It's true. We think our children will be happier when we're happy. When we're really alive."

Celeste's response had been a gift. "Robert. Remember how you always wished your parents had been divorced instead of being miserable together all their lives?"

"That was different," Bob's father pointed out. "Mother was a hypochondriac and Father was an alcoholic."

"Darling, things change." Celeste reached over to pat her husband's hand.

"Things always change," Robert grumbled.

Later, Blythe called her parents in Arizona to break the news.

"The divorce rate in the United States is about forty percent," her father told her. "I'm not surprised."

Her mother asked, "Are you okay? Do you need anything?"

"I'm fine," Blythe answered. "I'm better than fine."

Bob moved out of the house. Blythe watched and listened to her children carefully, trying to ease the shock of the change. The older ones had friends with divorced parents and took it in their stride, but Holly was sad and confused, and Blythe asked Bob if he could spend some special time with their youngest child. When Bob introduced them to his new friend Teri, they shamelessly bought the children's affections by giving them each the newest computer game or iPhone. After a few weeks, Blythe invited Bob and Teri to the house for a drink before the new couple took the four children out to dinner. The three adults sat in the living room drinking white wine and discussing the weather, the Red Sox, and the current British royal family scandal. It had been a tense but pleasant meeting, and the children gaped at the adults as if they were a new specimen from a lab.

Two years ago, Bob's father died suddenly. Bob and Blythe took turns flying to Nantucket to help Celeste. For the memorial service, Bob and Blythe attended together with their children. For the next few months, Bob went to the island to help his mother with estate matters, although his father had, not surprisingly, taken care to be clear and specific with his will.

After that, when Bob returned to his life with Teri, Blythe invited Celeste to stay with her and the children for a week or two. During that week, Blythe and Celeste hadn't talked about Bob and Teri, just enjoyed each other's company. But the night before Celeste returned to Nantucket, after all the children were in bed and asleep, Celeste sat at the kitchen table with Blythe sipping Irish coffees.

"You know," Celeste had said, "I'm going to have to be nice to Teri."

The alcohol in the coffee was making Blythe maudlin. "I'm no longer your daughter-in-law."

"No," Celeste had agreed. "But you are now the friend of my heart."

"Oh, that's lovely." Blythe tried to sniff back her tears.

"I'm also the grandmother of your children just as you are the mother of my grandchildren," Celeste had reminded Blythe.

surprise

Now, Blythe sat with her ex-mother-in-law at the round table looking out at the yacht club's dining room and foyer. Some people were still eating. Others were drinking coffee and chatting. The air carried the aromas of good food and the soft melodies of conversation.

Blythe leaned toward Celeste. "Talk to me. Pretend you're telling me something serious. For example, someone we know died this year."

Celeste understood immediately and turned her face to Blythe. "Who are you trying to avoid?"

"Sandy Green. She told me she's bringing a man to dinner tonight and he's widowed, and she wants me to meet him."

"Ah." Celeste quickly eyed the room. "I think that the man with the short hair is Hugh Green, Sandy's husband, which means that the man with them, the man with wide shoulders is— Goodness, Blythe, you should meet him. He looks awfully nice."

Blythe chuckled. "I'll meet him after you tell me if Roland Wilson is your boyfriend."

"We haven't slept together, if that's what you mean. We're companions. Good companions. We'll share a hotel room in Boston, but the room has two beds."

"Okay," Blythe interrupted Celeste. "Here they come."

Sandy, her husband, Hugh, and their friend Nick arrived at the table. Sandy introduced everyone. Nick bent toward Celeste and shook her hand, giving Blythe a moment to study him. He was tall and broad-shouldered, handsome, tanned, athletic. Kind of Superman with a Clark Kent vibe. His eyes were a shade of honey ringed with cocoa, matching his shaggy, sun-streaked brown hair.

"And this is my best friend Blythe," Sandy said.

Nick turned to Blythe. "Hello." He had a beautiful voice.

"Hello," Blythe said, and held out her hand. When she laid her palm in his, his fingers closed around her hand as if sending a secret code. Blythe blinked in surprise. Deep inside her, neglected chemicals woke up and raced around, rearranging and flinging themselves, ricocheting in her brain and body like sparkling jewels exploding from rocks. *Well, hello,* she thought.

"Won't you join us?" Celeste asked.

Nick took the chair next to Blythe, and when he sat, his knee skimmed hers.

"What have you been doing on this beautiful day?" Celeste asked.

"We spent the day sailing," Hugh said.

"That's why they've got sunburns," Sandy added.

That gave Blythe a reason to stare at Nick. He *was* sunburned, and he was beautiful, in an outdoor guy kind of way.

Nick's eyes met Blythe's and held. She felt warm all over, as if she'd just come in out of the cold.

"Nick's a middle school teacher!" Sandy announced, as eager as a mother introducing her child to a new classroom. "Plus, he's a musician!"

Celeste leaned toward Nick. "How wonderful! What do you play?"

Nick gave his attention to Celeste. "Guitar, mostly. Also, fiddle. I sing sea shanties. I'll be performing for the children at the club sometime this summer."

"Can adults attend?" Celeste asked.

"If they want," Nick answered, and he looked back at Blythe.

"I'm not attending," Hugh said. "My summer's already booked."

Sandy nudged Hugh. "Right. Golf. Tennis. Sailing."

Hugh extended his arm over the back of Sandy's chair in a playful hug. "You've reserved me for plenty of your evening activities. Cocktails. Dances. Parties."

How lucky they are, Blythe thought, watching her friend and her husband talk.

"Is *your* summer booked?" Nick asked. He looked at her as if she were the only person in the room.

Inside her torso, just above her belly button, those chemicals were still fizzing around, ricocheting off her heart. They made Blythe coo, "Well, I know I'm going to attend a concert." She sounded so flirtatious, she shocked herself. She reined herself in. "I mean, Sandy probably told you, I've got four children to feed and chauffeur, so that will keep me busy."

"Maybe you can find some time to show me the island," Nick said.

"I'd like that. But won't Hugh be showing you around? You're staying with the Greens, right?"

"I am. But Hugh's island will be different from your island. I mean, we each have our own versions of the island."

"I hadn't thought of it quite that way," Blythe said. If she leaned any closer to Nick, she'd fall right into his lap. She straightened. "I do have some favorite spots." She blushed. *Did that sound sexual?* Because for the first time in months—years!—she felt sexually awake. "How long will you be here?"

"I hope to come back often. I live in a suburb of Boston, so I can come and go whenever I want."

He had long eyelashes, the sort of eyelashes women always said should belong to a girl. He had a cowlick at the back of his head. Why were cowlicks so adorable?

"Let me give you my phone number," Nick said. "And if you'll give me yours, we can make some plans."

"Good idea." Now she knew she was blushing. When was the last time a man asked for her number? She reached into her small evening clutch and took out her phone.

"Give me yours and I'll add my number."

As they exchanged phones, their hands brushed. Blythe knew she was glowing like a candle. *I have to stop smiling,* she thought.

But she couldn't stop smiling.

At her side, Celeste straightened in her chair, placing her napkin on the table. "I'm sorry to cut the evening short, but I need an early bedtime tonight." She rose. "Sandy and Hugh, it's great to see you again. Nick, I'm pleased to meet you. I hope you'll come by the house often."

Nick rose. "It's been a pleasure."

"A pleasure," Blythe echoed, smiling.

The others at the table rose with Celeste.

Blythe pulled herself together. "Celeste, we'll walk you out."

Blythe strolled arm in arm with Celeste from the dining room into the large foyer with its walls hung with bulletin boards packed with sign-up sheets for doubles tennis and posters about the first summer dance.

They spotted Holly sitting by herself in one of the puffy navy-blue armchairs in the foyer.

"Everyone else went into town," Holly said. "Carolyn had to go home with her family. I guess I want to go home, too."

Celeste said, "Rose Waterstone's over there. I'll chat with her a little before I walk home." She kissed Blythe's cheek. "That was a nice turn of events, don't you think?"

"It was a lovely evening," Blythe said.

"And I haven't seen you glow like that for a long time." Celeste bent to hug Holly. "We'll talk more tomorrow."

"I *glowed*?" Blythe was amazed.

"You're still glowing," Celeste said. "Good night, sweethearts." She walked over to her friend and was quickly chatting and laughing.

Blythe wrapped her arm around her youngest child's shoulders. "It's just you and me, babe."

For a moment, mother and daughter waited and watched as several families with young children passed by. A small girl squealed with pleasure as her father swung her up onto his shoulders. A boy of seven or eight gabbled excitedly to his mother about the sailboat they'd just come from. A little girl in a blue gingham dress and braids skipped along, each parent holding a hand.

Blythe sighed, remembering the days when her children considered her their hero, their best friend. The days when Miranda was small and adored them both. And as the two oldest children grew more independent and less adoring, along came Teddy and then Holly.

One day when Teddy was three, he told Blythe that he was her *cuddlemum*.

"Where did you learn that word?" Blythe had asked her little boy.

"I didn't learn it! I *made* it! I made my own word!" Teddy had been wide-eyed with astonishment at his achievement.

Blythe remembered all the nights when she and Bob lay in bed sharing anecdotes about their children, their magical children. After a bath, when their hair was damp and fragrant with baby shampoo and they were wrapped in towels, when they giggled as Blythe played a game on their toes as she dried between them—such small things! Such small moments! Now she knew they had been some of the happiest moments in her life. And back then, when she was tucking her children into bed, she was probably thinking about whether or not she would still fit into her blue dress for the party she and Bob were going to that weekend. Her mind would be in two places at once, and often it still was, and sometimes she yearned to be back in that world, but then she'd remember how exhausted she'd been, trying to decide whether Daphne's rash required a visit to the doctor, or whether she should talk to Bob about buying a new dishwasher.

Beside her, Holly was chattering about the land turtles her grandmother had spoken about at dinner. "Land turtles are a brilliant idea, because they could be kind of like taxis for the sea gerbils, when they come out onto the beach to explore."

Blythe wanted to show her daughter that she was as interested in sea gerbils as Celeste.

"Maybe they could meet a seagull and he could fly the sea gerbils around the island," she suggested.

Holly broke into a fit of giggles. "Mom! That's crazy. Gulls would eat sea gerbils!"

"Right." Blythe pretended to laugh, but really, in a way, her feelings were hurt. If Celeste had made that suggestion, she thought, Holly would have loved it! But Blythe realized how silly it was for her to have her feelings hurt over a discussion of sea gerbils.

Then Blythe looked up and saw, backlit by the outdoor lamps, the first man she had ever loved.

Aaden Sullivan. Her high school crush. Even after she'd married Bob twenty years ago and loved him as well as she could, she'd disciplined herself to ignore any thought of Aaden from her mind. She hadn't looked him up on any social media or googled him. She hadn't asked anyone about him. She hadn't attended any of her high school reunions, but that was because she'd always been pregnant or rearing children. (And she'd always wondered why people said "*rearing* children" because that word brought to her mind an image of a horse on its hind legs, its forelegs waving threateningly in the air, about to come down on you and slash you or wheel around and gallop around the field in a fit of wildness. Which, she realized, could be a description of what some days with children felt like.)

"Mommy?"

Blythe looked down at Holly, who was no longer babbling on about sea gerbils.

"Why aren't we walking, Mommy?"

Blythe tried to laugh charmingly, in case Aaden heard her. "Oh, sweetie, I think there's a man out there who I knew so long ago in high school."

"Is he a nice man?" Holly asked. "Because you look weird."

"Well, thank you so much for pointing that out," Blythe said, making a face at Holly.

Holly giggled and made a face back. Usually, because she was eleven, she considered herself too old to act silly, but clearly Holly was as elated as the rest of them to be on the island at the beginning of summer, plus, she was alone with her mother, which didn't happen very often.

Blythe's mind was rushing with those thoughts when she heard a man say, "Blythe? Is that you?"

She knew that voice so well. The huskiness, the bass tone, the slight accent, woke up parts of her anatomy she'd forgotten she had.

"Aaden! My goodness! What a surprise!" *My goodness?* she thought. She sounded like someone's Great-Aunt Myrtle.

Aaden wore tennis whites. Blythe couldn't *not* notice his spectacular muscles and his perfect tan. She felt shivery all over, like a debutante being approached by a prince.

He walked up to her and kissed her quickly on her cheek. He smelled of warm cotton and sunshine.

"And who is this lovely person?" Aaden asked, smiling at Holly.

Before Blythe could speak, her daughter announced proudly, "My name is Holly Benedict and I am a graphic novelist, the fourth of four children and the third girl. My mother is divorced, but she owns our Nantucket house."

Aaden answered, "I'm very pleased to meet you, Holly Benedict. I'm Aaden Sullivan. I was a good friend of your mother in high school.

I have two daughters, but my wife and I are divorced and my daughters are traveling all around the world."

Holly said, "Ooooooooooh."

Quickly, before Holly hijacked the complete conversation, Blythe asked, "Do you have a house on the island, Aaden?"

"Unfortunately, I do not. Fortunately, I'm staying with a good friend."

Immediately Blythe envisioned his friend, a sexy, dark-haired socialite with a wicked backhand, a short tennis skirt, a flat stomach, and an aristocratic overbite.

Blythe cocked her head perkily. "You're staying for a month?"

"Yes. Arnie tells me I can stay as long as I want."

The toothy aristocrat vanished into thin air. Blythe beamed. "We should meet for coffee sometime."

"How about tomorrow?" Aaden still had black magic eyes.

"Um, I'm not sure . . . the kids have such complicated schedules—"

Holly interrupted, obviously trying to be helpful. "I'll probably be with Grandmother tomorrow."

"Why not come have lunch with us at our house?" Blythe knew she was being cowardly. If the children weren't around, if she was alone with Aaden, she would probably kiss him. They were both divorced! She would definitely kiss him.

What was going on with her tonight? Only a few moments ago, she was practically drooling over Nick.

Aaden raked his hand carelessly through his thick dark hair.

Blythe remembered clutching that hair when they were together, kissing passionately.

Aaden grinned, as if he'd read her thoughts. "I'd like that. What time is good?"

"Oh, any time around noon," Blythe told him.

"We live on India Street," Holly told him. "Number thirty-four."

"I'll see you then."

Aaden leaned forward and kissed Blythe's cheek again. She felt his breath, his nearness, and she wanted to take his face between her two hands and move his mouth to her lips.

Instead, she forced herself to smile. “Okay, then, see you.” She took Holly’s hand and walked away, out of the club, into the sensible air, and through the lot to their minivan.

Holly swung Blythe’s hand. “He’s cute.”

“Oh, you think so?” Blythe winked at her daughter. A moment later, she wished she hadn’t winked. Quickly she changed the subject. “How’s Carolyn?”

“Oh, Mom, she has a puppy! One of those poodle doodles, she has photos on her phone, he’s all fat and curly and I’m going over to her house tomorrow to see him, his name’s Buddy, because he’s her very own buddy, and I told Grandmother I’d go to her house for lunch tomorrow and then we’ll work on the novel, and *oh no*! If I have lunch at Grandmother’s, I won’t get to see Aaden Sullivan! Is it all right for me to call him Aaden instead of Mr. Sullivan? He told me his first name . . .”

Blythe smiled as Holly babbled on and on. She always tried to let Holly talk all she wanted because when she was smaller, and probably now as well, her older sisters and brother spoke so loudly Holly could never get a word in. They referred to Holly as “the child.” If she’d told them the house was on fire, they wouldn’t have paid attention.

Only now was the light slipping away from the sky. Streetlights and house lights blinked on, and in the gentle dusk, the world magically became smaller, like a stage light shrinking the world down to a circle around the two of them, going home in the minivan, past lawns bordered by flowers whose perfume grew stronger with the arrival of darkness. Blythe remembered how it had been with Aaden, in his car, wrapped around each other, and nothing else in the world had mattered, all of the meaning of life had been right there, enclosing the two of them as they touched.

crushes

When Blythe woke the next morning, the children were all up, running through the house, talking on their phones, playing video games. It was their second day on Nantucket. It was June, with the normal pleasant temperature hovering around seventy-five, so Blythe put on her favorite shirt in all the world, a large cotton button-down in faded blue, and white shorts.

Aaden was coming for lunch today.

But first, Brooks was arriving.

She'd met Brooks several times before, and she liked him. He was dangerously handsome with blond hair and blue eyes and a slim build. He was on the football team and the soccer team and he was smart, too. He carried himself with a gentle confidence instilled in him from birth. His parents were executives at an international bank, and Brooks had traveled in several countries and spoke three languages, counting English.

Blythe tidied the kitchen. She went into the family room with the television and the couches. Here the large antique cupboard stood, full of board games and playing cards and, on the bottom shelf, sheets, blankets, and pillows for overnight guests. She was certain they would use them at least once more this summer when Holly had a sleepover with her friends. But tonight, and for the next month, Miranda's boyfriend, Brooks, would sleep here.

Miranda came crashing downstairs, wearing a cropped T-shirt and low-rise shorts that showed off her belly button with its fake diamond.

"Mother! Teddy is still *sleeping*! Brooks arrives on the ten-thirty ferry and Teddy will come slobbering down at noon, half-naked, burping, pouring his cereal all over the table!"

Blythe hid her amusement. She knew how important Brooks was to Miranda. How could she not? She'd been thinking of her own first love. She put her hands on her daughter's shoulders, steadying her.

"Miranda, Brooks knows how guys are. Brooks is staying here for a month, so he'll see Teddy all the time. But the only thing Brooks will be looking at is you, and you are always beautiful."

Miranda blinked back her tears. "Thanks, Mom. Sorry I'm such a freak-out. I just love him so much."

Blythe gave herself a moment of peace before saying, "Everything's ready for Brooks to sleep in the family room tonight?"

In an instant, Miranda transformed into a monster. She jerked away from Blythe's hands. "*Mom!* We have two guest rooms!"

"I don't want him sleeping on the second floor where our bedrooms are."

"That is *so insulting*! Do you actually think he'll come sneaking down the hall to get in bed with me?"

"Miranda," Blythe said softly, "we've discussed this. And you're so emotional, I'm worried about you."

Miranda collapsed onto a kitchen stool and sagged over the counter. "I know. I'm sorry, Mom. It's just, I haven't seen him for two days and it *kills* us to be separated from each other." Her face was tragic when she gazed up at her mother. "I don't think you can understand the intensity of our feelings. I don't think you and Dad ever felt like this."

Blythe was quiet. In truth, she hadn't felt like that for Bob. She'd loved him, in a way. She'd admired him sometimes, and she'd cared for him. But she'd never loved Bob the way she loved Aaden, and that was something her daughter didn't need to know.

Blythe changed the subject. "Are you walking down to the boat to meet Brooks? Or do you want me to drive you?"

"*Mom.*" Miranda was insulted again. "I can drive. I have my license."

"I just thought it might be nice for Brooks to put his luggage in the car and then you can walk into town with him." Blythe spoke pleasantly, offering peace.

"I don't know. Maybe that's a good idea. I know, I'm a mess this morning."

"I made you cinnamon toast."

Blythe opened the oven door and pulled out the rack holding two pieces of toast thickly buttered and sprinkled with sugar and cinnamon. She didn't do this for all her children, and that was the point. Early on, probably after Daphne was born, Miranda had become sullen. Pouty. Disagreeable. Blythe had discussed this with Bob, who had said, "She's just jealous. She'll get over it." After that, Blythe had made it a point to give something special to her oldest child, even if it meant—*especially* if it meant—not giving the same treat to the other children.

When she talked this over with her friend Sandy, Blythe had said, "I'm probably giving all my children some kind of complex, some emotional issue."

Sandy had laughed. "You'll be giving them emotional issues whatever you do."

Blythe had always thought Miranda was more sensitive than her other children. Almost anything could make her burst into tears. If she couldn't tie her shoelaces or find the blue crayon and if the new baby, Daphne, screamed when her diaper was being changed, Miranda would cry. When she was in school, she'd return home in tears, because some other girl snubbed her or she hadn't known the answer to a question or she hadn't been able to control a cough that made the other kids stare at her.

It helped that she was beautiful. It helped a lot. Her light brown hair, streaked by the summer sun, was glossy, and she had large turquoise-blue eyes. Sometimes Blythe and Bob would lie in bed and speak in wonder about the gorgeous little girl, how had they managed to produce such a lovely child? As she grew older, she had several close friends, and she was always invited to birthday parties, and wonder of wonders, she made excellent grades, even in math and science, which had been Blythe's downfall. Miranda could become a model or president of the United States or the scientist who discovered the cure for cancer. Those were the things they said about her, and she'd shrug and look miserable when they said it, and finally Sandy (Lord, what would Blythe have ever done without Sandy?) suggested that they were putting too much pressure on her. They should let her know she didn't have to be extraordinary, she could be whatever she wanted and she didn't have to decide that so early in her life, and they would still love her.

Blythe's second child, Daphne, had been so different. Early in her first year, she turned her head away from Blythe's breast and drank from a bottle. She insisted on dressing herself. She even insisted, for a few years, on cutting her own hair, even though she went around looking like an orphan right out of *Oliver Twist*. Her grades were excellent, she had plenty of friends, and her favorite pastime seemed to be pretending she and her friends had been abandoned on an island. At the far end of the backyard, they would collect leaves to stuff into old pillowcases to make beds and scrape the bark off of fallen branches to turn into bowls for collecting rainwater. For Christmas, Daphne asked for field glasses—she called them *field glasses,* not binoculars—and a sleeping bag and a Swiss Army knife. She wasn't given any kind of knife, and she sulked until Valentine's Day. At some point, she decided she would save the world, or at least the animals. She would only wear clothes bought at the thrift shop. She was independent and often critical of her parents, those great consumers, but she still enjoyed snuggling with them on Saturday night, sitting under a blanket, watching a movie, and eating popcorn. (They had to buy an air popper to pop the corn because most microwave popcorn bags were lined with perfluorooctanoic acid and diacetyl and hydrogenated oils.) Daphne was such a serious, studious, brainy child that Blythe was surprised (although she tried to hide it) when, in eighth grade, she brought home her boyfriend Johnny, who was also smart and impossibly handsome, with thick brown hair and slightly hooded eyes that Blythe had once called *come to bed* eyes, but never did after meeting Johnny. With Johnny, Daphne was lighthearted and relaxed. She was nice and friendly and warm. And, they finally realized, Daphne was also beautiful. Even so, she scorned cosmetics and last Christmas she asked for a subscription to *Scientific American.*

A year ago, Johnny had moved away. Daphne hadn't seemed upset, but Daphne held her feelings close.

Their third child was a boy, and Blythe couldn't decide if Teddy was so relaxed and amiable because of all the coddling and attention he got from his sisters or if he was simply an easygoing kid. He had dark hair, dark eyes, and a lanky build. He was a soccer star at his school and excelled in English as well as science. He had many friends, including friends-who-were-girls, and occasionally girlfriends, but nothing serious. He was only thirteen. Blythe didn't worry about him, although she knew from one of the other mothers that the boys had tried smoking for a week and then gave it up, probably because they were too busy to remember to do it.

And finally, Holly, a surprise, like the sunniest day in the spring.

She was happy in a crowd or alone in her room. She was almost a doll or a pet to her older siblings. If she cried, someone rushed to console her. Miranda loved dressing her, Daphne loved reading to her, and Teddy loved teaching her to play softball. When she was left alone, she happily went to her room to play or color and now to write her graphic novel, which Blythe considered a sign of creativity, except that sea gerbils were creepy. Was she raising a female Stephen King?

For now, she focused on her first child, who had eaten only a few bites of cinnamon toast.

"Thanks, Mom. I'm not hungry. I'm just so excited to see Brooks. I don't want anything to go wrong."

Blythe was swept through with love and sympathy. First love was so hard. "It will be fine."

Miranda said, "Sorry, Mom. I'll try to be better."

"Good. Here. Take the keys. Why don't you drive there and I'll drive home?"

"Cool. Thanks." Miranda took the keys with the blue whale key chain. "Oh, wait. He's coming on the Hy-Line. I want to be on the dock when the ferry arrives and there's never any place to park."

Would they stand in the kitchen all day, unable to decide who would drive? Blythe felt like she was caught in a television comedy.

Blythe said, "I'll drive."

They rushed to the car. Blythe drove while Miranda, in the passenger seat, took a call from Brooks, who said the high-speed passenger ferry had arrived and the crew were putting out the landing ramps.

"Oh, I won't be there when he gets off the boat!" Miranda cried.

Blythe concentrated on weaving through the traffic. The Hy-Line docked at Straight Wharf, which was always crowded in the summer, when the Stop & Shop parking lot and Lower Main Street were jammed bumper to bumper with cars and trucks and taxis making their way along the narrow streets to pick up or drop off passengers.

They reached Main Street.

"I'll go meet him there, Mom!" Miranda tried to jump out of the car but had forgotten to unhitch her seatbelt and was jerked back against the seat. Struggling, she unfastened it.

"I'll be somewhere in this chaos," Blythe said. "You can have Brooks load his luggage in the car and then show him the town."

"Thanks, Mom. I *love* you, Mom!" Miranda freed herself from the seatbelt and raced away.

Miranda ran off. Blythe joined the line of cars snaking into the Stop & Shop parking lot—in the summer, no vehicles were allowed on the pier. She was in front of Jewel of the Sea, ready to do another pass, when she saw a blur of color.

"Open the trunk, Mom!" Miranda yelled.

"Hello, Mrs. Benedict!" Brooks yelled, and shoved his luggage into the minivan before being tugged away into the crowd by Miranda.

As she drove home, Blythe did a mental checklist of where each child would be today.

Miranda would be prowling the town with Brooks.

Holly had biked over to Carolyn's, sent a shot of her friend's new puppy, and texted that now she was at Celeste's. She'd be coming home later with Carolyn, and Carolyn's mother had agreed to let Carolyn sleep over at the Benedicts' that night. Holly had hidden her sea gerbil books because she didn't want Carolyn to think she was weird.

Daphne had biked over to the Maria Mitchell aquarium, where she was volunteering for the summer.

Teddy would go to the yacht club with his friends.

And Aaden was coming to lunch.

As she entered her house, Blythe felt all bubbly and excited, like a bottle of champagne shaken up. She was going to see Aaden again.

This morning, she'd made a chicken salad from two of the packets of cooked white meat chicken she'd brought down, with crisp cuts of celery and onion mixed with mayonnaise, salt, and pepper. She seldom drank wine at lunch, but she put a bottle of Whispering Angel in to chill because she thought she might need a glass of wine so she didn't have a heart attack simply from being near Aaden.

Yesterday at the yacht club, he had looked really *good*. He'd always looked really good, but now he wasn't a teenager, he was a man.

He'd been kind to Holly. Many adults simply ignored children as they spoke with the parents. But Aaden had been kind. He had always been kind.

He was divorced. She was divorced.

Suddenly she wanted to look through her high school yearbooks, but they were all at home. She had no photos of him on her phone, and why would she? High school was a long time ago. But her memories were crystal clear and they made her heart race.

She set the table on the back porch. With the long lush yard stretching to the neighbor's lacy wall of evergreens, she and Aaden would be able to talk unreservedly, without the intimacy of an enclosed room. She spread a retro tablecloth, white with red cherries falling everywhere, and used the real plates instead of the dishwasher-safe plates she'd bought when the children were young. Those plates were of different colors, and slightly scratched but still sturdy even though the children used them as Frisbees.

Should she pick some of the tulips to put in a vase on the table?

No. This was not the beginning of a high school romance or the beginning of any kind of romance. This was simply lunch.

Whisking up to her bedroom, she changed into a blue sleeveless sundress. Sandals. Pulled her hair back in a low ponytail. She took out a white gold Celtic trinity knot necklace and clasped it at the back of her neck. Aaden had brought it to her that last Christmas, that late January. Instead, that day, they broke up.

The truth was, she had known since their first kiss that she would love him all her life, but she had never believed they would spend their lives together. She brought her hand to her necklace and held the small knot between her fingers.

Her phone buzzed and someone knocked at the front door. She hurried down the stairs so fast she thought she might trip and break her heart. No, no, not her heart, her *head*. Her emotions were flooding through her.

"Aaden!" Blythe hurried to answer the door.

"Hi." He seemed almost shy, standing there in a red rugby shirt—red always was the best color for him—holding a sheaf of daffodils in his hand.

Blythe felt completely giddy at the sight of him. He was so real, thick dark hair, intense dark eyes, as handsome as he'd been in high school. She wanted to inhale him.

Aaden said, "I know it's past daffodil time, but every yard had tulips and I thought roses might be too sentimental."

Blythe regained her wits as she took the flowers. "Such complicated decisions to make! Thank you. Come in. Follow me. We're eating out on the back porch today."

She sensed Aaden glancing around the rooms as she stood at the kitchen sink filling a vase with water. It was cluttered, it would always be cluttered, but it was a good, solid house. Comfortable.

"Would you like a glass of wine? Lemonade? Ice water?" She was proud of herself because her hands weren't shaking.

"A glass of wine would be lovely. And maybe ice water, too."

"Same." She poured the wine and filled tumblers with ice and water, handed his to him, and led him out the back door. "You sit there. I need to be closer to the door to get the food."

Aaden sat, set his glasses on the table, and swept his eyes over the yard. "You've got a beautiful garden. A beautiful home."

He was older, and somehow more perfect. Laugh lines at his eyes. A touch of gray in his hair. How did he stay so handsome over twenty-five years?

"It's all mine," she told him. "My grandmother left it to me. I'm sorry you never got to come here when we were in high school. You always spent your summers in Ireland."

"And I'm sorry you never got to visit me in Ireland. Although, there's still time."

Visiting him in Ireland? That was more than she could deal with right now. "This house is our second home. The children have come here every summer of their lives."

"Lucky kids."

"Yes." Blythe studied his face. "And you have been living in Ireland?"

"Not completely." He took a sip of wine. "Eileen, my ex-wife, and I had an apartment in Boston. Since the divorce, she's kept the house in Ireland and I have the apartment here."

"Where are your daughters?"

Aaden chuckled. "In Europe. Their grandfather, Eileen's father, gave them the money to spend a year traveling the continent. Like students, mind, not living in posh hotels."

"How wonderful." Blythe wondered if she could ever be so relaxed about any of her children wandering loose in Europe.

"The truth is, the girls needed to get away from Eileen and me. They told us—our daughters told us—they couldn't live with us because we were dull and uninspiring."

Blythe threw back her head and laughed. "Oh, Aaden! Aren't daughters the *worst*? They are so critical and cruel! Miranda, my oldest, told me that I've become 'intolerably earnest.'"

Aaden laughed, too, and it was a laugh Blythe remembered, rolling out like kettle drums, rumbling and strong.

"Ah, well," he said, "that's probably true. How do we raise children any other way?"

"I suppose you're right. Miranda is almost seventeen. She thinks she's discovered sex, which is nothing old people like me could have any idea about . . ." Blythe gazed down at her hands. She wore no wedding ring. She'd taken it off three years ago, wrapped it in tissue paper and bubble wrap, and carried it up to the attic to store in her grandmother's old jewelry box.

Now she murmured, "Sex. Love."

Aaden said, "What they don't know is that you and I invented it."

Blythe met his eyes and a shiver of memory passed through her. "I suppose it feels like that for every couple."

"No," Aaden said. "It doesn't. What we had was unique. *Is* unique."

Blythe glanced away. Aaden could say things like that because he was Irish, but she was hopelessly a New England colonial, probably with strands of Puritan in her DNA.

"Aaden—"

"Hel-lo-o!"

The front door slammed. Footsteps raced down the hall to the back door, and Bob's sister, Kate, appeared, stepping out onto the porch with the enthusiasm of a showgirl jumping out of a cake.

"*Oh!*" Kate nearly elevated into the air in her pleasure at finding Blythe with a man. "I didn't know if you were home but I saw your car in the drive and thought I'd take a chance."

Blythe was so full of words she wanted to say, none of them pleasant, that she went completely numb.

Aaden rose and held out his hand. "Hello. I'm Aaden Sullivan. An old friend of Blythe's."

Kate studied him as she allowed her hand to be enfolded in Aaden's. Kate was pretty, Blythe realized, with her brother's dark coloring and her body tuned by years of exercise classes.

Blushing, Kate told Aaden, "I'm Kate Barnes. Her sister-in-law."

"*Ex*-sister-in-law," Blythe said.

Kate didn't pay attention to Blythe. She seldom did.

"I need to borrow Blythe's slow cooker."

Blythe ducked her head to hide a smile. *Slow cooker.* The words recalled the languorous, measured way Aaden's hands had slid over her body.

Kate took that moment to say, "Oh, you're having lunch. Blythe makes the best lunches. She can make normal meals look expensive."

Okay. That was enough of Kate's insults veiled in compliments. "I'd invite you to join us, but I haven't seen Aaden since high school and we have a lot to catch up on that would bore you terribly."

"Oh, well, of course, I'll come back another time. I know where you keep your slow cooker. I'll get it on the way out."

Kate walked reluctantly back to the door, ears perked like a hunting dog in case one of them said anything to her, and when they didn't, she slowly left the porch and went into the kitchen.

Blythe and Aaden sat in amused silence as Kate banged and clanged pots around until she found the slow cooker and walked down the hall and out the front door.

"Sorry about that." Blythe took a sip of wine, and then another. "She's Bob's sister. My ex-sister-in-law. I don't hate her, but she's always sneaking around, trying to catch me doing something awful, although I can't imagine what that would be, with four children around."

"She's jealous," Aaden said. "It's obvious."

"Oh, I don't think so. She's married to a perfectly nice husband, and she has two children in college."

"You're beautiful," Aaden said.

"I'm older." Blythe raised her eyes and allowed him to see her face, wrinkles and all. "I've had four children. I love them like crazy, but they're exhausting."

"How are your parents?"

"Oh, dear." Blythe laughed. "They're fine. They live in Arizona now and yet they're somehow still exhausting, too. How are *your* parents?"

"My father has passed on. Mother spends time playing cards with her friends and telling everyone in the family what to do."

"And your business?"

"Still flourishing. Over the years we've downsized, had to lay off employees, but truth to tell, most of them were so old they were ready to retire. The internet has opened a whole new group of customers, and our younger staff is genius with technology. Also, Ireland has had quite the boost from the film industry—*P.S. I Love You, Leap Year, Wild Mountain Thyme*. And now from streaming. We're fine. Tell me about you."

"No, wait. Tell me about your family first. Your wife. How did you meet her? Is she Irish?"

Aaden leaned back in his chair. "Ah, I wish I still smoked. Eileen Kelley. Gorgeous as a movie star, wild as a Kerry Bog Pony. Flaming red hair. Eyes as green as shamrocks. A mouth on her pretty as a rose to see, rude as a sailor when she gets mad. Different from you, Blythe. So different. Eileen has a bit of the Irish Traveller in her. Doesn't enjoy being settled. Dances like a whirlwind, faster than a wave in a stormy sea. And she sings like an angel come down from heaven. When she sings, you want to catch the breath of her and make it into jewelry."

Blythe was both fascinated and wounded. When she was in college, she'd been rule-abiding and studious. The wildest she'd ever been was when she loved Aaden, and she'd loved him then like the sea needing the sun, craving his presence, glittering only in his radiance. She'd never been as wild as a Kerry Bog Pony.

She wanted to wish something terrible on Eileen, this woman Aaden had loved so fiercely, this gorgeous, singing, angelic woman, but she was too aware of karma to wish anything really terrible on her, not death or even an accident, so she wished that Eileen Kelley Sullivan had bad teeth.

Across the table from her, Aaden looked amused. "What are you thinking?"

Blythe said, "I hate her."

Aaden threw his head back and laughed, his irresistible rolling thunderous laugh. "Ah, Blythe, you're wonderful."

Blythe shook her head. "I'm an idiot." She rose. "I'll get our lunches."

Aaden reached out and put a hand on her arm. "No. Wait. Let me tell you more. Sit down."

Blythe sat.

"Eileen drinks and sleeps around. She's never satisfied. Her parents live in Kerry and they told me when I first met her that I'd never be able to trust her. I laughed at them. And Eileen was a good wife and a good mother, but after a while she got bored. The company's headquarters were in Dublin, still are, that's a two-hour drive from Kerry, and once our daughters were away in school, Eileen took to driving back to Kerry for the weekend, and then the week, and she said she was staying with her parents, but after a while I learned she was staying with a man instead. To be honest, for a few years I was glad she was away. I had an affair." Aaden shook his head. "Patricia was, well, she still is, English. Proper English, an earl in her family, a solicitor who was married to a solicitor, all shirts tucked into her expensive skirts and pearls around her neck. It was the difference from Eileen, I think, that attracted me. I think I attracted her because she thought I was wild. Ha. I've always wished I could see Eileen and Patricia in a room together for fifteen minutes." He sighed. "So that's the story."

Blythe said, "I hate Patricia, too."

Aaden laughed, and Blythe found herself laughing along with him, and for a moment, there on the back porch with its white railings and porch table covered with a cherry-sprinkled tablecloth, with the bright sun and the full promise of a new day spread around them, for a moment she and Aaden were together again as if they'd never been parted.

Quieting, Blythe took a sip of wine. "*Now* I'll get our lunches."

Aaden said, "No, woman, you stay put. You tell me about you."

"The whole story? It's not as colorful as yours."

"How could it be? You're not Irish."

She nodded her head. "I went to university. Lived in a dorm. Had a wonderful time. Made decent grades. Made some good friends." A memory struck her. "After midterms or finals, a bunch of us would go to a bar and celebrate. We drank too much. We laughed too loud. We made fun of our professors. We told terrible jokes. We flirted with every man in the bar. We drank a lot and stood on our table and sang 'My Heart Will Go On' from the movie *Titanic* with heartbreaking passion even when we weren't in a relationship."

"Did *you* ever stand on the table and sing?"

Blythe laughed. "Oh, Lord, I did."

Aaden said very quietly, "I wish I had seen you."

Blythe said, "I wish you had, too." She glanced at him quickly, a challenge. "Maybe I would have taken your eyes off your Eileen."

For a long moment, Aaden didn't speak.

Then he said, "Ah, no, Blythe. I've heard you sing, and you're a terrible singer."

Oh, he's good, Blythe thought. "Damn, Aaden, you're right."

He reached across the table and took her hand. She leaned forward and closed her eyes, giving in to the sensation of his strong, familiar, never-forgotten hand.

The front door slammed. Footsteps came down the hall.

"It's just me again!" Kate yelled. "Do you have any cinnamon?"

Blythe and Aaden quickly withdrew their hands and sank back against their chairs.

Kate came out on the porch, raving with indignation. "Do you have any cinnamon? I have to have it for this ridiculous recipe I'm taking off the internet for a beef stew and I have to add cinnamon and cloves, plus I'm supposed to use *lard* or *clarified butter*!"

"I brought cinnamon with me from home," Blythe said. "But I'll want it back. I often make cinnamon toast for the children on rainy days."

"Fine." Kate scanned the table. "Haven't you eaten yet? Good Lord, it's after one o'clock."

Kate went into the kitchen. A moment later, she called out, "Where do you keep your spices?"

Blythe rose. "I'll show you."

She went into the kitchen, opened a cupboard, and found the glass bottle of cinnamon.

Kate said, "It would be easier to find if you had a spice rack like a normal person instead of keeping them hidden on a shelf."

"You're welcome," Blythe replied sweetly.

Kate followed Blythe back out to the porch. "I'll give you a spice rack."

"I don't want a spice rack." Blythe sat in her chair and picked up her wineglass, giving Kate a visual hint that she needed to leave.

"You need a spice rack." Kate spoke to Aaden, as if he were a referee. "Blythe is a person who always has spices around."

Aaden smiled politely. "I'm not surprised."

Blythe didn't argue.

"Well, I have to go." Kate waited for them to ask her to stay, then went through the back door, and trotted down the hall. The front door slammed.

"Well," Blythe said, "there's a passionate woman for you."

"She's frighteningly passionate," Aaden said.

"Now I'll get our lunches." Blythe rose.

"I'll help," Aaden said.

Together they went into the kitchen, which was shady and cool after the sunny day outside. Blythe handed Aaden the basket with the crusty baguette in it and carried out the two plates nicely set with chicken salad and sliced tomatoes sprinkled with basil.

As they sat, Aaden asked, "Sorry, but do you have any cinnamon? I always put some on my chicken salad."

"Sorry," Blythe told him. "All out."

They smiled at each other, and it was as if years had never passed between them, as if they were there together, fully, profoundly, everlastingly together, as they had been when they were young. As if during all the years they had lived they had still carried their love like the breath of their bodies and the poetry of their souls.

Blythe broke the spell. "Kate's husband is a real estate broker. Nice, but boring. He would never argue with Kate. And my ex-husband, Bob, Kate's brother, often comes to Nantucket with the children to stay with his mother over Easter holidays or Thanksgiving. He'll be here with his girlfriend later this summer. Celeste, his mother, is completely wonderful. I truly love her and trust her, and my children adore her, love spending time with her."

"Where did you meet Bob?"

"In Boston. At a graduation party. You know how it is. Spring. Set free. Finally starting our real lives. We met and talked . . ." Blythe leaned her cheek on her hand and went quiet. After a moment, she said, "I really did love him, in a way. I know he loved me, in a way. We both wanted a home and children, and we wanted to stay in the Boston area. I met his family. I got my teaching certificate, he got his law degree. We got married. We had four children and got divorced a few years ago and that's that."

Blythe studied Aaden's face. "You were gone. You were living in Ireland." Sighing, she gazed at her plate, the little hill of chicken salad, the nicely cut tomato, the crisp lettuce. The plate, Portmeirion china, part of the set she'd bought when she inherited this summer house. For a moment, none of it seemed real.

Lifting her head, she remembered. "I raised the children and did substitute teaching. Bob worked hard, enjoyed his work at the Boston branch of his father's law firm, and we were both caught up in bringing up the children. We were good parents, but failures as husband and wife. After a while, we were like a couple who see each other when they're running a company, and they go to separate places to sleep at night."

Aaden said, "I've read that we live too long, and that's why so many people get divorced. When people died at thirty or forty, they didn't have time to change their lives."

"Oh. Sad. They didn't get to see their grandchildren."

"Tell me about your children."

She counted her children off on her fingers. "First, Miranda. Beautiful. Turquoise eyes. Light brown hair. Almost seventeen. Madly in love with a guy named Brooks who's staying with us for a month.

Miranda's angry because I'm making him sleep in the family room, on a different floor from the bedrooms."

"They'll find another place," Aaden said.

"Maybe, but it won't be where my other three and I can hear them. Next, we've got Daphne. Fifteen. Dark hair, dark eyes, braces, *and* glasses, my poor darling. She's brilliant and she'll be just as gorgeous as Miranda, but right now she's extremely serious about the state of the world. She's volunteering for the Maria Mitchell Natural Science Museum this summer.

"Next, Teddy. Thirteen. Oh, he's wonderful. Kind, thoughtful, funny . . . I worry about him, though, because the divorce hit him hard. And Bob's father died, so Teddy tries to spend a lot of time with Celeste, his grandmother. He's very uncomfortable about Teri, Bob's girlfriend. She's young and sweet, but she embarrasses him. Teri's very demonstrative with her affection. Sits on Bob's lap, nuzzles his neck, that sort of thing. When Teri hugs Teddy, he looks mortified. Basically, though, he's a happy kid."

"And number four?"

"Holly, you met her last night. Eleven. Sweet girl. Lives in her own world. She's artistic, and her art teacher told me she's talented. So that's my four." Blythe paused to take a sip of her wine. "Now. It's your turn. Tell me about your daughters."

"Ah, yes, my beauties."

Aaden dabbed his mouth with his napkin but missed a small spot of chicken between his mouth and his nose. For some reason, it made Blythe feel close to him.

"Shannon and Aisling. Eighteen and seventeen. They might as well be twins, they're together all the time, both as gorgeous as their mother. The good thing is they both are planning to take over Awen someday, and they want to update our knitwear and jewelry. Shannon has become a fine weaver and Aisling has learned all about the business side of things. They're traveling now, getting ideas, and getting away from me and Eileen. We're divorced, we are, but Eileen has become . . . not unstable, but *unreliable*. She was one of the managers of the gift shop in Kerry, but since the divorce, she doesn't always show up and sometimes when she does, she's in one of her . . . flamboyant . . . moods."

Blythe murmured a neutral "Oh." She didn't want to be unkind, but she did enjoy hearing that Aaden's ex-wife was a problem.

"How are your brothers and sisters?"

"Well, let me think. You know Donal, my older brother, escaped from the family long ago and has his own construction business in Boston. Niamh, my younger sister who adored you—"

"Oh, sweet Niamh."

"You gave her one of those American Girl dolls—"

"Kathleen! And I gave her all sorts of accessories—"

"Niamh worshipped you after that, and my mother did, too."

"I always liked your mother. She was so warm and loving and nothing fazed her. Remember when your little brother, Joe, was at the dinner table—he was about ten—and he asked me if I knew there was a one-eyed sex monster in the neighborhood, and I said, no, and he closed one eye and grinned at me. He was so cute."

"Ma hit him over the head with a magazine for that."

Blythe laughed with Aaden. Then she turned serious.

"Shouldn't you be in Ireland in the summer?" she asked. "For your business?"

Aaden chuckled. "I've got a foreman, Del, for the textiles, who's been with me forever, and an impressive young woman, Nora, for the shop. I needed to visit Awen's Boston office, and I haven't had a vacation for years and years, and when my friend Arnie invited me to Nantucket, I couldn't turn it down. I'm glad I came."

"I don't believe I know Arnie."

"Arnie McDougal. He's a great sailor. Plus, he's divorced."

"Oh, dear, is it only you two old bachelors roaming around his house?"

"You haven't seen Arnie McDougal's house. Out in 'Sconset. Massive. He's got a housekeeper and caretaker living there year-round, keeping up with things. Whenever he comes, Janice turns into a cook. Tim is a great jack-of-all-trades, and if we go sport-fishing, Tim comes along and deals with the fish. Cleans it and all, so we can eat it fresh that night."

"You're a lucky man," Blythe said.

Aaden gave her a long, serious look. "I am now." He reached out and took her hand.

Blythe's heart took a bungee jump. She knew this hand so well, yet it seemed like the first time he had touched her.

She asked, very quietly, "But your home, your real home, is in Ireland, isn't it?"

"That's true, yes. But I have an apartment in Boston. And I think you'd enjoy visiting my ancient house in Dublin." His eyes were dark.

"Aaden . . ."

"MOM!"

The front door slammed.

Teddy came dashing down the hall and out to the porch. His friend Eric came right behind him. They were both wearing tennis whites and Red Sox baseball caps. They smelled like the ocean and the things swimming in it. Teddy had hair on his legs. She couldn't keep from glancing at Eric's legs in shorts instead of jeans. No hair.

Teddy skidded to a halt. He looked at Blythe. He looked at Aaden.

"Hi," Teddy said to Aaden, and before Aaden could respond, Teddy said to his mother, "Eric and I are biking out to Surfside and we're taking all the bananas and two water bottles and the box of Cheez-Its."

"Hello, Eric," Blythe said.

"Hello, Mrs. Benedict," Eric said politely.

"Teddy . . ." Blythe softly touched Teddy's shoulder. "I'd like you to meet my dear old friend, Mr. Sullivan."

Aaden rose and held out his hand. "Hello, Teddy."

"Hello, Mr. Sullivan. This is my friend Eric."

Teddy shook hands with Aaden and then Eric shook hands with Aaden. The boys waited as if they were poised at a starting gate, eager to race out, away from the adults.

Blythe smiled at them. "Be careful. Mind the lifeguard. There might be sharks in the water."

"Cool!" both boys yelled.

"Okay, bye!" Teddy yanked his friend's arm. They disappeared into the kitchen where they made rustling noises as they gathered their provisions. Then came the pounding of their feet on the floor and the slamming of the front door.

"They're animals," Blythe said.

Aaden leaned back in his chair. "Ah, they're gorgeous. I remember those days, when I was a new teenager and still young enough to spend the entire day outdoors. I don't think I've ever been happier."

Blythe smiled at the memory of him as a teenager. His hair was shaggy and curly, no matter how often he had it cut, and his nose was sunburned and peeling.

Aaden's cell buzzed. He slipped it out of his pocket, checked it, and mouthed to Blythe, "I have to take this."

Blythe carried their plates and wineglasses into the kitchen to give him some privacy.

Soon Aaden followed with their utensils. He opened the dishwasher and put them in their little basket.

"Aaden, you don't have to do that," Blythe said.

"It was very strenuous, but I managed anyway. Anything to impress you, Blythe." Aaden straightened and stood close to Blythe, and inside the kitchen, in the cool shade, he seemed bigger than he had been on the porch, and more substantial.

"Sorry. Work. Listen, Blythe . . ." Aaden moved closer. He bent forward and kissed her mouth.

Her knees went weak. She said, "Aaden."

He stepped back. "I'd like to kiss you more, but the truth is, I'm wary of your front door opening and closing again."

He'd made her laugh. He always could. Blythe gazed at him in wonder. "You are real. This is real."

"Yes. When can I see you again?" Before she answered, Aaden said hopefully, "Tonight?"

"I don't think so. It's our second day here and Miranda's boyfriend just got here. I'll figure out everyone's schedule and call you."

They walked to the door together.

"Thanks for the lunch," Aaden said.

Blythe paused. She hoped Aaden would surge forward and press her against the wall with hungry kisses. He would have, once. But they weren't teenagers now. They had families. Responsibilities. They had to go slowly.

"Thanks for coming," Blythe said. "And thanks for the flowers."

Aaden left. As he went down the sidewalk, he turned, looked up at Blythe, and waved.

Blythe watched as Aaden walked away, along the brick sidewalk, past the hedge shaped like a whale, past the house with the blue door and the widow's walk, past the house with the Mercedes convertible sitting next to the Range Rover in the driveway. Then he turned the corner and was out of sight. She wanted to sink down onto the steps, lean back on her elbows, and remain right there, in the air where Aaden had been.

conversations

Blythe had learned to keep the refrigerator, pantry, and shelves stocked with food. Seedless grapes, bananas, watermelon slices would disappear in one day as various kids swarmed the kitchen, grabbing whatever they could eat without having to sit down. Once a week Blythe made meatloaf and cut it into thick slices so it could be eaten in a sandwich or warmed on a plate with chips. She made a large pot of macaroni and cheese every week, and a rice salad tossed with vegetables, a bottle of the ranch dressing her children preferred placed next to it. Bowls of Brussels sprouts roasted in olive oil, sea salt, and, sometimes, parmesan cheese. Towers of carrots, cucumbers, broccoli, red peppers, cut fresh every day. She seldom bought cookies or chips, knowing they wouldn't last twenty-four hours in her house, but she bought mozzarella sticks and yogurt with fruit and salted nuts. She refused to buy sodas but made pitchers of fresh lemonade. Her kitchen was a kind of free twenty-four-hour cafeteria.

Tonight, Miranda would have dinner at home with Brooks and some, if not all, of her siblings. Blythe told Miranda it was the proper thing to do. It was a way to welcome him into the household. Any other evening, Miranda and Brooks could eat lobster rolls and hot dogs from the Sandbar restaurant at Jetties Beach, and enormous pizzas from Sophie T's, and probably Sunday dinner at Celeste's. But this was Brooks's first night here.

Blythe entered her kitchen, the funny old kitchen they'd never gotten around to renovating. It had red tiles on the floor, supposedly to look like bricks, and a wide double porcelain sink and cupboards with flowered knobs put on by the previous owner, and a new refrigerator, stove, and microwave. The ugly cousin in the kitchen was the rolling dishwasher that sat in the corner and had to be pushed over to the sink and hooked up to the faucet with a long black hose and to the electric socket with a long black cord. Blythe had considered getting a new dishwasher installed with the hoses directly connected to the sink, but the kitchen would have to be completely torn apart and rearranged, and there had never been time.

She didn't mind. Nantucket cherished its history and the buildings, streets, and houses that had come with it. The room was small, and it certainly didn't have an island, but she didn't mind that, either. There was enough room for a wooden table under a window where two people could sit, eating breakfast or helping to peel potatoes.

She brought out the large casserole dish from the cupboard and began opening tin cans of tuna fish. It was fun to make this retro dish that she could remember her own mother and grandmother serving.

She realized she was singing as she worked. She stopped for a moment and gazed out the window.

She was happy because she'd seen Aaden.

But more than that, she was happy because at last she felt free to *be* happy.

The first couple of years of her divorce had been hard on the children. Bob had moved out. They sold their big house in Arlington and

Blythe bought a smaller one in the same school district. They'd talked together with their children, explaining that their lives would be different, but better. The kids went through a period of slamming doors and yelling fiercely critical remarks at Blythe and Bob. After a while, everyone settled down.

Sometimes in those first months, Blythe would hear Miranda crying while she took a bath with the bathroom door locked. Teddy became obsessed with throwing things in the backyard—sticks, plastic bottles, shoes—until Blythe had a basketball hoop put up on the garage door. She gave Teddy a basketball, and that had really seemed to help to use his turbulent energy. Holly had regressed a little, finding the baby dolls she'd packed away in the attic and tending them. She would wrap her babies in blankets and rock them, singing softly to them, saying, "It's okay. Shh, now. It will be all right." Daphne had been angry. She had a passion for justice and lots of energy fueled by her emotions, but no place to use that energy.

In October, when the weather was bright and crisp and the leaves were beginning to turn, Blythe rallied her four children and forced them to hike with her up the unfortunately named Gibbet Hill. She confiscated their phones and sang old camp songs that embarrassed them so much—it wasn't the songs, it was their mother's singing—that they promised not to complain if she would promise not to sing. Afterward, she took them for cheeseburgers and ice cream and felt victorious as she saw her children eating heartily.

Every weekend that fall, Blythe went climbing. Often the children had better offers. Overnights. Parties. Time with their father and Teri. Most of the time, only Daphne joined her on the hike, and as the weeks passed, Daphne's fury diminished. Blythe felt better, too. She saw how her daughter was beginning to notice what was along the trail. Blythe would stand gazing in awe at a maple blazing with red leaves, and Daphne would kneel at the tree's trunk, studying a mushroom—or was it a toadstool? Blythe began to explore websites, looking for the best parks. She bought Massachusetts field guides that described where and how to find turtles, bugs, frogs, and snakes. She was only slightly surprised when Daphne saved her allowance and bought *The Secret Pool* and *The Secret Bay.*

But, Blythe thought, this was *this* year. A new year. A new *summer.* Anything could happen. Anything had already happened—Aaden was on the island.

And so were her children, and their friends. Holly was having Carolyn for a sleepover tonight, and Miranda would stay home to have family dinner with Brooks on his first night on the island. Other than tonight, who knew when they'd all be together at the table. Blythe had released her children and herself from the rule of eating dinner together every night. The four didn't exactly roam wild on the island, but every day was different, with friends meeting at the lawn at Children's Beach for a game of soccer, or to see an extravagant animated epic movie on the big screen at the Dreamland, or a rainy day with board games and popcorn and apples for dinner.

She hummed as she worked, wondering if she'd have time before dinner to call Aaden and deciding she'd do that and make a plan to meet him later on Straight Wharf.

She took a foolish moment to brush her hair and apply fresh lipstick before sitting on the side of her bed and calling him. She got his voicemail.

"Aaden, it's Blythe. Would you like to meet later at the gazebo at Straight Wharf? We could check out the yachts."

Around five-thirty, the children stormed back into the house, talking, arguing, kicking off their sneakers, staring at their phones, and the Great Tracking In of the Sand began. It would take place every day for the entire summer. In earlier years, when the children were young, Blythe had made herself crazy trying to sweep up every sneaky tiny grain of sand that came in on the children's shoes, clothes, and skin. Blythe made rules: Take your shoes off at the door. If you've been swimming, go around to the back, drape your towel over the porch railings, and use the outdoor shower before you enter the house. That helped. But nothing could prevent shifty bits of sand from making it into the house to lie on the floor, on the sofas, and, finally, in the sheets.

Well, she wouldn't worry about that today. She had other things to think about.

Miranda and Brooks arrived, both of them with sunburned cheeks and noses.

Blythe kissed her daughter. Miranda was glowing, and not only from the sun. Blythe pulled Brooks in for a hug. Miranda had told her how lonely Brooks was, how a housekeeper named Mrs. Jones took care of Brooks when his parents had to go abroad. Mrs. Jones was nice, and a reasonably good cook, but she wasn't a motherly type, more of a formal person.

Brooks said, "I'm really glad to be here."

"Mom," Miranda said, "I'm going to show Brooks where to keep his stuff."

"We'll have dinner in about ten minutes," Blythe said.

She was starting to set the table when Daphne wandered in, carrying a book with her finger holding her place.

"Oh, good," Blythe said. "You can help me set the table."

"Why do I have to be the one who always helps," Daphne asked, sighing.

"Because you're the child I like to be with the most," Blythe told her daughter, because that was what she told all her children when she was alone with them.

"Oh, Mom." Daphne rolled her eyes, but she smiled.

Finally, all the food was ready and everyone was seated and Blythe made them hold hands and say a quick grace and then she passed the bowls around. Already the children looked rosy and flushed from the sun and all the time spent outdoors. They ate quickly, as if they hadn't been fed all day, and the humble tuna casserole vanished. They gave up and played at eating their salads—why didn't children like salads?—all the while arguing about *Dune: Part Two* and how could the dainty Timothée Chalamet possibly be cast as a warrior and why was Christopher Walken so cool even if he was, like, *ancient*?

Blythe sat eating quietly, sipping her wine, wondering when Aaden would return her call. Holly's friend Carolyn was at the table, picking at her food, and needing to eat it all, because the girl was too thin, but it wasn't Blythe's place to insist she eat, and Holly would be embarrassed if Blythe tried. Brooks was debating the strengths and weaknesses of *Dune: Part Two* with Teddy, while Miranda listened with miraculous patience to Daphne talking about the cnidarians and ctenophores on display at the Maria Mitchell aquarium.

Voices drifted from the front door.

"Yoohoo, Blythe!" Sandy called. "I'm here with Nick. Can we come in?"

"Of course," Blythe called.

Sandy entered the dining room. "The girls have gone off with friends on a sunset cruise. What are you doing this evening?"

Nick was there, behind Sandy, just inside the doorway, looking uncomfortable and also heart-stoppingly attractive.

Be normal, Blythe ordered herself. "We were just finishing dinner. I made sugar cookies—"

Before she completed her sentence, the children jumped up from the table as if they'd been zapped by an electric shock.

"Wait!" Blythe said. "Have some manners and say hello to Sandy and Mr. Roth."

As if directed by a choir leader, the children chimed, "Hello, Sandy. Hello, Mr. Roth."

"Now," Blythe directed, "take your dishes to the kitchen. The cookies are for dessert. Help yourself."

"Then we can leave?" Miranda asked.

"Yes," Blythe answered dryly. "I've officially unlocked your shackles."

"Great!" Miranda took Brooks's hand. "Come on, let's walk into town for ice cream."

Brooks rose—Miranda was gently pulling him to his feet. "Thank you for the dinner, Mrs. Benedict."

"You're welcome, Brooks." Smiling at Sandy and Nick, Blythe invited them to join her at the table. "Sit with me while the kids sort themselves out."

For the next few minutes, it sounded like middle school when the last bell rings. People ran up the stairs and back down, called out names and questions, raced out the front door, thundered back into the kitchen to grab a few sugar cookies, raced out the back door, and all at once, blissfully, it was quiet in the house.

"We're on our way to Straight Wharf to get ice cream," Sandy announced. "We thought you'd like to come with us."

Blythe couldn't think of a reason *not* to join them. Her children had gone off, and Aaden hadn't returned her call, and if he did come to Straight Wharf, well, Nick was with Sandy, wasn't he?

"That would be fun! Give me a moment to get organized."

She took her plate into the kitchen, dashed into the downstairs lavatory, brushed her hair, swooped on some lipstick, and checked her phone, in case Aaden had left a message. No message.

She stood in the lavatory, which she and Bob had decorated several years ago with cream wallpaper patterned with seashells and pale cream woodwork, and gave herself a moment to think. What if Aaden came to Straight Wharf without phoning her back? Or what if he phoned? She imagined introducing him to Sandy and Nick, and everyone would get along fine, but it would change the emotional tone of the evening, at least for Blythe. It was too soon for her to consider herself romantically linked with Aaden, even though in a way, she'd been romantically linked with him since she first saw him. But even if the two men shook hands and were friendly, Blythe would silently freak out. Blythe loved Sandy and she was sure that Nick was a great guy, but she didn't want to deal with Aaden seeing her with another man, which was ridiculous, but a powerful thought.

Also, she was insanely attracted to Nick.

Blythe took a deep breath. She walked down the hall and found Sandy and Nick sitting in the living room.

"Sorry I took so long," Blythe apologized. "Would you mind if we stayed here and sat out on the back porch and had iced tea and sugar cookies? It's just that it's been such a circus getting all of us out of the Arlington house and down here and unpacked and so forth. I'd love to sit and catch my breath."

"Of course," Sandy said.

Blythe led them to the kitchen. She poured iced tea for her and Sandy and a Scotch and soda for Nick and carried the plate of sugar cookies—there were four of them left—out to the back porch.

"Oh, this is lovely," Sandy said as they stepped out onto the porch. "I want the swing."

"It's all yours." Blythe set the plate of sugar cookies on the small wicker table and sank into the wicker rocking chair.

Nick sat on the wicker settee facing the flowers and lush green lawn. "Nice garden."

"I hope the cushions don't reek," Blythe said. "We keep them in the house in the winter, tossed in with the boots and snow shovel in the back hall, but I haven't had time to wash the slipcovers."

Sandy stretched her arms over her head. "The only thing I smell is summer. Isn't this a perfect night!"

"How long will you be on Nantucket?" Blythe asked Nick.

He said, "I've got three months of vacation. I'll be here off and on all summer."

"Nice." Blythe couldn't keep from reappraising the man on the wicker settee. Nick was big like a football player, but as well-dressed and charming as a diplomat.

Nick smiled. "It is nice. Your home is beautiful."

"I work hard to keep it that way. The most challenging job is to make my children do their assigned tasks. Mowing the lawn. Watering the flowers. Doing laundry. Sweeping, vacuuming, and that most heinous task, cleaning the bathroom."

"If you can inspire your children to do all that, then you must be a remarkable teacher."

This time his smile reached his eyes. He was very handsome, and Blythe saw that he was kind. It was easy to talk with him. She was comfortable in his presence.

There was that heart flutter again. Maybe she was more than comfortable.

"How did you get into . . . teaching?" she asked.

Nick said simply, "It's a family thing. My grandfather taught history at St. Mark's in Southborough. My father was principal at Arlington High, and my sister teaches there now."

"Wow. Impressive."

"I like teaching. I like the challenges." He shook his head. "Not all of them."

Sandy pushed the floor with her feet, bare now that she'd kicked off her sandals, and the wicker swing creaked as it went back and forth.

Blythe agreed. "It's hard work, I remember. But when they get something right, when *we* get something right, it's dazzling."

Sandy interrupted. "Okay, enough. Life can't be all about teaching. You don't know it yet, but Nick can get awfully boring and dreary."

"Thank you, Sandy," Nick said with a smile.

Ignoring him, Sandy continued. "That's why Hugh invited him here for a few weeks."

"Do you sail?" Blythe asked. "Sandy's husband is a great sailor."

Before Nick could answer, Sandy spoke up. "If Nick goes out with Hugh on his boat, I'm going to make Hugh swear not to force Nick to crew. Nick's our guest. He should lie in the sun and relax."

"Like now," Blythe said. "Look."

The sun had dropped beneath a cluster of puffy white clouds, their rippling edges glowing pink. From the apple tree at the back of the garden, a robin sang, his tail flicking among the fresh green leaves. A gentle gray dusk passed on to the porch, so the light was dimmed and it felt that, for a moment, the world held its breath.

They were quiet for a while, and the silence seemed to be a way of speaking to one another, and to the evening, to the moment, this moment of peace.

Then another bird swooped onto the branch where the robin sat and they chirped and flew off. Someone called for someone named Corker from a house down the street. Someone else yelled, "Coming!"

The world began again.

Nick said, "I'd like to rent a spot on this porch every evening."

Sandy pretended to be indignant. "What's wrong with our porch?"

"It doesn't face west."

"I suppose you're right." Sandy slipped off the swing, stepped into her sandals, and said, "I have to go home. I'm suddenly yearning for my new mystery novel."

Blythe was used to her friend's quick changes. "That's a good idea. I haven't read a book in two or three days. It was such a mad dash packing to get here. It always is."

Nick rose, too. "Thank you for the cookie and the drink. I hope we can get together again."

"I'd like that," Blythe told him, trying not to sound too eager.

She walked with them through the house down the hallway, and the entire time she admired the long span of Nick's back, his wide shoulders, his thick honey-brown hair. No male-pattern baldness here, she thought, and she knew that shouldn't matter, but right at that moment, it did. When they stepped out onto her front porch, Nick turned and shook her hand.

"Thanks again, Blythe."

She wanted to say: *Don't leave.*

"I'm so glad you came," she told him.

They smiled at each other and kept holding hands. Blythe had forgotten how delicate the skin of her palm was, and the trick it had of sending shock waves through her body.

Behind Nick, Sandy stood grinning.

"I'll see you soon," Nick said, and gently released her hand.

Blythe returned to the kitchen. She realized she was humming. And she hadn't thought of Aaden for the past hour.

She checked her phone.

Aaden had texted: *Sorry. I was out with my host for drinks with his neighbors. Raincheck?*

Before she could stop herself, Blythe texted, *Maybe*. Because it was fun to flirt with Aaden even though he probably knew she'd run to him in the pouring rain or the wildest wind.

Immediately, his text popped up. *Tomorrow? Dinner?*

Blythe texted *Yes* and hugged herself.

The summer was beginning to be more interesting than she'd imagined.

Now Blythe waited for her children to come home. The three younger ones had to be in by eleven. Miranda and Brooks had a curfew of midnight. Blythe settled herself in an armchair in the living room and opened one of the Agatha Christie mysteries someone had left in the bookshelf. What was it about Agatha Christie books that was so unexpectedly comforting?

Not that she needed comforting. She hadn't been this excited since—since high school? Could that be true? It could be, because never before had she been interested in two men at the same time. She closed her eyes, lay her head against the back of her chair, and pictured the two men. Aaden, dramatic like lightning spearing her heart. Now Nick, as sweet and tempting as a spoon of honey.

She was being silly, and she knew it, and she loved it! How many times did a woman in her forties who had children to raise and feed and protect find her entire body awake and astonished by her own desires and pleasures? For pleasure was what Blythe had experienced with Nick, and with Aaden, too. What a surprise!

What a revelation.

"Mom! We're back!"

Holly and Carolyn were the first to come in through the front door. They launched themselves into the room, both talking at once about the handsome young Irishman who played the fiddle on Main Street and the adorable little girl who spontaneously danced to his music and were any cookies left and they were going to get up early tomorrow and run down to Jetties Beach to watch the sun rise.

Blythe managed to squeeze in a motherly reminder. "Be sure to brush your teeth before you go to bed."

"Okay, Mom!" Holly started to run up the stairs, but in a quick change of mood, she raced back into the living room, and hugged Blythe. "Thanks, Mom. You're the best."

Blythe returned to her mystery, listening with half an ear to the sounds coming from the second floor. Bathroom door opening and closing. Laughter. Bedroom door opening and closing. Muffled laughter.

She remembered being that age, when everything made her laugh. At eleven, Blythe had considered the world incomprehensible and surprising, with something unexpected happening every day. Tonight, Blythe felt that way again.

When Daphne arrived, she was talking on her phone.

"Hang on," she said to whoever was on the other side. "I've got to check in." She stuck her head into the living room. "Hi, Mom. I'm going to bed now."

"Don't spend all night on the phone," Blythe said.

"I won't." Daphne trudged up the stairs to her bedroom, still talking on her phone. "But I like the pale pink skirt."

It's a friend, Blythe thought. *Daphne has a friend, and how could that be anything but wonderful?* Daphne could be a loner, an introvert, and Blythe knew she couldn't change her, and sessions with her therapist taught her that she *shouldn't* change Daphne. She might not want to be popular, but she had been close to Johnny before he moved away. Now she had a few serious friends like Lincoln, plus her ongoing passion for saving the world, and what parent could object to that?

Blythe's own parents adored Daphne above all Daphne's siblings, and they often sent her important books about world problems needing solving like *Maid: Hard Work, Low Pay, and a Mother's Will to Survive* and *The Soul of an Octopus*. Blythe wished her daughter would read some of her older sister's romance novels with knights and peasants and wishing wells to balance out the harsh realities.

Blythe's ears perked up when she heard two male voices coming toward the house. Had Teddy invited someone to sleep over? The guys were comparing Minecraft and Fortnite, two video games Teddy played at home. The front door slammed and Teddy and Brooks entered, engrossed in their discussion, and Miranda followed.

Teddy and Brooks went down the hall to the family room. Miranda came into the living room and threw herself right onto Blythe's lap. She was taller than Blythe, but much slimmer, with long, long legs. Blythe felt like she was embracing a flamingo.

"Honestly, Teddy is driving me psycho. He talked with Brooks all the way home. I think Brooks has forgotten I even exist." Miranda put her arms around Blythe's neck. "Mommy, make Teddy go away."

Certain things Blythe knew at once. One simple breath produced a small explosion of information in her thoughts: no hint of alcohol or pot or even cigarettes.

Blythe kissed Miranda's cheek. "What would you do without me?"

She gently shoved her daughter off her lap and stood up. After smoothing her wrinkled shirt, she went into the hall.

She called out, "Teddy? Wherever you are, Teddy, you need to go to bed. Tennis tomorrow morning."

"Going, Mom!" Teddy burst out of the family room and up the stairs to his bedroom.

Miranda approached Blythe and hugged her from behind. "You're so cool, Mommy."

"I love you, too." Blythe slipped around to face Miranda. "Now you have to help Brooks get settled for the night. And then go up to your own room. No dawdling. It's late for all of us."

"Okay." Miranda drifted away down the hall and into the family room.

Blythe double-checked the kitchen and the porch lights at the front and back doors.

At the door to the family room, she said, "Miranda. Now."

Miranda detached herself from Brooks, who was standing in his black sleep shorts and red T-shirt with a silk screen of Patrick Mahomes bellowing like a moose.

The pullout sofa bed was already made up with cotton sheets, a blanket, and a pillow.

"Do you have everything you need, Brooks?" Blythe asked.

"Yes, thank you," Brooks replied.

"Brooks travels all the time," Miranda said. "He knows how to pack. Someday we're going to backpack through Europe."

"But now we're all going to bed," Blythe said.

Miranda sighed dramatically and went up the stairs to her room.

Yawning, Blythe flicked off all the downstairs lights. As she went up to her own room, she thought how these teenagers, so full of energy and plans for the future, had no idea how beautiful they were, or how time would slowly burnish the honeyed smoothness of their limbs and their thoughts until their faces, their bodies, their hearts would be marked with life's answers to their desires. The answers would not always be *yes*.

But sometimes the answer would be *yes,* and at the most unexpected moments.

complications

The next evening, Aaden took Blythe to the Brant Point Grill, where they drank cocktails on the porch overlooking Nantucket's inner harbor. Ferries, private yachts, and sailboats came and went, passing one another easily through the calm waters. A Sunfish with a bright orange sail loitered near Monomoy.

Aaden wore a navy blazer and a white shirt that set off his new tan and his dark eyes. Blythe wore her most daring summer dress, with a necklace that dipped down into her cleavage.

It was a wonderful meal. They dined on oysters and sea bass. They sipped cold white wine. And for dessert, strawberry shortcake with mounds of real whipped cream. They talked about Nantucket matters—there was always so much to discuss about Nantucket. Rising seas. The new money. Traffic congestion. They were moving through a conversation maze, searching for each other.

"Where are your children tonight?" Aaden asked.

"The younger three are either having dinner at a friend's house or with their grandmother. Miranda and Brooks are going to a new Marvel movie, so I don't have to worry that they're having sex in the house while I'm gone." She paused. "Not that I know whether or not they're ever actually having sex."

And here they were. Their eyes met and held. His gaze on her face was so gentle, so warm. Just this, meeting his eyes, was like kissing. With each breath, a memory moved through her. Their first kiss so long ago. Such a sweet, yearning kiss that broke Blythe's heart open to a hint of what a woman and a man could have together. Their quick pecks after they were a couple and passed each other on the street or when she slid into his car at the beginning of a date. The heated smash of their mouths when they were alone and desperate for each other's touch.

The waiter approached.

"Would you care for anything else?"

Without looking away from Aaden, Blythe said, "Yes, please. I'd like a cup of coffee."

The waiter went away.

She sighed. "I haven't had a night like this for weeks. Months. Years."

"You haven't gone out to dinner?"

"Well, of course I've gone out to dinner. With my kids to Five Guys or with my friends to restaurants to eat more complicated meals than our children could tolerate. I've even had a few dates in the past three years, and at best they were pleasant, but sometimes—" Blythe shook her head. "I don't even want to think about those times. I'm here on the island, it's June, my children are well and happy, the food was perfection, and most of all, Aaden, I'm giddy to be sitting here with you." Embarrassed, she covered her mouth with a hand, but it didn't cover her smile. "I can't believe I said that last part."

"You always did talk a lot," Aaden said.

The warmth in his eyes sent her heart racing.

"You always talked a lot, too," she responded.

"I know. That's one reason we're so good together."

She gave him a skeptical stare. "Present tense? You said 'that's one reason we're so good together.' Not one reason we *were* good together." Blythe didn't know if she was teasing him or encouraging him. Well, of course she knew, she was encouraging him. He was irresistible.

Aaden crossed his arms on the table and leaned toward her. "We're pretty good together right now, wouldn't you say?"

"Yes," Blythe agreed. "We are."

"And we don't need to account for our actions to anyone else. Not our parents. Not our children—"

Blythe interrupted him. "My children are sometimes around, and they're impressionable."

"Very well," Aaden said. "I won't ravish you in your living room."

Blythe shivered and crossed her arms where goosebumps were spreading at his words, at the thought of what Aaden had said, what he would do. *Ravish me.*

She suggested mischievously, "Maybe you could stage a pre-ravish display if you ever hear Kate bursting into the house again. That might teach her to knock."

His voice was low. "I'm not sure if I could stop ravishing you once I began."

Butterflies fluttered beneath her rib cage. She had given birth to four children since she'd last made love with him. She'd nursed four children. She was more than twenty years older and had the cellulite to prove it. But maybe in the dark . . . but could she restrain herself from wanting more than a few nights with him before he left this island for his own island home across the ocean?

"How soon do you leave Nantucket?" Blythe asked.

"Does it matter?"

Blythe blinked. "We always were more to each other than fast sex."

"We were," Aaden agreed. "We always will be. More to each other than fast sex."

Blythe hugged herself. "This conversation is making me sad. I don't know why. I'm sorry." She rose. "I'm going to the restroom."

She held herself steady, wearing one of those slight smiling faces people wear when they pass through a dining room, as if invisible voices were complimenting her.

She entered the bathroom and swung the door open to a private stall. Shut the door and leaned against it.

She had to center herself. She had to slow down. She hadn't been prepared for this when she began her summer. She probably had never been prepared for seeing Aaden again, and her emotions were in turmoil. Their love had been so deep, so complicated, spiritual as well as sexual, and they had been best friends as well as lovers. Often, back then, when she left him after an evening, she fell into a state of panic. When would she see him again? How could she make the hours pass fast enough for her to be with him again? She wanted to superglue her body to his, and remembering that, remembering when she'd told him that, Blythe laughed out loud. She was laughing, crying, hyperventilating. If another woman entered the restroom, they'd think a madwoman was in this stall, and she *was* a madwoman, because she absolutely wanted to make love with Aaden, and being with him made her realize she had never stopped loving him. Beneath all the love that she'd once had for Bob, beneath all the love she had for her children, her love of Aaden was still there in the deepest part of her heart. She had been struck by lightning. The mark would always remain.

Dashing out of the stall, she washed her hands and caught sight of herself in the mirror.

"Damn, I'm like a teenager again!" Blythe said.

A voice from another stall said, "Enjoy it, honey."

Blythe skittered out of there before the woman saw her.

By the time she returned to the table, Blythe had recovered her sense of humor.

She slid into her chair and inclined herself across the table to whisper to Aaden. "I was talking to myself in the bathroom, and I said I was acting like a teenager, and a woman from a stall—I didn't see her—called out, 'Enjoy it, honey.' "

"That's good advice if I ever heard it," Aaden said, grinning. "Shall we go?"

Blythe drew back. "Oh, Aaden, I didn't mean . . . I'm not ready—"

"Don't look so alarmed, woman. I'm not going to ravish you. I want to get to know you again first."

Relieved, Blythe said, "Me, too. I mean, I want to get to know you again, too."

They left the restaurant and stood for a moment on Easton Street. It was after ten o'clock and the sky was polished silver above them.

"Let's walk to the lighthouse," Aaden suggested.

"Yes, let's."

Aaden reached for her hand and held it as they walked down the long, beautiful street, lined on one side with summer homes facing the water and on the other side a large open field. They had the sense of being in the town and the country at the same time, and then they came to the beach, which curved out and around, and on the expanse of sand, right at the corner, the squat white Brant Point Lighthouse stood, only twenty-six feet high, a welcoming sight to travelers as they rounded the corner into the harbor.

Blythe steadied herself on Aaden's shoulder and bent to slip off her heels.

"Ah," she sighed. "The sand is still warm."

Aaden had kicked off his topsiders. Taking her hand again, he led her past the ramp from the beach to the closed lighthouse door and around to the sloping shoulder of sand. They settled with their backs against the lighthouse, looking out over the harbor, with its gathering cluster of big and small boats, and to the beach at Monomoy with its summer houses and lights glowing like lanterns.

After a while, Blythe said, "I didn't know if I'd ever see you again. I certainly never dreamed I'd be sitting in the sand on Nantucket with you."

"No? Because I dreamed of you often, especially when I was stressed out, when Eileen was a screaming terror and I had no love for her or she for me."

"I'm sorry. Do you want to tell me more? Maybe about the worst times? Not so that I can judge. I'm sure I've been a terror myself."

After a moment, Aaden said, "Sure, the poor woman was probably driven mad by me. I was never home, it's an old story, the man works day and night to keep the business thriving while the wife is alone with two wailing babies. There I was, working nineteen hours a day and giving no help to Eileen, but I was pulling the company out of the grave and into the light."

He paused, picking up a pebble, throwing it into the water.

"That happens a lot," Blythe told him. "Women with the home and children, men with the work."

Aaden asked, "Is that the way it was for you?"

Blythe steadied the back of her head against the lighthouse. "No. And not because I was the perfect mother. No, I had plenty of help. Wonderful friends and babysitters at home. On Nantucket, Celeste, my mother-in-law, and her husband adored them and helped so much. And Kate, my sister-in-law, well, you've met her. She's highly efficient and extremely dictatorial. And I was glad. Back then, I was grateful for her support."

"And Bob?"

Blythe chuckled softly. "In the beginning, he came home in the evening and helped out. He diapered our children and walked the floors with them at night. As they grew older, he was busier with work, and of course he was being paid more, handling harder cases. We became sort of a partnership. Thank heavens for his parents. They love our children, and Celeste often came up to take over when I had the flu or was overwhelmed. I love Celeste. I've learned so much from her."

"What about your parents?" Aaden asked.

"Oh, you remember my parents, Aaden. They were busy with their own careers. My father was a doctor and Mother taught. They were fond of Miranda and Daphne, but they were philosophically opposed to my having four children. They were shocked and disapproving." She sighed. "For their birthdays my parents send the children one annual subscription to *National Geographic* to share. For Christmas, they donate money in the children's names to several charities."

"And now?"

"The children will be in school. I could continue to substitute teach. But I've been offered a job teaching English full-time in seventh grade."

"Are you going to take it?"

"I don't know. The children are growing up so fast. I want to make sure I can be there for them."

"I understand. Still, I wonder, with Bob and Teri in your children's lives here on Nantucket . . . what if you could get away and come for a week or two in Ireland?"

It was as if he'd reached behind his back and magically brought out a beautiful box with a golden latch. All she had to do was open it. For a few moments, Blythe couldn't think. Two weeks away from her children? She thought of Pandora's box. They had been clever, those old storytellers.

She reached over to put her hand on Aaden's arm. Oh, what a warm, strong arm. "That is a *shocking* suggestion. Truly, Aaden."

"You've never been away from them?"

"No, not really. I've never even thought about it. I've never even had the time to think about it." Suddenly, she shivered, as if she were on the very edge of a cliff high in the air and if she took one step forward, she would plunge into a vast unknown. "I don't think I could, or *should,* leave my children for two weeks."

Aaden said, his voice very low, "Blythe, I'm sorry. I didn't mean to shock you or frighten you. It's too soon for me to ask such a question."

Blythe forced herself to do the deep breathing she was counseled to do when she was confused. "Aaden, aren't we too old for a . . . a fling?"

Aaden was quiet. Then he said, "Sure, that's possible. But we're not too old for a relationship."

She felt trapped, caught, torn between hope and fear. "Oh, you Irish," she said, almost angrily, "you and your bewitching words."

"I want to bewitch you," Aaden told her. "But I'm in no hurry. I've waited twenty-four years for you. I can wait for a while longer."

The clock on the Old South tower chimed eleven times.

"I need to go home." Blythe scrambled to her feet. "The children . . ."

Aaden rose, too, and he didn't touch her, but he stood close to her. She could feel his warmth.

"Blythe. I had no idea you would be on the island when Arnie invited me. When I set eyes on you at the yacht club, I felt an electric shock. It was as if my eyes had been opened and I could see my future."

Anxiety made her insolent. "You saw all that in one moment?"

Aaden did not back down. "I did."

"That's . . . a lot. Aaden, I think I should go home. I think I need to take a moment." Blythe tilted her head back, studying his face. "I still love you. But I love my children . . . I love my life. I don't think I'm ready to go to Ireland yet."

He reached out his hand and cupped her cheek. "No. Of course you aren't. I've gotten all ahead of myself. I apologize. But it's true, Blythe, what I said about first seeing you here."

Blythe slowly moved her head so that her lips touched the palm of his hand. She kissed him, and felt him tremble, and tears stung her eyes.

Then she pulled away from him. "Aaden, I'll think about it. But it might take some time."

"I'm here," Aaden said. "I have time."

Screams interrupted the air as a pack of adolescents swarmed over the sand around the lighthouse.

"I'll take you home now," Aaden told her.

He took her hand in his, and they walked together up the beach, away from the dark, lapping water, to his car.

time to see the roses

Blythe woke in the morning and allowed herself to lie there, snug beneath her blue duvet, relaxed and dreamy and in a rare poetic state of mind.

It was early, and the rising sun felt like hope. She lay idly, allowing herself to gaze lazily at the wide sweep of sky. A few clouds floated past, diaphanous, like wedding veils.

She thought that summer light on Nantucket was different from any other light in the world, because the island lay between the vast Atlantic Ocean and the much smaller Nantucket Sound. Nantucket light carried the mist of clashing waves, fumes from the ferries coming and going daily, and whirlpools of air as the gulls swooped and shrieked for food. The heart of the island was wild hilly moors stretching for miles, so the air was also filled with scents of low bush blueberries, beach plum bushes, and wind-twisted pine trees. The busy, invisible air absorbed the authentic perfume of warm earth from the warrens of field mice, the cautious trails of deer through the brambles, and the nests of hawks and doves. Their scent joined that of coconut oil, beer fumes, spicy chips, and sizzling meats from the beaches and yards of all the homes and rose to glide in the sky.

Also, the kisses and whispers of lovers, a sweet hidden honey, drifted in the island air.

She wished she could be a bird just for an hour, swooshing through the summer sky.

"Oh, Lord," Blythe said aloud. "I've gone poetic."

She plumped her pillows and sat up, leaning against them, not ready to leave the dreamworld of her bed.

Aaden had invited her to visit Ireland. Hope and fear shot through her. She felt excited and nervous and *guilty,* which was ridiculous. She hadn't gone off and left her children.

But seriously, she told herself. She couldn't go to Ireland with Aaden for two weeks!

And yet, why not? When Bob and Teri came to stay with Celeste, the four children could stay with them and be perfectly cared for.

Although, what would Blythe feel like if the children wanted to stay in her house? True, it was where all their summer gear was stashed. True, Bob had lived here before, when they were married, but the house her grandmother had left her had always been totally, legally, hers. The thought of Teri being able to look through her drawers and closets made her feel rather sick. Although she was pretty certain that Teri wouldn't be interested in her old lady clothing.

Her phone pinged, breaking into her thoughts.

Nick.

"I've had an idea," he said when she answered the phone.

"That's impressive," Blythe joked. "I haven't even had my coffee yet."

He had a good baritone laugh. "Sandy told me you like to hike. Let's go walk the bluff path at 'Sconset and have lunch at Claudette's. I've never walked the path before. Also, I hear this is the time to see the roses."

His deep, smooth voice made Blythe snuggle into her pillows. "This is the time to see the roses," she echoed. "Nick, that sounds lovely."

"I'll pick you up at eleven?"

"Please."

"See you then."

Smiling, Blythe rose, padded downstairs, and made herself coffee. She went out to sit on the porch. She had so much to think about she couldn't think at all. And it was too beautiful a day for thinking.

She heard slight noises and Daphne stepped into the doorway.

"Daphne. Sweetie. Come snuggle with me." Blythe patted the wicker swing.

"I'm already dressed." She wore a bathing suit with shorts and a long T-shirt.

"Come on." Blythe held out her arm.

"Mom." Daphne was a very serious fifteen. Obviously snuggling with her mother was out of her range of acceptable activities. Oh, Lord, was Blythe infantilizing this child? Was she holding Daphne back from being the person she could be? Daphne could cure cancer or bring world peace!

"We're on vacation," Blythe reminded herself and Daphne. Didn't even the smartest person need a vacation?

Daphne trudged across the porch, kicked off her flip-flops, and sat on the swing.

Blythe pulled her second-oldest child close to her. Daphne snuggled into her arm.

"You smell good," Blythe told Daphne.

"It's soap. Just Ivory soap." Daphne rejected all perfumes and most cosmetics, worried that testing on animals was part of the process of production.

Blythe smoothed Daphne's uncombed hair. "Do you have plans for today?"

"Yeah. Lincoln and I are going to bike out to Cisco and pick up plastic and stuff."

"Oh, sweetie, we just got here. Can't you take a day or two to enjoy yourself?"

Daphne bristled. "I could if people recycled or at least picked up their trash and stuffed it in a bin. How can I enjoy myself if I know some poor baby seal out in the ocean is choking on the plastic bread wrapper some family let wash out to sea?"

"I'm sure you know that there's an official Nantucket Clean Team that goes out every morning to pick up trash."

"I do know that. But they can't be everywhere."

Blythe said, "Well, I am proud of you." She tried to earn one more minute with her daughter. "Want me to pack up a lunch for the two of you?"

"Thanks, no. I've got bananas and water and there are food trucks at the parking lot."

"Do you need some money?"

"Please. Can I get some out of your purse?"

"Of course. Take a twenty." Blythe could sense Daphne's eagerness to get started. "Be sure to take your phone."

"Mom. I'm fifteen." Daphne sat up, slipping her feet back into her flip-flops.

Blythe said, "Daphne. You do know you don't have to fix the world all by yourself."

Daphne gave her mother a very grown-up look. "Someone does."

As her daughter went out the door, Blythe called, "Take a sweater in case it rains."

No answer. After a few minutes, the front door slammed.

Blythe sometimes thought that her children were breaking away from her like rocks in a landslide. Of course they had to leave, to grow up, to be their own people. Now the question was: What would she do with herself? Go to Ireland for two weeks? Teach full-time?

Her morning calm was gone. Blythe went upstairs and into the en suite bathroom for a quick shower. It was a luxury to have all the hot water she wanted because Miranda, who could shower for hours, was still asleep.

Dressed in capris and a blue-and-white striped rugby shirt, she headed downstairs. She heard voices coming from the family room.

Ah, she thought. *Miranda has come down to wake Brooks.*

She hoped that was why Miranda was in the family room.

She walked down the hall and looked in.

"So, the sea gerbils leave their caves at the exact moment the sun disappears, which makes it impossible for people to see them. They gather beneath the water and flash out like shadows."

"I see." Brooks was listening carefully to Holly as she explained a page in her graphic novel.

Holly was dressed in a swimsuit and shorts. Brooks was dressed in swim trunks—Under Armour dark gray with compression liner—she'd bought a pair for Teddy—and a T-shirt. Brooks had folded his sheets and blanket and put them in a corner with his pillow on top. His blond hair stuck out in all directions, and bristles covered his jaw. He would have to shave, Blythe thought, and soon Teddy would be shaving, too.

Brooks spotted her at the doorway. "Good morning, Mrs. Benedict."

"Hi, Brooks. Hi, Holly." Blythe waved and turned to leave.

"Hi, Mom," Holly said, but she didn't look up from her sketchbook. She had a captive audience and she wasn't going to let him go just yet.

Blythe went into the kitchen and set out boxes of cereal and a dozen pastries she'd bought at Born & Bread yesterday. Only when it was raining or windy did she make a full eggs and bacon breakfast. The children rarely all got up at the same time. Food would grow cold. And sometimes someone was in a hurry to get to the beach or the tennis court and skipped breakfast entirely. She topped off her coffee and went back to the porch.

Through the open door, she heard laughter, and then she heard

Holly, Miranda, and Brooks enter the kitchen. She could tell by his voice that Brooks was happy. She knew he was an only child, and probably often lonely when his parents traveled to other countries and left him with the live-in housekeeper, even though she was perfectly nice.

"MOM!"

"I'm here!"

Miranda stepped out on the porch. "I couldn't find you anywhere."

"Well, now you have."

"Can me and Brooks have the car to drive us out to Sesachacha? We want to pick up a couple of friends and spend the day there. We'll stop at Something Natural and get food on the way."

Blythe took a moment.

"Mom." Miranda was using her sweetest voice. "You know we're both good drivers."

"Give me a minute. I'm trying to think whether I'll need the car today. Wait—when will you be back?"

"Well, me and Brooks want to stay out there at night, I don't mean all night, I mean until maybe ten o'clock? Or eleven?"

"If I let you have the car, Miranda, will you promise me that next time you will say 'Brooks and I'?"

Miranda frowned. "Brooks and you what?"

Teddy, fully dressed in white shorts and T-shirt, burst out onto the porch. "I'm going to the club to play tennis and stuff."

Blythe asked, "Have you had breakfast?"

"Yeah, cereal. Bye."

"Teddy, stop!" At least, Blythe thought, she could still get him to pay attention to her. "You have to give me a hug."

"Jeez, Mom." Teddy rolled his eyes but gave her the world's quickest and fiercest hug—for a moment Blythe couldn't breathe.

Teddy was stronger than he used to be.

"Mom," Miranda said.

"Fine. Take the car. But promise me you'll call me when you get there and check in sometime in the evening."

Miranda shook her head. "You are so weird."

"Yeah, but you love me anyway," Blythe replied, and in a moment of happiness, she hugged her oldest daughter tight and kissed her cheek. "Have fun."

"Weird," Miranda muttered as she returned to the kitchen. "Just weird." But she was smiling.

Blythe was smiling, too.

Nick arrived at her house in a big red high-clearance Bronco.

"I didn't know the Greens had a Bronco," Blythe said, hauling herself up into the vehicle.

"They don't. I rented this. I plan to drive out to Great Point this summer, and I need four-wheel drive."

Blythe fastened her seatbelt. "Have you been there before?"

"Several times. I grew up in Boston and we spent many summers and holidays here."

"So did I! I inherited my grandmother's house, the one I lived in all summer."

"You're lucky to own a house here. We only rented. And not every summer."

"Still, it's surprising we haven't met before."

Nick glanced over at Blythe. "I'm glad we're meeting now."

"Me, too." Blythe suddenly felt shy. "Have you always lived in Massachusetts?"

"I took a semester abroad in France my junior year of college."

"That must have been fun."

"Oh, it was." Nick laughed. He was quiet as they made their way around the rotary and onto Milestone Road. More seriously, he said, "That was where I met my wife."

"She was French?"

"Yes, but she wanted to study in Boston. She was another college student. A chemistry major. Very bright. Brielle."

"Sandy told me you are widowed."

"Yes. Five years ago."

Blythe waited a moment. She sensed he would be okay with her question. "How did she die?"

"Cancer. All of medicine's knowledge couldn't save her."

"I'm so sorry."

Nick nodded. "It was a bad time. But she did it with such grace. Our son, Seth, is a cellist. She often asked him to play for her in her last days."

"Sandy said you have another child."

"Jason."

"Is he a musician?"

The question amused him. "Oh, no. He's tone-deaf. He's a jock. He's greased lightning on the field but in Bre's bedroom, he couldn't move without knocking something over. Brielle said she liked having him around. He provided comic relief."

"Where are the boys now?"

"Jason's on the practice squad for the Kansas City Chiefs."

"Impressive."

"Seth plays with the Boston Symphony Orchestra."

"Wow. Music must run in your family."

"Probably. Dad coached sports and Mom taught music, both at the same school." Nick laughed. "My sister, Nora, is a teacher."

Blythe gave him a brief summary of her own family, mentioning that she'd always wished she'd had a sibling.

"Sometimes a friend is as good as a sibling," Nick told her. "Plus, you never have to beat them up."

"You beat up your sister?" Blythe asked, faking horror.

"I wanted to. We're only two years apart, and we fought a lot. When we were little, she'd sock me and I'd pull her hair. We had some legendary shouting matches. Also, I might have put a frog in her bed."

"At least it wasn't a snake," Blythe said.

Nick fake-cringed. "Well . . ."

"You put a snake in your sister's bed?"

"It couldn't hurt her. It was dead."

"Ugh! Nick Roth, that's terrible!"

Looking mischievous, Nick recalled, "It was brilliant. She was *so* mad! Don't worry. She got over it. We're good friends now. I've mellowed since I was six."

Blythe was laughing as Nick went around the 'Sconset Rotary and parked in front of the Sconset Market. This village was a different universe from the town of Nantucket. Small, quiet, it was like stepping back into the past.

They strolled through the lane of small cottages, their roofs covered with roses. When they got to the Bluff Walk, they went single file, stopping now and then to comment on the view of the Atlantic, rolling peacefully today. They passed sprawling mansions on their left and on their right, stairs zigzagging down the steep cliff plunging to the beach.

By the time they reached the end and followed the trail back, they were both hungry. At Claudette's, Nick bought them roasted turkey sandwiches with the works and bottles of water and they settled at one of the tables on the deck.

Blythe caught her breath and tilted her head back to the sun. When she straightened, she saw Nick studying the view of vine-covered mansions and the road slanting down to the beach.

She studied him. He was fit. All that hiking, she guessed. His face was tan, with white creases fanning from his eyes. His shoulders were wide. He looked sturdy. She wanted to put her hand on his chest, right where his heart was.

Nick felt her gaze and turned to her.

"I have to confess something," Blythe told him. "I'm not a serious hiker."

"Well, that was not a serious hike."

"Oh, and what's a serious hike?"

"The West Highland trail in Scotland. It can take six or seven days."

"Have you hiked it?"

"I have."

"I bow down to you, O Serious Hiker," Blythe teased, not exactly kidding.

"Stop it. Listen, have you hiked up Mount Greylock? In western Massachusetts?"

"No. I've only hiked with the kids, and we've stayed close to Boston."

"How about Mount Washington in New Hampshire?"

"I have not. Haven't even considered it. You must really like to hike."

"It's cheaper than therapy." Nick put his bottle of water on the table and was quiet. Then he raised his eyes to meet Blythe's. "When Brielle died, I lost part of myself with her. I've never been strictly religious, but I've always believed in *something*. I don't think you can be a musician and not believe in something. Those days were so hard, for her and for our sons. It was five years ago. The boys were in high school. I took a leave during Brielle's last few weeks, but we made the boys continue at school. Jason with sports. Seth with music. They took Bre's death hard, but they had more of a balance than I did. I was kind of lost. I still taught, but I wasn't myself. I was a robot. A minimum-functioning teacher and father."

Nick closed his eyes. Blythe sat with him in silence. No one else was on the deck and the only sound was the cry of the gulls.

Nick continued, "The boys went off to college. I still had casseroles from kind friends in the freezer, but eventually I had to cook for myself. Worse, I had to eat by myself. When I was teaching, I began to enjoy being with the students. I even enjoyed the endless faculty meetings. In the fall and winter, I attended the symphony and other venues where Seth played. The music has it all, the beauty and the grief. It helped. But the summer was long and lonely." He cleared his throat. "Loneliness is a killer, isn't it? I was lonely for someone to hold me and laugh with me and dream with me. I miss the touch of loving hands, the warmth of someone else's skin next to mine. I had plenty of friends and I loved teaching, but at night I was so lonely . . ."

Blythe was quiet, waiting. Understanding.

"Then Jamie, who taught science at my school, insisted I start hiking with him." Nick smiled and rolled his eyes. "He told me I was sadly out of shape. So I started hiking. I liked it. The world looks different from a mountain trail. It's all so much bigger. When you look down from a mountaintop, you can believe anything exists. Plus, it always seems like an achievement. I asked my sons to go with me, but they have their own lives. Last summer I went with Jamie to Scotland. We hiked and drank Irn-Bru and ended our evenings with Scotch. I came home believing in something again."

"I'm glad," Blythe told him.

Nick turned to her. "I've talked too much. Tell me something about yourself."

Blythe took a moment to gather her thoughts. "I know about loneliness. I was lonely during my marriage to Bob. We were kind of like workers on a conveyor belt, dutifully taking care of our children. The children were the center of our marriage, and they were happy, but we were miserable. When we began to talk about divorce, it was as if we could see the sun rising after a long dark night. We've been nicer to each other after divorcing than we were before. I've been less lonely."

Nick said, "Good."

After lunch, they walked down to the beach and waded in the cold Atlantic water. The sun was high and strong.

"You'd better take me home," Blythe told Nick. "I'm afraid I'll lie down on the sand and fall into one of those snoring, twitching, drooling sleeps that happen when salt air and sunshine combine."

"That sounds intensely attractive, Blythe," Nick joked. "I'll have to bring you out here again."

Laughing, they walked back to the air-conditioned Bronco. As they rode home, Blythe closed her eyes and simply relaxed in the pleasure of the day.

"Thank you," Blythe said when they returned to her house. "I had a great time."

"So did I," Nick said. "We'll do it again."

"I hope so." She unsnapped her seatbelt.

"And some night we'll go to the theater or a movie."

"I'd like that a lot."

He had such beautiful eyes. She couldn't look away. "I have to get out of this car, don't I?"

"Unfortunately, yes. But you can come sit in it anytime you want."

"And the Greens won't think I'm odd, sitting out on the drive in your Bronco?"

"No. Because when you're sitting here, I'll join you."

He made her so happy! Impulsively, Blythe moved toward him and kissed his cheek, then jumped out of the Bronco before she did anything else.

Nick waited until she was in the house, then drove away.

No one else was home, so Blythe took a cool shower and pulled on a sundress.

She was glad she'd told Nick about her marriage, but she hadn't told him everything.

Blythe and Bob had had terrible, bitter arguments. They'd always waited until the children were in bed, and they'd always shut themselves into the den, but did they shout? Maybe. Did they call each other names? She wasn't sure.

Blythe had wanted to teach full-time. Substitute teaching was so hit or miss.

Bob had told her she should focus on their own children. He was making enough money, God knew, for them to live on.

Blythe had snapped that money wasn't all their children needed. When had Bob ever helped any of the kids with their homework? Or attended a recital or soccer game?

Bob had reminded her that he was involved in a legal suit against a company that had dumped toxins into Boston Harbor and did she want him to stop working?

Of course not, Blythe said, but Bob wanted to buy a sailboat to moor on Nantucket. Blythe didn't enjoy sailing and thought it wasn't right for the expensive boat to be bought with their family income. But, she continued, if she taught, she could help support the family.

Bob had snorted with laughter. With her teacher's salary? And what about him? When did she ever support *him*? Sure, she made all the meals and picked up his dry cleaning, but when did she ever ask about his work? When did she ever initiate making love?

Blythe went out and bought a sexy pair of crotchless lingerie and appeared in the den late one night when he was watching the Red Sox. She'd wrapped a robe around her in case the children woke. She made a dramatic appearance in the den, tossing her robe off and posing seductively against the door.

Bob looked at her and gave her the first sincere and loving smile he'd given her in months.

"Oh, sweetheart," he said sadly, as if he were consoling a child with a hurt finger.

Insulted, hideously embarrassed, Blythe had raced back to her bedroom, ripped off the rather uncomfortable outfit, wrapped it in newspaper, pulled on the robe, and taken the lingerie out to the trash barrel. When she returned to the house, she hurried up the stairs, went into their bedroom, and locked the door.

That night, Bob had slept in the guest room. After that, he slept there so often that the kids asked about it. He told them he'd wrenched a muscle in his back and needed to sleep alone.

A few nights later, they'd talked again, seriously, about their lives. Bob told her she loved the kids first, him second. He'd said that she'd been beautiful in the Victoria's Secret lingerie, but that kind of sex wasn't what he wanted, and besides, her C-section cut had showed, and all he could think about was the night Holly was born.

"We have the children," Blythe had reminded him. "Are we supposed to be wildly passionate lovers, too?"

Bob had taken her hand. "Maybe not. But I would really like to have a wildly passionate lover before I die."

"Maybe we can't have everything we want," Blythe told him sadly.

"Maybe not. But I'd like to try."

That night, they hadn't made love.

They'd spent hours with a marriage counselor. They'd tried not to fight in front of the children. They'd been much nicer to each other when they decided to divorce. When they told the children, they spoke honestly but not angrily. The children were confused for a while, and upset, and worried. That was the worst thing about divorce, Blythe thought, your children were caught in between.

But here they were, on Nantucket as they had been every summer, and three years after the divorce, they were all comfortable with the situation. It was an enormous plus that Bob spent much more time with his children. It helped that Blythe had the Nantucket summer house. When Bob and Teri spent a few weeks on the island at his mother's house, the children stayed there, too, often racing into Blythe's house for a forgotten sweatshirt or lost earring. Blythe loved how the children moved easily between the two houses. She was glad Bob was happy with Teri, and she hoped that someday she'd meet a man she could be glad to spend time with, although she had her doubts that that would ever happen.

It was miraculous, Blythe knew, that Celeste and Blythe remained close friends. When all the kids were off somewhere, Blythe would make iced tea or, if the time was right, a fizzing vodka tonic with lots of crystal-cold ice and slices of lemon. They would sit on the back porch and talk about the garden, Celeste's bridge club, and, sometimes, Teri.

One late afternoon, when it was uncomfortably hot and humid, definitely vodka tonic time, Celeste had said, "I have to give Teri credit. She's a lovely girl, and good with the children. But sometimes she acts as if I'm one hundred years old. Also, she doesn't *read*. She hasn't read *anything*. When I asked her if she'd like to borrow my copy of *Beloved* by Toni Morrison, Teri said, and I quote, 'I'll just wait and see the movie. I'm an addict of romantic movies.' "

"She makes your son happy," Blythe had reminded her ex-mother-in-law.

Celeste had lifted an eyebrow. "And you're happy without him."

"I am." Blythe had glanced down at her left hand, free of any rings. "And your son is happy without me."

"Mom!"

Blythe's memories were interrupted by Holly.

"Hi, Mom, I'm in a hurry. I've got to change clothes and go to Grandmother's," Holly called, thundering up the stairs to her room.

Blythe followed, a load of clean laundry in her arms. "Will you be gone long?"

"I don't know," Holly said. "I promised Grandmother I'd come over this afternoon to help make cheddar crisps for a small get-together she's having this evening."

Blythe leaned against the door, watching Holly whirl around the room. "Are *you* invited to this small get-together?" Blythe asked.

"Not as a guest, which—no thank you. She's only having four or five friends, but she asked if I would pass around the goodies, you know, like a caterer."

"I didn't know you were interested in catering."

"I'm not," Holly responded casually. "I want to check out this Roland guy she's dating."

"You want to check out the guy your grandmother is dating? How old *are* you?"

Holly shrugged. "*Somebody* has to watch out for her. I've talked it over with Teddy. We always hang out at her house, so it's natural for us to be around. And Grandmother is naïve. She hasn't dated a new man for probably *eons*. She owns a huge house on Nantucket, probably worth ten or twenty million. We don't want anyone marrying her for her money."

"I'm speechless," Blythe said.

"Actually," Holly politely pointed out, "you've just spoken. Two words. Three since it took two words to make 'I'm.' "

Blythe laughed. "You're getting way too smart. And so sophisticated. To think your grandmother is naïve! Really! Does she know you think that?"

"I don't think so. She just thinks we like to be around her, and that's true. We do."

No one had ever given Blythe advice on how to deal with this situation. She turned the problem over in her mind. "Celeste isn't senile, Holly. She's intelligent and capable and she has full use of her senses. It's sweet of you to look after her, but I don't think you need to *worry.*"

"Sometimes her hand wobbles," Holly said.

"Sometimes *my* hand wobbles," Blythe countered.

"Only after you've played tennis," Holly said.

Blythe gasped. "Oh, give me strength. Don't tell me you're inspecting *me,* too."

"Not as much now." Holly sounded as calm as if she were counting to ten. "When you and Dad divorced you had some difficult moments."

Blythe bit her tongue. *Difficult moments!*

"Gotta go!" Holly rushed past her mother. "Love you!" she yelled as she raced down the front steps.

The front door slammed again. The sound of voices came from the front hall and then a clatter, which would be Teddy dropping his tennis racket, and then Teddy and his summer friend Azey—his real name was Adam, but he was an identical twin, so one boy was called Azey and one Beezy—stormed into the kitchen.

Teddy had blood on his face and on his white tennis shirt. Both boys were red-faced and breathing hard.

Blythe held herself back. She knew if she fell to her knees and hugged Teddy, he would be mortified.

"What happened?" she asked. Did he fall on the tennis court? Did he get hit by a ball?

"I was in a fight," Teddy said. He stood in front of her with clenched fists and a recalcitrant expression.

Blythe almost sat right down on the floor. "You got into a *fight*?" She'd have been less surprised if Teddy had been bitten by a shark.

Azey explained. "Jack Winchester was making fun of Scarlett's glasses."

"And?" Blythe prompted.

"And," her son burst out, "she already has to wear braces, and Jack was calling her Cyborg and Android and Terminator, and she was crying and I told him to stop, and he didn't, so I shoved him away from her and he hit me and the tennis pro banned us both from the yacht club for two days."

"Wow." Blythe didn't know whether to praise him or scold him. She gestured toward the table. "Thank you. Azey, sit down. Teddy, you, too. You need to cool off and catch your breath. I'll give you both a glass of lemonade."

The boys sat, still radiating an almost visible energy.

Ladies and Gentlemen, Blythe thought, *the dreaded testosterone has arrived.*

"It wasn't a real fight, Mom," Teddy declared.

"Yeah," Azey cut in. "Jack was all up in Scarlett's face and Teddy pushed Jack and Jack slugged Teddy in the face and then Scarlett kicked Jack in the leg." Azey met Teddy's eyes. "She's sick, man!"

"Really?" Blythe sank onto a chair at the table. "Scarlett is sick?"

The two boys laughed like a pair of chimps.

Teddy crowed. "Mom, she's not sick, she's *sick*!"

"It's like slang. It means she's excellent." Azey was impressed with himself as translator.

"Scarlett's banned for two days, too," Teddy said.

Blythe's phone buzzed. She pulled it from her pocket, hoping to see Aaden's number.

It was the tennis pro, Zane. She answered the phone.

"Hello, Mrs. Benedict. The reason I'm calling," Zane said, "is to fill you in on the incident involving Teddy at the yacht club."

"Yes. Teddy is here now."

"Good. He'll have told you that he was the one who caused the altercation. He pushed Jack Winchester. Hard. Jack fell back against a table and hit his arm. It's not broken, but it will be bruised for a while. One of our waitstaff brought him ice wrapped in a napkin. Then Jack slugged Teddy in the face. Again, nothing broken, no broken nose. We gave him ice in a napkin, too. But our rule is, as the boys know, no fighting on yacht club property. Both boys have been suspended from the club for two days."

"But is that fair? Teddy was protecting Scarlett—" She interrupted herself, glancing at Teddy. "What is Scarlett's last name?"

"August," Teddy said.

"Scarlett August?" Weird name.

Zane continued. "We have a no-fighting policy. It's only for two days, and it's a good thing to happen at the beginning of the summer. Maybe this will be a warning example to other children."

"I understand," Blythe said. She wondered what would have happened if Bob had taken the call.

Zane said goodbye. Blythe studied the two boys, trying to decide what to say.

"That was Zane Lewis. He basically confirmed what you told me, and you are banned from the club for two days."

Again, the phone. This time it was Mrs. August. Blythe held her hand up to silence the boys, wanting to hear her son called a hero for protecting Scarlett.

The other woman sounded angry. "Mrs. Benedict? I'm Mrs. August, Scarlett's mother. I'm calling because of that very disturbing situation your son caused."

"Oh, it wasn't Teddy who bullied Scarlett—"

"I'm quite aware of what your son did. My husband and I have been extremely careful to teach Scarlett that violence is never the answer. Scarlett has been taught to take care of herself and to be strong and to ignore other children's silly remarks. Your son interfered. He acted with anger and violence. He made an embarrassing scene at the yacht club. Scarlett is still in tears."

Blythe felt like she'd just fallen down Alice in Wonderland's rabbit hole. "Mrs. August. My son was not trying to start a fight. He was pushing the other boy away so that he couldn't continue harassing your daughter. It was Jack Winchester who hit my son, and Teddy has a bloody nose. You should be calling Jack Winchester's mother."

"Suzanna Winchester is a dear friend," Mrs. August said. "I've spoken with her and she assured me that your son started the fight."

Blythe didn't know whether to laugh or curse. "*Mrs.* August, thank you so much for calling. I'm so glad you've raised such a composed daughter. And I'm sorry you were given the wrong information about the incident. Goodbye." She ended the call before Mrs. August, who obviously felt it would be disturbing to give her first name, could say anything else.

"Sit down and eat some cookies," Blythe told the two boys. "We need to have a little talk."

Blythe knew her son hated her "little talks." They weren't exactly the high point of her life, either. She knew that a person in the guilty seat tended to exaggerate all facts in his or her own favor. The wisest advice she'd ever been given was to make certain that whatever punishment was given, it wouldn't be as bad for the supervising parent as for the child. She decided to ban all screen privileges for two days. That meant he still had all of the island to explore. At night, he could read a real book.

She sat at the kitchen table with her son and his friend and pointed out the difference between the way Teddy had described pushing Jack Winchester and the way the tennis pro had. She reminded him to tell the truth. She listened to him moan and mutter when she laid out his punishment, and she wanted to moan and mutter herself.

Finally, she let the boys leave, and they shot out of the house as if escaping a dragon.

That left her alone with her thoughts. Her stomach was boiling with anger and frustration—it wasn't *fair* that Scarlett's mother was a good friend of Jack's mother! But Blythe had told her children so many times that life wasn't fair. She had to accept that and remind Teddy, when he returned, to stay away from Scarlett and Jack.

Next, she settled in to more serious thoughts. Was Teddy developing a tendency toward violence now that he was flooded with male hormones? Boys his age fought—wanted to fight. She'd taught middle school. She'd read the books. She'd heard the lectures. She'd actually stopped a few fights herself when she was substitute teaching. One of the first rules she'd learned was not to personally step in to end the fight. That would be a good way to get hit herself.

What should she do about Teddy?

He should have a man to talk to. Was it a problem for Teddy that he had three sisters and no brother? That his father figure was out of the house and not around to deal with problems? She would have to discuss this with Bob. Bob didn't like being strict or handing out discipline, but he was going to have to at least talk with Teddy.

Could she talk about Teddy with Brooks? *Should* she? Brooks was a seventeen-year-old male, so he would have insight into the moods and emotions of a thirteen-year-old boy. On the other hand, Brooks wasn't yet an adult. Maybe it wouldn't be proper for her to involve Brooks with Teddy's problems. Or, more accurately, with Blythe's problems because of Teddy's actions.

Other thoughts tumbled down on top of those thoughts, like heavy boulders in a landslide. Maybe this was the wrong time for her to become involved with a man, to bring a new man into her children's lives. But what about *her* life, *her* happiness?

Was she sex-starved, narcissistic, or simply perimenopausal? Did she have her own hormones flooding her system and drowning her judgment? Blythe worried that her common sense was trapped in a spaghetti-like maze. Right now, sea gerbils were the good news.

popularity

The next morning, Blythe woke early, full of worry and hope.

Her phone pinged. Lazily, she reached for it on the bedside table. "Hello?" Her voice was husky. She needed coffee.

"Good morning, Blythe." It was Aaden. *Aaden!* His voice was the background music to her adolescence. Hearing it now, over the phone, transported her back to those early days when they first fell in love and thought they'd be together forever. Sneaking a kiss behind their locker doors. Raking leaves together and diving into the pile, holding each other and laughing, gold and ruby leaves caught in their hair, on their sweaters, on their jeans. Snowy-night phone calls when a storm iced the pavements to slickness and she or Aaden had winter colds and they croaked to each other for hours about their love. The spring afternoon when they had taken their terrifying SATs and exploded out onto the elementary school playground to scream as they zipped down small people's slides and Aaden pushed Blythe's swing so high in the air she thought she could fly away.

The evening when Aaden told her he was going to Ireland for college.

Now, it was a future neither one of them had imagined. His voice was the same velvet voice she'd heard for so many happy months so many years ago.

"Could you have breakfast with me? Something has come up and I have to fly to Dublin today. I'll be back, but I want to talk to you before I go."

"Um, sure, I guess." She sat up in bed and tossed her covers aside.

"I'll pick you up in ten minutes."

"Please make it fifteen."

She quickly showered and dressed. All the children were in bed, Teddy snoring, Daphne reading, Holly tapping away on her laptop, and Miranda whispering on her phone.

Blythe left a message on the blackboard telling them where she was going and when she'd be home and they should get their own breakfasts.

Aaden arrived in Arnie's ancient station wagon with wood paneling. Blythe saw him and slipped out the front door, waving as she walked to the car.

He leaned over and kissed her cheek. She inhaled his Aaden aroma, a mix of mint and musk, which she'd always laughingly called "Irish Spring."

They talked lightheartedly about the weather, the traffic congestion, the sharks beginning to circle the island. At the restaurant, they placed their orders and settled back with their coffee.

"You look great, Blythe," Aaden said. "Salt air is doing you good."

Blythe thanked him and kept her gaze on her coffee, protecting herself from his charm.

She didn't look at Aaden, but stirred her coffee, as if she hadn't already stirred it. Now that he was here, so near her, she was confused. She'd been attracted by him the night they had dinner and attracted yesterday to Nick. She felt unbalanced, emotionally dizzy.

"You said on the phone that you're leaving."

"I've got to go back to Ireland. For a week or so. But I'll return to Nantucket as soon as possible. Arnie has invited me to stay with him whenever I want."

"I'm glad we got to catch up," Blythe told him, as if she didn't care if she saw him again.

"Whoa." Aaden frowned. "Blythe. I'm going to see you again. Absolutely. It might be ten days instead of a week, but I will return and I want to spend time with you. Lots of time."

Blythe lifted her eyes. She did love looking at the man. He seemed even more handsome now, with flecks of gray in his hair. His voice was as seductive as always.

She still loved him. She would always love him, in a way. But would she ever trust him? Really, the situation was impossible. He would never leave Ireland and she would never leave her children.

"Aaden, don't hurry back because of me."

"That's a little cold."

"No, wait. Let me say it. It is *lovely* seeing you again. But our lives are so different. I don't think we should imagine a future together."

Aaden reached out and held her hand. "I'd be happy imagining a full night together." The intimate touch of his skin, the charming lilt in his speech, woke memories.

She pulled her hand away. "Don't try to be seductive, please. I need to be realistic."

"What we had was real."

"That was years ago, Aaden."

"True. And here we are now, together, and I want you as much as I always did. Remember the time I kidnapped you from attending assembly and we hid in a supply closet and kissed for almost an hour?" He smiled his bad-boy smile, inviting her to join him in memories.

Blythe nodded. Remembering flushed through her.

Aaden leaned toward her, his voice low and urgent. "I was desperately in love with you. Have you considered what might have happened if you had come to Ireland with me? We could have lived all the times of our lives together. Blythe, I regret that every day. But we still have time. I *am* coming back to Nantucket. Fate has brought us together again, and I will not refuse to take a chance."

God, he was beautiful, Blythe thought. She had loved him more than any other man; even after she had lost him, she had loved him more than she'd loved Bob. Her heart cramped with guilt. She hoped Bob hadn't known.

She cleared her throat, sniffing back tears. "Take a chance, you say. You sound like you're gambling."

"Ah, sure, and what love isn't a gamble? Taking a breath is a gamble. Life is a gamble."

Aaden took her hand again, and this time she did not take it away.

"Gamble on me now, Blythe. I'm a sure bet." His smile blazed.

Absolutely like a lightbulb flicking on, a thought flared. Blythe was almost surprised when she spoke. "But can *you* gamble on *me*?"

She assumed he'd be shocked, even hurt. Instead, Aaden laughed.

"Ah, that's why I love you, Blythe. You can still surprise me. You always could. That's why we're so electric together. I want you to come to Ireland. Stay for two or three weeks. This summer. I'll show you around and I know it will call to you."

"I don't know . . ."

She remembered how she was with him, different, more carefree, even wild. In high school, they had egged each other on in small mischiefs like skipping assembly, kissing in the supply closet. Just being with him was like climbing onto a motorcycle, arms wrapped around him as they sped away.

But now she had children. She couldn't afford to gamble.

Aaden sensed her thoughts.

"Let's do this. Let's agree to text each other. Facetime each other. Get to know each other. I don't want to lose you again."

"Yes, let's do that." It was a good idea, Blythe thought.

They left the restaurant. Aaden drove Blythe home and kissed her chastely at the door to her house.

Not until Aaden was driving away did Blythe think, *But Aaden didn't lose me. He left me. He will always leave me for Ireland.* How could she compete with an entire country?

And did she even want to? Was she attracted to Aaden simply because he was attracted to her?

Their summer days fell into a pattern. In the mornings, the children slept in, spread like starfish on their beds or curled up into a lump in their covers, enjoying the luxury of free days. They took the bus all over the island, or Miranda drove them when everyone wanted to go to the same beach. Blythe washed sheets and beach towels, swept up the never-ending scatterings of sand, cut flowers from the backyard and arranged them in vases around the house. She made cakes with buttercream icing, and the cakes were gone in a day. She sliced peppers, carrots, and cucumbers, arranged them in a glass bowl in the refrigerator until, in the late afternoon, the kids came thundering back into the house, diving onto the food like gulls at the harbor.

She planted cherry tomatoes in several different plots, and geraniums with flowers like pink and white candy, and begonias and pansies. In a small room off the kitchen, once a pantry, Blythe had established a kind of office with a small desk for her laptop, printer, and Post-its scribbled with reminders. Each square on her large wall calendar was filled. Cocktail parties with old summer friends. Volunteer work for several non-profits. Nick called every day, and one night she joined him and Sandy and Hugh for a gala dinner for A Safe Place. She'd been glad to see him, but there was no chance for private conversation. When she was at the beach or as the children came in from a long beach day, Blythe snapped informal photos on her phone, printed them off, and stuck them to the refrigerator with the alphabet magnets she'd bought for Miranda seventeen years ago. She always knew when the kids saw the photos because she heard screams of laughter in the kitchen. Aaden texted her from Ireland, sending photos of the Ha'Penny Bridge and St. Michan's church and she sent back photos from the beach.

She was restless. Something in her life had changed. She wasn't frightened. She wasn't angry. She was . . . excited. Hopeful. Something was out of control. She felt like a woman waiting for the Powerball numbers to come up while she held her scratch ticket. Not that she'd ever played the lottery. She was too cautious for that.

Maybe she'd be less cautious this summer.

One morning, Nick called.

"Blythe," Nick said. "It's a nice day. Let's go rent a couple of kayaks."

If he'd suggested going up in a hot-air balloon, Blythe wouldn't have been more surprised. She'd never been in a kayak before, and the idea was tempting but worrisome. She'd been with friends in sailboats and motorboats, of course, but this would be the first time Blythe would, as Louisa May Alcott said, paddle her own canoe. What would happen if one of her children needed something? She reminded herself that their grandmother was here on the island, and so was their Aunt Kate. Nick wasn't inviting her to sail to Maine.

She said, "That's a great idea, Nick! Let's do it!"

She pulled on her bathing suit and covered it with a long-sleeved T-shirt to protect her from the sun. Nick arrived in the bright red Bronco, which made Blythe feel young and reckless.

"I brought sunblock. We should use it on our noses. On each of our noses. I mean, we don't have more than one nose. You know sun reflecting off the water can cause sunburns." Was she babbling? She was babbling. She laughed at herself, which didn't make any kind of sense, and behind the steering wheel, Nick smiled.

At the far end of the harbor, Blythe and Nick found Sea Nantucket Paddle Sports and Blythe was delighted by the "Sea Nantucket" pun.

The owner had life jackets, which made her feel even better. It was slightly creepy to slip her legs inside the shell sitting almost in the water, but after a couple of strokes with the paddle, Blythe's body adapted and as they slid through the water away from shore, she experienced a rush of pleasure.

"I feel like I've become a very odd fish," she told Nick.

"You're paddling like a pro," he told her.

They headed out to the harbor, carefully weaving around sailboats and fishing boats. A small yacht seemed to tower above them from their water-level view. They glided to the end of the harbor, which was too shallow for anything but kayaks. The ocean had flooded the marshes, making several watery trails that led them as if they were navigating a maze.

"It's so quiet," Blythe whispered.

"That's the pleasure of a kayak," Nick told her. "No motor."

He took a trail to the west. She headed east.

The watery path was narrow and shallow. She dipped her paddle and easily touched the bottom and the last of her disquiet faded away. Golden grass enclosed the salt marsh, so high she couldn't see over it. Birds occasionally swooped low, flashing past her silently moving boat. In the distance, a white heron stood at the end of a sandbar. The sun was strong. The air was still. This place was here all the time, Blythe realized. While she fretted about her children or laughed at a joke or sang in the shower, this still, silent place was always here, the end of the harbor, the beginning of the sea, a luminous world. She watched a crab creep over the sand between the seagrass. She saw flickers of small silver fish—minnows?—in the water. A bead of sweat trailed down her cheek. Her heart beat quietly. She closed her eyes and simply floated there in the brown, peaty water.

"There you are!" Nick came around the corner of one of the winding creeks. "Are you stuck?"

"No. Just enjoying the silence. Thanks for bringing me here, Nick."

"My pleasure."

Nick paddled away and Blythe followed. She knew she could easily get lost in these creeks and now she was hot, and her nose was burning.

Later, as they ate lunch at Lemon Press, Nick asked, "Have you decided about taking the seventh-grade job?"

"Not really. I've got so much going on with the children."

Nick nodded. "I get it. But when won't you have so much going on? When will you feel ready to teach again? I know your kids need you, but you've said you love teaching and so many other kids need you."

Blythe studied the shine of the sun on her fork as she thought. She couldn't remember a time when anyone had said what Nick had said, that the other kids needed her. Emotion welled up inside her, shoving against her heart, waking a pleasure she'd forgotten was there. She had been a good teacher, even as a substitute. A few times a teacher would be out for a month, and she'd been able to get to know the students, to sense their response to her, to see how their papers improved. Sometimes a former student would stop her in the grocery store or post office and thank her for forcing them to learn how to write, because she was now president of a company. Or a man with a baby in his backpack would yell, "'Sup, Mrs. Benedict? Found any dead mice lately?" and while strangers looked askance at Blythe, she would remember teaching a class a Billy Collins poem about loving a dead mouse, and her heart would swell with pride and joy because so many years later, that father remembered that poem.

At least he remembered the dead mouse.

But she was older now, and she had four children. She said, "I know you're right, Nick. I've got to decide. I *will* decide. I'm glad you're pushing me on this. It's so easy to get lost in family problems. And I know I'll be happier when I'm teaching."

She took the last sip of her coffee and stood up. "I'm going home. I'll call Krebs now. Thank you for this wonderful morning. I'm inspired!"

The late June light was strong, warming her shoulders and brightening the streets as she walked home. Her time with Nick always seemed to bring out a part of her that could so easily be forgotten. She remembered how much she'd enjoyed teaching. The silent focus on putting together a lesson plan. The honeybee swarm of energy she felt whenever she entered the classroom. The delight of talking with the class, the joy when some students really got it, and the exhilaration she felt when challenged by a student. The pleasure of intellectual fencing. The beauty of the young faces. Coffee and laughter with colleagues in the teachers' room. The windows framing autumn leaves, snowflakes, spring flowers.

But how would this affect her family? She wouldn't be home during the day, and she'd be busy at night grading papers, doing lesson plans. On the plus side, she'd have money of her own to help allow the children to take music lessons or buy wonderful Christmas and birthday presents. She could even take them all on a trip somewhere special—to Quebec or even, if she saved her money, to a play and a night in New York. And she'd be showing her children that a woman could have meaningful work and a family at the same time.

Oh, she was excited.

She found Harry Krebs's number and called.

When he answered, she almost hung up. But she said, "Hi, Harry. It's Blythe Benedict. Do you still need a middle school teacher for the coming year?"

That evening, Blythe invited Celeste over for a drink. They sat on the back porch, sipping icy cold vodka tonics, listening to the kids coming in and out. Blythe told Celeste about her return to teaching, and Celeste applauded.

"This is just the right time," Celeste told her. "Your chicks are learning to be self-sufficient, and you can return to a job you love. I'll bet you're a wonderful teacher."

Blythe glowed with pleasure. She was so grateful for Celeste's love and approval.

"Thank you, Celeste." She sipped her drink. "And how are *you*?"

"How am I?" Celeste seemed surprised. "I'm just fine, don't you think?"

"I think you're wonderful, but I worry because you're alone in your big house."

Celeste found a spot on her sleeve that needed ironing out with her fingertips.

Blythe waited.

Finally, Celeste cleared her throat and met Blythe's eyes. "Please don't worry. In the summer I'm never alone. In the off-season, I spend time with friends and serve on several town boards. Kate checks in on me every day in the off-season, and I am grateful, although I realize I'm another 'Must Do' on Kate's busy list of obligations."

"Oh, Celeste, Kate loves you."

"I know she loves me." Celeste spoke curtly. "But I know she considers me a responsibility, and that is very close to being a burden."

"Maybe she'll relax when Bob and Teri come to stay for two weeks," Blythe suggested.

Celeste laughed. "Maybe *she'll* relax. *I* won't. Bob and Teri absolutely *swarm* over me, insisting on taking me out to dinner, or worse, Teri wants to cook dinner at home, and Lord, she's a terrible cook. At some point, Bob will take me aside for a 'little talk' to remind me to put away the pictures on the hallway wall that have Bob grinning proudly with you and your newest baby or during a holiday. Bob tells me the pictures hurt Teri's feelings."

This was the moment, Blythe knew, when she could mention seeing Teri kissing another man that day in Boston. That moment had been so brief, and yet so enormous. Should Blythe have a private talk with Bob, or ask for a meeting with both of them? Should Blythe tell Celeste and ask her advice? But no, she didn't want to gossip, even though Blythe's worries scrolled out into fears that if Teri left Bob, the children would be even more hurt, certainly more confused.

Celeste was laughing. "I'm absolutely not taking the photos down. I always remind him that the children would be upset if I did."

Blythe was glad she hadn't mentioned Teri's kiss. She changed the subject. "You've also got a boyfriend. Tell me about him."

Celeste shifted in her chair. "Oh, he's really just a summer friend. Remember when you were young? I always lost my heart to some summer boy who vanished in September."

Intrigued, Blythe leaned forward. "Have you lost your heart to Roland?"

"Oh, heavens, no. I enjoy going out with him. But he's a summer person, and he lives in Florida in the winter. He's invited me to visit, but I know from the grapevine that he has plenty of girlfriends in Naples."

Blythe sat back in her chair, slightly confused. "At dinner with the children, you made it sound . . . more romantic."

"Yes, I did, didn't I?" Celeste gazed into the distance.

Blythe kept quiet.

Celeste looked down at her hands when she admitted, "The thing is . . . and this is for your ears only . . . I do my best to appear active and *interesting* to my grandchildren."

Blythe started to object. "Oh, but you—"

Celeste held up her hand. "Darling Blythe, one of the realities of old age is that I don't have any illusions. I don't try to diet because at my age I need a little fat to protect me in case I fall. And I'm certainly not trying to get thin for my summer grand events as I did into my sixties. I'm only trying to stay healthy enough to prevent my *last* grand event.

"I'm speaking honestly now, and you mustn't contradict me. I dread what will happen when I'm truly ancient and crippled and wrinkled and moving slow as a tortoise, with arthritic fingers like a fairy-tale witch. I might decide not to see the grandchildren then. I don't want them to remember me like that."

"I can understand," Blythe said quietly. "I only hope you know that my children adore you, and they'll adore you when you're ninety-nine and an arthritic tortoise."

"We'll find out, won't we?" Celeste responded. "If I'm lucky." Before Blythe could react, Celeste continued. "I hope you know how grateful I am that you have so many children."

Blythe chuckled. "We only did it for you." After a moment, she said, "Of course, Kate's kids are your grandchildren, too."

Celeste nodded. "Yes. But Chip is twenty-two and Melissa is twenty. They have their own lives, good, busy lives, off-island."

"Kate must be so happy with how they're turning out."

Celeste agreed. "True." After a moment's silence, Celeste said, "But to your concern about me living alone. When I was younger, like your daughters, even like you, I only thought about how I looked to other people. Clothes, hairstyle, exercise outfits. Now I really care less about that—I do try to look, at the very least, not insane—but now I find I care more about looking *out*. I don't just mean I like watching people, because of course I do, and I enjoy celebrity news as much as anyone. But I prefer sitting with the world. Listening to the wind. Watching birds sing and squabble. The way the sun comes through my chandelier and makes dancing rainbows on the wall. Einstein said, 'Either everything's a miracle or nothing is a miracle.'" Celeste laughed lightly. "I probably sound senile to you."

"No, Celeste, not at all!" Blythe put her hand on the older woman's arm. "The other day I was thinking about Nantucket light. How it's different from light anywhere else in the world."

"Oh, yes. I agree." Celeste took Blythe's hand. "Tell me, what else have you been thinking about?" She peered at Blythe with a smile.

Blythe stared down at their two hands. Celeste's skin was soft and spotted with brown age spots. Her knuckles were swollen from arthritis, but her nails were painted a pale pink, and she wore her heavy diamond engagement ring and wedding ring on one hand, and an opal surrounded by diamonds on the other.

Catching her gaze, Celeste said, "I know. The opal ring is stunning. Kate has insisted that she'll inherit it, and she hints that she doesn't want to wait until I die because I'm so obviously not ready to go yet. Most of my jewelry will go to you and your daughters and Kate's daughter. I'm sure I have enough to go around." She gently pulled her hand away from Blythe's and held it up, turning it this way and that to watch the fire opal flash.

"I don't wear my engagement ring and wedding ring anymore." Blythe looked at her own hands, tanned and ringless.

Celeste chuckled. "Of course not. You're divorced." Celeste paused. "Now. I'm happy to hear that you have a new man in your life."

Blythe froze, torn between telling Celeste about Aaden and fearing it was the wrong thing to do. "You mean Nick Roth?"

"Absolutely. I saw the sparks fly when you met him after dinner at the yacht club."

Blythe relaxed. "Yes, Nick is a friend of Sandy's husband. I've spent some time with him. He's very nice, and he coaches soccer and teaches history at a high school near where my children go. I find him . . . very attractive."

"Take some advice from an old woman. Go out with Nick Roth, if he's interesting to you at all. You don't have to be madly in love with the fellow. You can have fun. You can even have some pleasurable sex. When you're my age, you'll be glad for the memories."

Blythe knew her face had gone red. She wanted to blurt out that she was *seeing* both Nick *and* Aaden. And it was so confusing, but also kind of fabulous. Two attractive men in her life?

Fun?

Pleasurable sex?

Really?

She didn't know if she could actually have a relationship with a man. Ever since she held her first infant in her arms, she'd had a powerful fear caging all her thoughts. As a mother, she was responsible for the health and welfare of her children, and she believed if she ignored that in order to please herself, she would set a chain of events in motion that would somehow hurt her children. She knew it was irrational, but she couldn't shake the idea.

Celeste leaned forward. "While I'm so full of advice, I'll share one more insight with you. You'll discover when your children grow up and become adults that you will love them, but you might not like them."

Blythe laughed. "Oh, Celeste, I've already disliked my children more times than I can remember. And they have certainly disliked me."

Both women went silent when they heard Holly and Daphne enter the kitchen. Arguing.

"Holly, gerbils eat *insects*."

Holly sniffed. "You always know everything, but *my* gerbils are different. They are sea gerbils. Just look at my book, please?"

"Fine. But don't get mad at me if I criticize it."

The two girls stomped up the stairs, their voices trailing behind them.

"Oh dear," Blythe said. "Do you think Holly feels inferior to Daphne?"

"Of course," Celeste answered easily. "Daphne is older and whip smart. But Daphne is respecting Holly's work by discussing it. And isn't it a good thing for Daphne to have a younger sister who admires her?"

Before Blythe could answer, Teddy came through the house, yelling, "Mom! What's for dinner?"

Blythe smiled. "He doesn't even know if I'm in the house."

"But you are here, and he's hungry, and I need to go home." Celeste rose.

"Stay for dinner. I'm heating up a casserole."

"Thank you for asking, but I'm meeting Roland at the club."

Blythe kissed Celeste's cheek as she left. She heated the casserole in the microwave and made a salad, singing at the top of her lungs, which she often did to let the children know she was here, and preparing dinner. All the children swarmed in to set the table, pour glasses of water, and somehow everyone seemed to talk at once while also almost inhaling the food.

Then they helped clean the kitchen and disappeared in different directions. The front door slammed. The television blasted a Marvel movie into the air. Miranda and Brooks played badminton in the backyard, screaming with laughter.

Blythe called Nick and told him about her new job. They talked while the sun set and the moon rose high in the sky.

When she went to bed, she found a text from Aaden.

I miss you. I wanted to send a shot of me smiling on the Ha'Penny Bridge, but the rain has been constant and the sky gray, so I will wait. Here's Awen's office on Merrion Square. It's handsome, don't you think, even in the rain?

Please send me a photo of your lovely self so I can have some sunshine in my life. Love you.

Blythe started typing but erased her words and started again. To say that the weather was beautiful on Nantucket seemed mean. To tell him to hurry back would be misleading. To mention Nick would be wrong, and premature. Her feelings were in a whirlpool.

We've been busy here. I've gone kayaking in the sunshine (sorry). Good luck with your work.

She knew her message lacked warmth, but it was the best she could do. To soften the bluntness, she added XO.

She set her phone on the bedside table. She was smiling an absolutely silly smile, and she hugged herself.

"I'm so popular!" she said to the room, and laughed at herself, snickering as she nestled into her pillow.

fireworks

Over the next few days, Blythe was the perfect mother. She let Holly invite three girls for a sleepover and asked Brooks to sleep on the living room sofa for one night so the girls could take over the family room and television. She didn't tell the girls to quiet down until after midnight, and when they woke up at ten the next morning, Blythe treated them all to strawberry waffles with whipped cream. She allowed Miranda to take Brooks and her best island friend, Serena, and Serena's boyfriend, Riley, to dinner at the yacht club, just the four of them. She bought Teddy a new tennis racket and spent one morning with Daphne picking up beer cans and plastic bags from Cisco Beach.

Nick had to return to Boston for a couple of days, but he called her every night. Blythe snuggled into her pillows with the bedroom lights off as they talked about the music they loved: Miles Davis for Nick, and, unashamedly, Taylor Swift for Blythe. They discovered they shared the same taste in books: mysteries by Ian Rankin and Val McDermid, nonfiction by Nat Philbrick, novels by Carl Hiaasen. What favorite food would they eat all the time if they didn't have to worry about health or calories? Chocolate, of course, for Blythe. Beer for Nick. But was beer a food? They discussed this seriously. Nick's marriage, his teaching career. Blythe's marriage and teaching career. Nick had been seeing a woman named Elena who was a professional singer. Blythe told Nick about Aaden, her first serious boyfriend (she did not say her first true love), who lived in Ireland and sometimes visited Nantucket.

The evening Nick returned to the island, he took Blythe out to dinner. She went crazy getting ready. Did the cleavage on this dress dip too low? And on this dress, not low enough? Dangling earrings were sexy, but were they too sexy? Her legs were spectacular in her heels, but she didn't want to get stuck between the bricks on the sidewalks—that had happened once and she hadn't recovered from the embarrassment yet.

She stared at herself in the mirror. "What is going on?" she asked her reflection.

Her reflection didn't answer. But something was changing, as if a door she'd never seen before had opened, and she wanted to pass through, but was frightened. She didn't want to be hurt again.

But she did want to be loved.

She heard the Bronco pull into the driveway. Her heart danced. The sight of him at her front door gave her butterflies in her rib cage. She'd forgotten how tall he was, and now he was very tan, which made his eyes gleam like melted chocolate.

"Hello," she said, and grinned like a love-struck kid.

"Hello," he said back and bent forward and kissed her, right there in the doorway.

She wrapped her arms around his neck and softly kissed him, and they maneuvered into the front hall and shut the door and Blythe leaned against the door and Nick leaned against her and they kissed and kissed.

"We could go to bed now," Blythe whispered, flushing red, shameless as a hussy and glad. "No children here tonight."

She was surprised when Nick pulled away. "I never sleep with a woman on the second date." His eyes were dancing.

"Maybe now's the time," she told him.

"We have a reservation for dinner at the Languedoc," he reminded her.

"Oh, if we *must*," Blythe sighed, smiling.

They walked into town, holding hands, talking all the way. Their table at the restaurant was on the second floor, and the restaurant was full of happy, good-looking people. Blythe felt happy and good-looking, too. They talked about their early days of teaching, and what things had changed and what had stayed the same. They enjoyed oysters on the half shell and white wine, and salmon caught in Scotland, and more white wine, and bittersweet chocolate pot de crème, which made Blythe close her eyes and lick her lips.

"I could take a photo of you right now and blackmail you," Nick teased.

"If you bought me another pot de crème, I'd let you," Blythe replied. "But you know I don't have much money."

"It's not money I'd want," he told her, smiling.

When they left the restaurant, the sky was high and pale with a curved moon above them. They walked around town, stopping to listen to the street musicians. They went into Mitchell's Book Corner and Nick ushered Blythe up to the poetry section.

"What poets do you read?" Nick asked.

"I'm stuck in the nineteenth century with the Romantic poets like Coleridge and Keats," she told him. "And you?"

"Oh, I'm much more in the here and now," Nick said, grinning.

He pulled out a slim volume of poems by Mary Oliver.

Blythe read one of the poems. "How have I missed her?" She held the book tight to her breast.

Nick held a book of poems by Mark Doty. "Read 'Spent,'" he said.

Blythe read it. "Thank you for showing me. I'll buy this, too. Don't show me more. Not tonight, I mean. I'm overwhelmed with emotion. I'd forgotten the impact of poetry. I feel as if I've been hit in the stomach. How do you know about the poems? Nick, all I want to do for the rest of my life is read these poets."

"I hope that's not *all* you want to do," Nick said with a grin.

They bought the books and a new novel and went back out onto the street. Now the sky was dark, but shop lights shone, illuminating their way. They strolled into the library garden and sat together on a bench beneath a tall, swaying magnolia tree.

They talked about poetry and poets. Nick told her about Ogden Nash, an American poet and humorist. He brought up Nash's poem "Just Keep Quiet and Nobody Will Notice" and Blythe burst into laughter.

"That one!" she said. "I'll use that one in class."

They spoke about favorite movies and actors and if streaming was a gift or a curse. They compared musicians and artists and novels. They shared memories of their childhood pets and made a pact to adopt a rescue dog or cat when they returned to their real lives in the fall. They discussed what they should do on Columbus Day weekend. They agreed they should all come to Nantucket.

It was after midnight when Nick walked Blythe back home. She quietly worried that such a blissful evening would mean she'd find chaos and drama back in her house, but she was wrong. Holly's bike was halfway into the garage. Teddy's enormous rubber sandals were left at the front door as Blythe had insisted he do to stop tracking entire dunes of sand into the house. Daphne's Red Sox baseball cap had been tossed onto the hall table. Only signs of Miranda were missing.

Blythe and Nick stood in the front hall, holding each other.

"The kids are here," Blythe told Nick. "We've missed our window of opportunity."

"True," Nick answered. "But I'm sure we'll have many opportunities in the future."

Something magical shivered inside Blythe, all the way down.

On the Fourth of July, Nantucket morphed into an island carnival. Blythe and the children usually trekked down to Jetties Beach with hundreds of other people, to spread blankets on the sand and lie back to watch the spectacular fireworks display the town provided.

This year was different, and Blythe realized with a pang that from now on all summers would be different. Miranda and Brooks left to join a group of friends at the beach. Celeste and Roland were invited to the home of a friend who had a deck that provided a perfect view of the fireworks, plus comfortable chairs to sit in while watching.

"My days of lowering myself to the ground to watch the sky have passed," Celeste told Blythe. "And my days of getting up off the sand have absolutely gone by." She began to laugh. "If Roland tried to help me, we would both fall over each other like a pair of circus clowns. No, I'm delighted that I'll be sitting in a chair."

Teddy was spending the evening and night with his friend Azey, which left Blythe alone with Daphne and Holly. Blythe was trying to think of a way to make this holiday special—for so many years, the family had spectacular cookouts, with Bob displaying his manly skills by flipping hamburgers, hot dogs, corn on the cob, lobster tails, and often fish wrapped in foil with butter and veggies, on their very large Weber grill. After Blythe and Bob were divorced, even though the Nantucket house belonged to Blythe, Bob insisted on taking the grill to his mother's house because for years the family had called him "Grill Tsar" and had gifted him with an apron and a chef's toque printed with that title. When Blythe reminded Bob that he could always buy another grill, rather than hauling their old one over to Celeste's house, he told her that his grill was seasoned, perfect now for grilling.

Loyal sister Kate, standing by, had chimed in, "He's right, Blythe. Men and their grills are a thing."

So, three years ago, Blythe had bought another grill and barbecued on it, but she didn't really have the knack. The burgers were black on the outside, bloody on the inside. The next year, Teddy had bravely attempted to grill on the Fourth of July, but he couldn't get it right, either, although the family ate his blackened on the outside, raw on the inside burgers and pretended they were delicious.

This year, Blythe made reservations for them at the yacht club, and it was the perfect thing to do. Sandy invited Blythe and her children to join her and her husband for dinner and the fireworks. Miranda and Teddy were with friends for the night, down with the crowd at Jetties Beach.

Blythe walked to the club with Daphne and Holly who discussed with elaborate emotion what they would choose to eat for dinner that night. Holly remarked that the cheeseburgers weren't as good as they used to be.

They entered the club's dining room.

Holly eagerly announced, "The Greens are over there, Mom."

Yes, Blythe saw the Greens sitting at a round table on the porch. And she saw that Nick was with them. She knew he would be, but even so, when their eyes met, heat flared through her.

At the table, she kissed Nick on the cheek, easily, one friend greeting another. He smelled delicious, suntanned skin, tart aftershave, warm man. He was so large and muscular and male, she wanted to press herself against him and kiss him properly. Or did she mean improperly?

Before one of her daughters could take the seat next to Nick, Blythe slid onto the chair, smiling, she hoped, innocently.

Sandy noticed. She widened her eyes at Blythe and nodded slightly, a secret acknowledgment of Blythe's crush on Nick. Immediately, Sandy ran interference for Blythe.

"Holly, Daphne, sit next to me. Holly, what have you been up to?

Oh, and Daphne, Hugh wanted to talk to you about joining a committee to prevent environmental pollution."

Hugh had been studying the menu. Hearing Sandy's words, he looked startled but began a conversation with Daphne.

Blythe gazed up at Nick. Why was she so happy to see his face? What was going on here? "Hello."

"I think the secret's out," Nick said softly.

"The secret?"

"That I'm attracted to you."

Blythe went warm all over. "Me, too. I mean, I'm attracted to you. Oh, good grief, I can't believe I said that with my daughters so near."

"Why? Will they disapprove?"

Flustered, Blythe replied, "I don't think so. I don't know. They haven't seen me with any man other than my ex-husband. I mean, not like I'm with you. I don't mean I am *with you,* but . . ." What *did* she mean?

"I'd like it very much if you were *with me,*" Nick said.

Under the table, his knee touched hers.

The waiter arrived to take their drink orders.

Blythe straightened and smiled at her daughters. Daphne returned to her conversation with Hugh Green, but Holly was watching Blythe like an alligator spying prey.

Blythe put on her public face. "How was your time in Boston?"

"It was great. Seth performed Elgar's Cello Concerto with the symphony. He received a standing ovation."

Before Blythe could speak, Holly piped up, "I want to learn to play the cello!"

Blythe was surprised. "You do?"

"Yes, very much." Holly directed her words to Nick. "I have always been the musical one in the family. When I was younger, I learned to play the recorder. I considered the flute, but I prefer the lower notes, so the cello would be perfect for me."

"Have you heard recordings of cello concertos?" Nick asked.

"I've seen videos. My favorite is the Piano Guys playing the theme from the movie *Frozen*."

Blythe held her breath. So much was happening here. She didn't know that her youngest daughter even knew what a cello was. Nick might think she was silly for liking the famed animated movie music.

Nick smiled. "I've watched that. It's set in an ice cave, right?"

Holly lit up. "Yes! That's the one! In many cello songs, the music is sad, but in the Piano Guys, it's exciting, like horses galloping."

"You should go to YouTube and watch videos by 2Cellos."

"*Two* cellos?" Holly's eyes went wide.

Was there anything more endearing than seeing a friend being interested in your child? Blythe was flooded with affection for the man next to her. For a moment she thought she might burst into tears. Holly was a generally happy girl, but only Celeste seemed to connect with Holly like Nick was doing now.

If sweet, imaginative Holly liked Nick, couldn't Blythe like him? Publicly? Bring him to meet her children as Blythe's boyfriend?

Behind Holly's head, Sandy mouthed "Wow!" at Blythe.

Nick and Holly continued to discuss music—*cello songs*, as Holly called them.

Blythe just sat there smiling.

Their drinks arrived and the waiter asked for their dinner orders, breaking up the musical discussion. Sandy mentioned the trouble the Steamship Authority was having with employees, and everyone chimed in, recounting their most horrible incidents on the ferries. This led to the discussion that happened every year about how the island was changing and what could they do to make people on electric bikes stay off the sidewalks and who owned the biggest yachts in the harbor.

"Speaking of change," Blythe said, "I've decided to teach next year." She'd broken the news to her children one evening while they were all home for dinner. They hadn't been too surprised because she'd often substituted over the past few years. Miranda had found a way to suggest she get her own car, so she could help do errands and take her siblings to play dates.

"I'll think about that," Blythe had promised.

Now Hugh said, "Good for you. Schools need good teachers. And teaching has changed, too. Schools started using Chromebooks about ten years ago. Now add TikTok, Instagram, Snapchat, ChatGPT."

Before Blythe responded, Daphne spoke up. "Mom knows all about technology. She's learned everything from us."

Blythe wondered if she'd been accidentally transferred to heaven.

Their food arrived. Everyone ate steadily, realizing that the light in the sky was fading. They passed up dessert and went out to the lawn to watch the fireworks.

The first fountains and pinwheels exploded in the sky, a starburst of sparkles.

People cheered. Blythe watched the sky. After a moment, she leaned toward Nick and they stood with their shoulders touching.

summer heat

In the summer, over the lazy span of days, there was always laundry, mostly beach towels and bath towels. Blythe enjoyed this humble task. The warmth of a towel taken from the dryer. The pile of folded towels, like a cotton rainbow.

In the kitchen, Brooks was helping Miranda pack sandwiches, small bags of chips, and a banana or pear, into the brown paper bags that each child would tuck into their backpack. They filled thermoses with cold water, exchanging sultry glances as they worked. They were in that state of romance when they would have exchanged sultry glances if they'd been digging ditches. When all lunches were made, the couple planned to walk together down to Steps Beach, with backpacks full of beach towels and food and sunblock.

Carolyn's mom picked up Holly and took the girls to Surfside Beach. When they called, Blythe would pick them up and drive them home.

Daphne spent the mornings at Maria Mitchell and in the afternoon her friend Lincoln biked out and met her at the Madaket Beach.

Teddy played tennis with his friends at the club and often joined others to crew on a sailboat. He promised Blythe he always wore a life jacket. She didn't press the issue. She had her spies at the club, friends who looked out for one another's children.

It was July, and summer unrolled before them like a golden carpet.

One morning, Sandy called.

"Blythe, want to go to the beach today? Just us girls? I've got green grapes and cheese and a beach umbrella."

"That's a brilliant idea! I've got crackers, a million cold cans of fizzy fruit drinks, and caramel chip cookies."

"I'll drive. I'll be there in ten minutes."

"I'll be ready. I've just got to put on my bathing suit."

It was exactly what Blythe needed, she decided. Time for herself to swim and sunbathe, time to talk with her good island friend. She hurried upstairs and slipped into her Speedo, hurried downstairs and filled a cooler full of ice, drinks, and a couple of peaches. She flapped on her straw beach hat, double-checked that she had sunblock, and chose from the dozen sets of sunglasses she and the girls kept in a bowl by the front door. Her colorful beach bag, woven in Guatemala, held her small wallet with credit cards and phone. From the pile of clean beach towels in the laundry room, she collected her favorite, a long thick cotton towel striped navy blue and white.

For a moment, she felt like a young girl again.

Sandy arrived in her handsome black Toyota RAV4 and high-fived Blythe as she got into the car.

"Ain't it grand to be alone, without any men around," Sandy said as she drove away from the town.

"How are the girls?" Blythe asked.

"Lara's competing in the club tennis tournament, and Anne is teaching sailing at the yacht club and sailing when she's not working. I know they come home to sleep, and sometimes they raid the refrigerator, but mostly they're out living their lives."

"My lot are at the beach, too," Blythe said.

"Okay, good. Now, talking about our families is banned for the next few hours. We're solo for a while."

At Dionis, they lugged their gear out to the beach and found a nice empty space. The day was perfect, hot and clear, with only an occasional breeze. The shoreline was spotted with other people, swimming, sitting in beach chairs, lying on blankets to tan.

"Let's deal with this later," Sandy suggested, dropping her beach bag and umbrella onto the sand.

"Great!" Blythe anchored the blanket to the sand with her cooler and joined Sandy as she raced into the water.

They both screamed, "It's cold!"

Sandy was content to paddle and float near the shore. Blythe was not a strong swimmer, but she loved floating, with her eyes closed and sounds muted by the water. It took her a few moments to surrender, but soon she was relaxed, supported completely by the transparent magic of what she could not hold or control, the sea.

Later, they dried off and ate lunch beneath the beach umbrella. They talked about books, television shows, clothes, food.

Blythe took a deep breath. "Sandy, I want to ask your advice about something."

"I'm all ears," Sandy said. She took another long pull of cold water and stuffed the empty bottle into her backpack. "Go."

Nervously, Blythe folded her paper napkin into smaller and smaller squares. Finally she met Sandy's eyes and blurted, "Just before we came to Nantucket, my friend Jill and I were shopping at Copley Place in Boston. We accidentally spotted a couple right there in the mall, crushed up together, kissing passionately. They were kind of tucked into a corner, but we could see through the shop windows. Jill and I both watched them and we realized the woman was *Teri*. Bob's girlfriend. We didn't know who the man was. But we were both certain it was Teri."

Sandy frowned. "That's bizarre. I'm not Teri's biggest fan, but I can't believe she'd be kissing another man out in public."

"I know. I agree. But I can't stop wondering about it. I'm thinking I should talk to her, alone. Just to hear her deny that was her."

"Why would you believe what she said?" Sandy asked.

Blythe sighed. "That's a good point."

"Did you take a photo?"

"What? No!" Blythe slapped her hand to her forehead. "So stupid! I didn't even think of it! My phone was in my purse. Damn!"

"I think you should confront her."

Blythe shook her head, unsure.

After a while, Sandy asked, "Could you tell Celeste? Maybe she could confront Teri."

"I don't think so. It would only confuse her as much as it confuses me." Blythe yawned. "The heat is making me drowsy."

They lay face down on their beach blankets, and for a while they were quiet, enjoying the sun on their backs.

A beach volleyball landed next to Sandy's head. Two boys raced up, apologizing, spraying sand as they picked up the ball and ran off.

Sandy sat up and drank from her water bottle. "I don't think I have any kind of solution."

Blythe sat up, too. She shrugged. "I don't, either. I have to let it go."

"You have really let *Bob* go, haven't you?" Sandy asked.

Blythe brushed sand from her arms. "I have. I think we're doing all right with the children. It helps them a lot to be able to come here for summer and the holidays. And thank heavens I'm still friends with Celeste. She means so much to me. I think she loves me, too."

"And what about men?" Sandy asked.

"What about them?" Blythe couldn't talk about Aaden yet.

"Well, what about Nick? He likes you, Blythe. I can tell."

"I like him. A lot. It's kind of terrifying."

Sandy grinned. "Good. Keep me informed and let me know if I can help."

They swam again, and finally gathered up their beach bags and went home.

Blythe took a long shower, admired her new tan, and pulled on a loose turquoise caftan. She coiled her hair into a messy twist, fastening it with a claw clip. She settled on the living room sofa. She'd had enough sun for one day. She picked up her book. It was compelling, exciting, but suddenly laughter interrupted her mood. Pipes groaned and water exploded as the outdoor shower was turned on. It was right at the corner of the house, hidden by flowering bushes, and the only way anyone could see who was in the shower would be to go into the kitchen and stand on tiptoes and peer out the window.

Blythe closed her eyes. She could tell by the sounds of the voices and the laughter that two people were in the shower. Miranda and Brooks.

Okay, fine. They were both seventeen, or almost. She trusted them not to have sex in the outdoor shower where anyone could hear them.

My God. Sex in the outdoor shower. Had she and Bob ever had sex there? A person would have to be as supple as an octopus even to try it.

She checked her watch. It was five-thirty. Time for a little vodka tonic. She put her book down, entered the kitchen, and found a fresh lime. Just as she had it on the cutting board, her phone trilled.

The caller ID showed that it was Hilda Tillingham calling.

"Hello, Hilda, how are you?"

"Hello, Blythe, we are fine, thank you. How is Brooks behaving himself?"

Hilda's speech was always slightly unusual, but why wouldn't it be, when the woman spoke at least seven languages.

"Brooks is perfect. We're enjoying him so much. We—"

"I am glad. Blythe, I have an enormous favor to ask. Max and I need to be at a conference in Zurich and then a trade meeting in Rome.

We'll be away from home for at least another month. Maybe even a few days longer. Our housekeeper, Mrs. Jones, fell and broke her leg. She won't be able to walk until September at the earliest. So you see, we would have to let Brooks return to an empty home. Do you think it would be possible for him to stay with you for a few more weeks? We can always reserve a hotel room for him so he can remain on the island."

Blythe didn't think twice. "Oh, really, we would enjoy having Brooks stay with us. We have plenty of room, and he fits right in with our family." Why was Blythe so receptive to this idea? It wasn't simply that Brooks made Miranda happier. Part of it was that it was nice to have another male around. Only yesterday, she'd seen Brooks throwing the Frisbee with Teddy in the backyard.

"You're so kind. We will send you some money to help pay for his food. He eats like a starved bear."

"Please don't send money. We're fine, really. Maybe Brooks would like some spending money—"

"Brooks has his own money and a charge card. Thank you, Blythe. This is extremely kind. We are very thankful. Give Brooks our love."

Before Blythe could respond, Hilda Tillingham clicked off.

Well. Blythe's thoughts went in all directions. Miranda would be thrilled to know Brooks would be here all summer, but Blythe had learned that it was good for her children to have some kind of routine, even if only an hour a week. She would have to sign Brooks up for a sailing program, or maybe tennis. And really, Miranda should get some kind of job.

Blythe forced herself back to the here and now. A lime, sliced and fragrant, lay on the cutting board. Oh, yes, she was going to have an icy vodka tonic.

She was just settled on the back porch when her phone pinged.

A text from Aaden.

Oh, Blythe, how you like to tease me. The photos you've sent with you and your children make me long to be with you. I know you would worry about how your children will fare when you visit Ireland, but remember you could always fly home anytime. I'm dealing with a major crisis at Awen, so I don't know when I'll be back to Boston. I really need to see you.

He had attached a photo of himself wearing the high school letter jacket taken years ago, when they were in high school. And another photo taken of Blythe wearing the jacket, which was huge and fell almost to her knees. Aaden was standing by her, his hand on her shoulder. They were both smiling.

And another photo was attached, of Aaden now, grown and handsome, wearing that same high school letter jacket. He'd captioned the photo: *It still fits*.

Blythe allowed herself a moment to sink into the pleasure of memory. They had belonged to each other back then. They'd believed the world lay open to them, a smooth path through countless happy days. They'd believed their young love was eternal.

She straightened her shoulders. It was not the same now. It could never be the same. But Aaden had an apartment in Boston. He had to be there, sometimes, for business. That made a relationship seem possible.

But was that what she wanted?

Her desire for Nick was real and important. Did that mean it would be long-lasting? They hadn't talked about a long-term relationship, and they hadn't known each other for more than a few weeks. She wasn't sure she could trust her own instincts right now. She'd been living a perfectly happy divorced life with her children, and soon she'd begin teaching. Was this the right time to even think of having a long-term relationship? She trusted Nick, but they were too old to go steady, which she wasn't certain was even a thing now. Aaden was exciting, but she had to remember he'd left her before.

And, when she was honest with herself, she knew *all* this was way out of her comfort zone.

She tied on an apron and began making stir-fry chicken. She was putting together sliced fresh fruit for dessert when Daphne burst through the front door.

"*MOM!* I got to lead a group of kids on a beach walk today. By myself!"

"That's wonderful, Daphne! Tell me about it. Which beach did you go to?"

Before Daphne could answer, Holly and Carolyn came in.

"*MOM!*" Holly waved a book in the air. "Guess *what*? Carolyn and I found two copies of *Shipwrecked* at the library! Do you think we were awful to take both copies? But now we can read it at the same time and it's the third in Mary Alice Monroe's *Islanders* series and they have a boat."

"I think it's fine that you both checked out the same book," Blythe said, but before she could say more, Teddy rushed in.

"*MOM!* Azey and I took the bus home and I'm starving! When do we eat?" Teddy clearly had been swimming all day. His hair was so coated with salt it stuck out all over his head like a porcupine's.

"It's almost ready. Take a quick shower first. Here—have a carrot."

Teddy groaned and slumped away.

"*MOM!*" Miranda and Brooks strolled in from the family room where they'd been playing *Call of Duty: Modern Warfare,* a popular video game for Miranda's age group and one Blythe disliked. She'd given in to her oldest daughter's pleas but set a limit on the time they could play each day. "Me and Brooks found a brand-new game of *Zombie Kittens* at the Thrift Shop and we want Serena and Riley to come over and play after dinner, okay?"

"Brooks and I," Blythe said.

"You don't want to play this game." Miranda drifted into the kitchen. "Smells awesome, Mom. Here, Brooks, put the plates around. I'll do the silverware."

Somehow all the children and Blythe managed to get settled at the table. At the last minute, Blythe heated two heavily buttered and garlic-salted baguettes for what seemed like a crowd of children.

Blythe told Brooks about his mother's phone call.

Brooks said, "Cool. Thanks."

Miranda's face lit up. "Oh, Mom, you're the best. We'll be very good. We'll do our own laundry, right, Brooks?"

Brooks said, "Um."

Miranda whispered, "I'll show you how."

All these children, Blythe thought. The younger ones were truly stuffing their faces, as if they hadn't eaten for days. Daphne continued to explain the beach tour: clamshell, skate's egg case, and seaweed. Blythe listened, nodding, agreeing with anything Daphne said, because her second daughter knew much more about the beach life than Blythe ever would.

But Blythe knew more about human life. Children's lives. This was her specialty, and now as she sat at the table, she had one of those sudden moments of grace, when she was amazed and humbled by all the healthy, tanned, energetic, mysterious life around her. How lucky she was. She had all she needed right here.

Later that night, after everyone else was in bed, Blythe wrote a brief note to Aaden.

Aaden, You look wonderful in that high school photo and you look wonderful now. Please give me time to think things through.

Love, Blythe

music

A few days later, Celeste phoned.

"Tomorrow night is Family Night at the club. Open-air buffet dinner. Sandy's friend Nick Roth is performing out on the patio, so little kids can run around on the grass. I'd love it if you'd go with me, and any or all of your children."

"What a great idea!" Blythe already planned to attend because Nick would be performing. "I'll be there and I think most of the kids will want to go. Let me pick you up."

"Lovely," Celeste said.

The next evening, Blythe fetched her ex-mother-in-law at five—Family Nights started early because most of the club's sun-exhausted little children needed early bedtimes.

"Don't you look lovely," Celeste said as she slipped into Blythe's van. Blythe wore a blue-and-white striped sleeveless dress with a light cerulean-blue silk shawl. Celeste had given her the shawl for her birthday a few years ago, and it slid against her arms like summer air.

"You do, too," Blythe said. Celeste was wearing a blue and lavender caftan and dangling earrings of coral and turquoise that set off her dark eyes. Blythe had given Celeste the earrings last Christmas.

"Miranda and Brooks have gone to another party," Blythe told Celeste, "but Teddy, Daphne, and Holly played tennis this afternoon. They promised to reserve a table for us."

"I'm glad," Celeste said. "It's always such a crush."

When they arrived at the club, Blythe had to park in the back lot because the main parking lot was full.

"Oh, dear," Celeste said. "I hope they have enough tables for all of us."

Blythe glanced at her ex-mother-in-law. It wasn't like Celeste to worry like this.

They walked through the clubhouse and out onto the patio, saying hello and waving at friends as they went.

"Oh, look!" Celeste said. "The clever darlings!"

On the far side of the patio, near the small outdoor stage, Daphne, Holly, and Teddy sat at one of the larger round tables.

"You are geniuses to get this table," Blythe said.

"Because of this, I'm leaving you all my money in my will," Celeste promised.

Celeste said this every time her grandchildren did something extraordinary, so they had heard it many times before. Blythe realized how this made her children become used to the fact that their grandmother was mortal, while at the same time, because she said it so often, it seemed that Celeste would never die.

Across the lawn near the clubhouse, large outdoor grills and picnic tables were set up. Teddy went with Blythe to fetch drinks for everyone—tonight it was all self-serve. Blythe convinced Teddy to choose water for himself and his sisters, reminding him that a sugary drink now would weaken the taste of his food. Teddy agreed, probably because they were in public. While Blythe prepared vodka tonics with ice and a slice of lime, Teddy concocted three glasses of soda water with a slice of lime, a slice of lemon, and a cherry for himself and his sisters.

As Celeste and Blythe enjoyed their drinks, the three kids wandered off to see their friends, but soon they all joined the line of hungry people waiting to fill their plates with hamburgers, hot dogs, potato salad, corn on the cob, and fresh fat sliced tomatoes.

Blythe saw Sandy and her husband sitting with Nick and another woman Blythe didn't recognize. *I don't like her,* Blythe thought, surprising herself. How could she dislike a woman on sight? Was she *that* interested in Nick? For a moment she couldn't concentrate enough to eat.

"Is everything okay?" Celeste asked.

Blythe turned her attention to Celeste. "Of course. I can't get over how delicious all this is."

She talked local gossip with Celeste for a while, and when she noticed a man join Sandy's table and bend down to kiss the woman Blythe already didn't like, she suddenly felt happier.

By the time everyone had finished their strawberry shortcake, the buffet tables had been taken away and a stool and a mic were set on the stage. Some children flopped down on the grass. Teddy, Daphne, and Holly stayed at the table, licking their spoons.

The head of programming for the club, Janice Allen, welcomed everyone and introduced Nick. He thanked her, settled on the stool, adjusted the mic, and began to sing.

"Farewell and adieu to you, Spanish Ladies," Nick sang out and continued singing the old sea shanty about sailors leaving Spain to sail to England.

From the very first moment, Nick's voice was clear and strong, and as rich as rum, as sweet as honey. History seemed to flash over Blythe as he sang. She could almost see the sailors roaring as their boats rolled and reared over the stormy seas, wave-drenched men heaving on the ropes to the rhythm of the songs. Her hands flew to her chest, as if her heart were about to burst and she needed to protect it. This happened to her often when choirs sang Easter hymns or even when a soloist sang the national anthem at the beginning of a football game. She'd forgotten the power of one voice, the rise and fall of melody, the enchantment of strange words—"Haul up your clewgarnets, let tacks and sheets fly!"—which conjured up visions of older worlds, wilder seas.

Next to Blythe, Celeste was wiping her eyes.

"Mom!" Teddy said. "That's the theme song to SpongeBob SquarePants."

Celeste said to her grandson, kindly, "Darling, I'm sure that isn't true."

As the sky paled from blue to a smoky lavender, Nick sang "Drunken Sailor" and "Sloop John B." He told the audience he was adding a few modern sea songs that weren't proper sea shanties, but belonged to the deep waters. He sang "The Wreck of the Edmund Fitzgerald" by Gordon Lightfoot.

Afterward he told them, "The depth of Lake Superior is greater than the depth of most oceans. Long before it was called Lake Superior, the Ojibwe named it Gicgi-gami, meaning 'Great Sea.'" Next came Billy Joel's "The Downeaster 'Alexa,'" and finally John Denver's "Calypso," about Jacques Cousteau and his research ship.

When he finished, the audience rose to their feet yelling and applauding.

Blythe looked at her ex-mother-in-law. "Celeste, I think I'm in love with Nick."

Celeste smiled. "Darling, tonight *everyone's* in love with Nick."

The event was ending. Families gathered together to walk or ride home. It was only nine o'clock, so Blythe allowed her three children to go into town to buy ice cream, even though she couldn't imagine how they could want it after all they'd eaten. But then, of course, they were children.

Nick walked across the patio to Blythe. Heads turned to watch him. Blythe noticed various women whispering and for a moment she felt like a fangirl being chosen by a rock star. Nick stopped in front of Blythe, smiling.

She couldn't help herself. Throwing her arms around him, she kissed him solidly on the mouth. He put his hands on her waist. He had large, warm hands. Blythe nearly fainted.

Celeste cleared her throat.

Blythe dropped her arms. "Nick, you were amazing."

"You have a beautiful voice," Celeste said. "Your songs made me remember that we're all out here on an island, with shipwrecks all around us caused by shoals that have drifted away generations ago. I thank you."

"Thank *you,*" Nick replied.

Blythe stepped back as people crowded around Nick to thank him, to talk about the memories his songs had brought. She returned to her chair next to Celeste. The evening was cool, and they adjusted their shawls over their shoulders. The club's strings of tea lights came on.

Celeste leaned to whisper in Blythe's ear. "I'm so proud of him I feel like I'm his mother."

"I'm proud of him, too, but I certainly don't feel like his mother," Blythe said.

Celeste grinned and nudged Blythe's shoulder.

At last, the crowd dwindled.

"Let us take you for a drink?" a lovely young woman asked Nick.

Nick said, "Thank you, but I already have plans."

Celeste knocked her shoulder against Blythe's again and they exchanged a conspiratorial smile.

How odd and wonderful, Blythe thought, that her ex-mother-in-law could enjoy Blythe's attraction to Nick.

The waitstaff was folding chairs and carrying them away. Nick shook hands with the final admirer.

Nick smiled at Blythe.

Before he could speak, Celeste said, "I'm in the mood to walk home."

"I'll drive you," Blythe offered.

"Thanks, but I'd rather walk. It's a beautiful night."

Celeste kissed Blythe's cheek and strolled across the patio, exchanging goodbyes with the others on her way out.

"Well," Blythe said, peering up at Nick from beneath her lashes, "now I'm all alone. My children have gone into town for ice cream. I wonder what I should do."

Nick grinned, acknowledging Blythe's flirtatiousness. "Why not come for a walk with me? We could head down to Brant Point and watch the boats come and go."

Blythe thought that if he'd suggested swimming to Hyannis she would agree.

"I'd love that."

They left the club and strolled along the busy island streets. They passed an old woody station wagon, a banged-up Jeep with the soft-top down, a red Ferrari, and a silver Jaguar, all stalled by the holiday traffic, sandwiched between SUVs. Laughter floated out of Lola 41. They turned onto Easton Street, walked past the White Elephant hotel, and continued until they arrived at the beach sloping down to the water.

The sand was still warm from the day. The Brant Point Lighthouse stood steadily at the curve of sand that all boats rounded to enter the inner harbor. Its red light flashed every four seconds. Blythe and Nick settled on the sand and gazed out over the yachts and rowboats, Boston Whalers and sailboats, lying lightly in the calm water, their cabins bright with lamps.

"Nick," Blythe said, "you have such a beautiful voice. Did you ever sing professionally?"

"No. First I wanted to be an astronaut. Seriously. Then, a major league pitcher. Typical boy dreams. In high school, I formed a band with some friends, and for a while I wanted to sing professionally. But our band broke up when we went to college. I didn't know what I wanted, so I drifted through the required courses. When I was a junior, I met Brielle. She sang, too. She had a lovely voice." Nick was silent for a while. "Anyway, we were realistic about our futures. Brielle was planning to teach chemistry, so I got my degree in education. We thought that way we could have the same holidays." He paused, remembering. "And we did have the same holidays. We taught in the same school district and raised our sons. When Brielle was dying . . ." Nick cleared his throat. For a moment, it seemed he couldn't go on.

Blythe remained silent, respecting his sorrow.

"While Brielle was dying, she asked me to sing for her. I sang for her, and this made her happy. She was too weak to sing with me, but I saw by the way she closed her eyes and rested that I was helping her. Somehow, I was helping her. She made me promise never to stop singing."

After a few moments, Blythe said, "Nick, that's beautiful."

"Now." Nick's voice was gruff. "Tell me about you."

"All right. Let's see . . ." Blythe gathered her thoughts. "I was an only child. I was shy. I was lonely. In high school, I met a wrestler named Aaden, and for a couple of years, he was the center of my life. He went off to Ireland, so that was the end of us. I came to Nantucket to live with my grandmother and work at a summer camp. I loved it. I loved the kids. I knew I wanted to become a teacher."

"Go on," Nick prompted.

"I studied education in college. I met Bob at a graduation party. We married, I taught for a while, and then we had the children and I became a very happy stay-at-home mom. The past few years I've worked occasionally as a substitute teacher."

The nine o'clock Hy-Line fast ferry ruffled the water as it headed for the dock. Blythe and Nick went quiet, watching.

"Also," she confessed, "I love to read. I live to read. If I have a good book, I'm content. More than content, happy. You know how you feel when you enter a house and it seems to already be yours? You like the way the light comes through the windows and the warmth of the rooms? That's how I am with books. I have my tough times, bad times, like everyone else, but I've made it through hard days by knowing a good book was there waiting for me by my bed." Blythe laughed. "That probably explains why Bob and I are divorced. After getting four children to bed, I wanted a book more than I wanted Bob."

"I get that," Nick said. "I'm like that about music."

"Any kind of music?"

"Every kind. Waltzes, rock, rap. All of it."

"I've never waltzed before. I've always wanted to. It looks so dreamy."

"I'll waltz with you sometime," Nick promised.

Happiness bubbled through her. "I'd like that."

The clock on the Unitarian church chimed eleven times.

"Oh, dear," Blythe said. "I should go home. My children will think I've gotten lost."

"Or kidnapped," Nick said with a gentle smile.

Blythe rose, unsteady in the shifting sand. Nick caught hold of her and they stood looking at each other and finally they kissed.

And kissed.

Blythe thought she'd forgotten this kind of greedy, delicious kissing. She wrapped her arms around Nick. He put his hands on her hips and cradled her against him, and she pushed into him so forcefully they almost fell over.

Nick pulled away. "We need to stop. This is too public. Everyone can see."

"Let's go over into the bushes," Blythe pleaded. She laughed, slightly hysterical. "I don't mean that, I don't want to go over to the bushes, but I want . . ."

He smiled. "I do, too. But not tonight."

"Soon?" Blythe asked, laughing and teasing.

"Soon. Now let me walk you to your car."

The next morning, Blythe made Teddy and Holly go with her on a major grocery shop. When every brown paper bag had been emptied and folded, every bottle of milk and quart of yogurt put in the refrigerator, and all the fresh bananas and grapes draped like works of art in their large white bowl, Blythe told the children they were free to go. As if their tails were set on fire, they raced out the door on their way to the club.

"I'm having lunch with your grandmother," Blythe called after them. "If you'd like to come . . ."

"No, thank you," Teddy and Holly called back, not slowing their pace.

Blythe smiled like the Cheshire cat. She was completely fine with their answers.

Celeste had arranged their lunch on her back lawn and it looked like a scene from a Merchant Ivory film. A white lace tablecloth had been spread over the table, and a bottle of rosé sat in ice in a silver bucket. The plates, Blythe knew, were Celeste's mother's Limoges china with gold rims, and Celeste had brought out the heavy silver. Roses and hydrangea perfumed the air.

Blythe kissed Celeste's cheek.

"This is all very *Downton Abbey,*" she said as she sank into the wicker chair.

"It's a perfect summer day, isn't it?" Celeste lifted the bottle of rosé and poured them each a glass.

"Oh, dear, wine at lunch." Blythe was glad to see platinum-rimmed crystal glasses full of ice water, too. "I usually don't drink wine at lunch. It makes me too sleepy."

"But what is sweeter than a summer afternoon nap?" Celeste asked. She raised her glass. "Cheers."

"Cheers," she echoed, and drank. The effervescent liquid was cold and bright.

Egg salads mixed with watercress were on the plates next to the thickly sliced tomatoes.

"This is a treat," Blythe said. "Thank you."

As they ate, they discussed local news. Sharks seen off the south shore. The authors who spoke at the Nantucket Book Festival. The extravagant prices of meals at restaurants.

Then, leaning back in their chairs, nibbling on the grapes Celeste had set in a small silver bowl as a centerpiece, they talked about more personal things. Teddy growing taller every day. Holly creating her sea gerbil book. Bob and Teri, who would be staying with Celeste in a few weeks.

"I'd like to share something with you, Blythe." Celeste put her hand to her throat, a telltale sign that the something was private and difficult.

Blythe sat up straight, wiped her lips, and lay her hands in her lap. "Of course."

"It is a delicate matter."

Blythe nodded.

"Teri came to me this May, when I was visiting them in Boston."

Blythe waited. The air was warm and humid. Bees hummed among the heavy-headed roses and birds swooped busily from tree to tree. She was aware of her light floral sundress and Celeste's silver heirloom bracelet that caught the sun and winked as Celeste moved.

Celeste picked up her wineglass, sipped, returned the glass to the table.

"Teri told me she wants to have a baby with Bob." She held up her hand: *Wait*. "She can't seem to conceive. She's tried for months. She's seen specialists and she's fine. Everything's in working order."

"Oh." Blythe bent double, pretending to fix a twisted strap on her sandal. A sense of guilt surged through her, followed by a blast of anger—why should *she* feel guilty? Because when it happened, Bob had made her promise not to tell anyone, and she hadn't.

But now she had to.

She straightened. “Celeste, Bob had a vasectomy right after we had Holly. He said he didn’t want any more children.”

Celeste put her hand over her heart. “Oh, my Lord. I didn’t know.” She sent a helpless look at Blythe. “What should I do?”

“Really,” Blythe began, thinking her way through the problem, “Bob is the one who should tell her.”

“But obviously he hasn’t.”

Blythe shook her head. “It’s not fair to Teri.”

“You genuinely like Teri.” Celeste nodded. “I understand.”

“I do. I think she makes Bob happy and she’s nice to the kids.”

Celeste’s mouth quirked in a sad smile. “So, no chance that you’ll get back together with him.”

“No chance at all,” Blythe confirmed. “Sorry to be blunt.”

“No, no. I get it. But I still don’t know what to do. I don’t want to betray a confidence. I don’t want to seem unkind to Teri.”

“All right. Well—” Blythe tossed down a sustaining gulp of wine. “I want to tell you something about Teri.”

“I’m listening,” Celeste replied.

Blythe cleared her throat. Was she really doing this?

“First of all, I want to assure you that I’m not telling you this out of malice. In May, just before we came here, I was at the Copley Place Legal Sea Foods having lunch with my friend Jill. As we left the restaurant, we saw . . .” Blythe hesitated. “We saw Teri kissing a man. The man wasn’t Bob. He was taller, and younger, and they had their arms around each other and were kissing . . . passionately.

“I didn’t know what to do, so Jill and I left, almost running away. We were shocked. I’m still shocked. Teri was not kissing the man as if he was a relative or good friend. I’m telling you because I’ve been worrying about this all summer. I didn’t know if I should tell Bob or ask Teri about it. I’ve tried to believe it was a one-time event, but the way they were holding each other . . .”

“Oh, my.” Tears trembled in Celeste’s beautiful dark eyes.

It surprised Blythe, how pale Celeste was. The older woman put her hands to her chest, as if Blythe had struck her there. In that moment, Celeste's beautiful face seemed to age and wither.

When she spoke, her voice quavered.

"I don't know what to say." Celeste leaned against her chair for support. "I believe you, Blythe. I do believe you that Teri was kissing another man. But she's always been—demonstrably—in love with Bob. He hasn't seemed unhappy or worried."

"I couldn't decide whether to talk to you about it or not. I'm sorry I told you. I don't mean to be . . . tattling on Teri, but . . ." Blythe's entire body felt cringy. "But I don't know what to do. And you always know exactly what to do."

Celeste didn't speak. She bowed her head and smoothed the hem of the embroidered white napkin lying in her lap.

"This time, dear Blythe, I *don't* know what to do," she said, her voice soft. "This is a lot to take in."

"Oh, Celeste, I'm so sorry I upset you. I shouldn't have told you."

Celeste raised her head. "You did the right thing. I'm glad you told me. I'll think about it and let's talk more tomorrow."

Alarmed, Blythe hurriedly said, "Or not. We can just forget it."

"No, dear. We can't forget it." Celeste slowly rose from her chair. "Let's take the lunch dishes inside. I think I need a little nap."

"Oh, please, Celeste. Let me deal with the dishes. Go ahead and lie down. Please."

"Thank you." Celeste walked to the open porch door. She turned to Blythe. "It's fine, Blythe. Don't worry." She walked very carefully as she entered her house.

Blythe took the dishes inside and washed them carefully. When she'd finished, she went to the bottom of the stairs to the second floor and stood there, listening.

Quiet.

Blythe left the house, taking care to shut the front door gently. As she walked, her thoughts stumbled around one another. What had she done? How could she fix it? Should she talk to Teri about it? Or Bob? Was it a terrible, spiteful, gossipy thing she'd done, telling Celeste about her son's girlfriend? Blythe hadn't felt gossipy. She certainly hadn't thought it would shock her ex-mother-in-law so much.

But, come on, she thought, *why hadn't Bob told Teri he'd had a vasectomy?*

He needed to tell her! The poor woman. Blythe had friends who had suffered from infertility. It had wrecked marriages.

If Bob didn't tell Teri—what should Blythe do?

the hospital

She entered her house and found it quiet. The children had scribbled messages on the chalkboard.

She could tell by the writing that it was Holly who had written: *Mom. You left your phone on the counter when you went to Grandmother's.*

Beneath that, Miranda had added: *Ya u r so absentminded these days.*

Before Blythe could pick up her phone, it pinged.

Her heart almost stopped.

Blythe, I'm flying into Boston today. Arrive at Logan airport six this evening. Could you come meet me? Stay the night in my apartment. We have so much to talk about. Aaden.

His words swam before her. Aaden was back. He wanted to see her. It would mean a scramble to get ready, but she could do it. But *should* she do it? Spending the night with Aaden felt like a big leap, especially when she was beginning a new and lovely relationship with Nick. She didn't want to endanger that. But how could she go on with her new life if she didn't settle the emotional storm she'd been in since Aaden had come to her house for lunch? And when he'd taken her to dinner, she'd felt such *joy* in his presence. She'd enchanted herself with memories of Aaden for years. She couldn't let this chance go by.

She needed to settle down. To go slowly. To be an adult. As she often told her children, she needed to finish a task before starting a new one.

Not that Aaden was a *task*.

She remembered the winter of their senior year in high school, when they'd been at Blythe's house. Her parents weren't home, so Aaden built a fire in the living room fireplace and Blythe made real hot chocolate. They cuddled on the sofa, knowing they couldn't kiss without wanting more, because Blythe's parents might walk in any moment.

They had laughed together, warm in the firelight, safe in their love.

Aaden was the love of her life. *Then.*

But what did that mean for the rest of her life?

His arrival on Nantucket this summer had been like a miracle, like Fate placing him right in front of Blythe. She needed to see him again, and this would be a good time, while her children were busy with summer plans.

They would talk tonight. Just talk. She'd fly back tomorrow morning. Celeste or even Kate could take care of the children for one night.

In her Nantucket bedroom, Blythe texted Aaden. *I'll fly up this evening. Lots of planes this summer. I'll text you when I know what time I arrive.*

Immediately after pressing send, Blythe wanted to take it back. Because—what about Nick? What would he think if he knew she was flying to Boston to see another man? Would he be jealous?

Was she still in high school?

Her thoughts were interrupted when she heard her children pillaging through the house, slamming doors, arguing.

"Don't get snitty with *me* because Brooks wants to play tennis with Harrison!"

Ah, Blythe thought. Holly was squabbling with Miranda.

"I'm not being snitty with you," Miranda retorted. "Believe me, you'll know when I get snitty."

"Randy—" Holly began.

"Don't call me Randy!"

"Miranda, help me dye my hair pink. It will take your mind off Brooks."

"I can't. I'm busy."

"Yeah, you're busy. You'll watch your phone and chew on your hair and drive yourself crazy about Brooks."

Blythe smiled. Brave little Holly, who could take on her older sister.

Miranda forced a laugh. "Holly. Don't be such a child."

"But I *am* a child."

A bedroom door slammed. Holly ran down the stairs.

"I'm going to hang out with Grandmother for a while."

"That's nice," Blythe said. "Where's Miranda?"

Miranda came down the stairs. "I'm here." She sauntered into the kitchen, chewing on a stick of red licorice.

"Miranda, I have to fly up to Boston this evening. I'll be home tomorrow, but I'm going to ask Grandmother to stay here tonight with you all. You can have dinner at the snack bar and ice cream later. I want everyone in the house by ten. I'll call to check. You can watch *A Quiet Place: Day One* with everyone, but you have to watch something happy and fun after—*Hannah Montana* or something. I'm phoning Celeste now."

"Mom," Holly interrupted, "I can deal with the *Quiet Place* movies."

"You're only going to be in Boston for overnight? What's up with that?" Miranda asked.

Blythe knew that whatever she said would be shared with Celeste, Kate, Bob, and Teri.

"I have to sign some paperwork and they need it today." Blythe headed up the stairs, away from any further questions. "I've got to shower."

"See you later, Mom!" Holly called as she left the house on her way to Celeste's.

In her room, Blythe sat on her bed and called her former mother-in-law.

"Hello, Blythe," Celeste said. Her voice was strong.

"Celeste, I have to fly to Boston this evening to sign some papers. I'll be back in the morning. Could you spend the night here? They'll have dinner at the snack bar."

"Yes, of course. I'd love to stay with them." Celeste hesitated. "Is everything all right?"

"Everything's fine. This trip is a nuisance, but I need to do it," Blythe assured the other woman, and what she said was not a lie. She did need to do it. "Holly is coming over now. I'll call to check in."

"Safe trip!" Celeste sounded happy, almost excited. Being with her grandchildren always cheered her up.

Blythe took a quick shower, wondering what to wear to meet Aaden. She wanted to look both irresistible and untouchable. No matter what he said or how enticingly he said it, she was not having sex with him.

Or maybe she was. This would be a test.

She changed out of her silk blouse and pants and put on one of her most expensive, alluring summer dresses. Checking her watch, she saw that it was a little after four o'clock. At this time of year, flights were going to Boston almost every twenty minutes. She'd catch whatever she could. She checked her makeup. Her summer tan was flattering. She needed only mascara and lipstick.

She put her toothbrush in her purse.

Down in the kitchen, she scribbled a note on the chalkboard, telling everyone what she'd already told Miranda. Dinner at the snack bar. Celeste would come to spend the night. She'd be home in the morning.

The house was quiet as she walked through it. Why did she feel so guilty? Her children adored their grandmother.

It took ten minutes to drive to the airport. She parked in the long-term lot and walked toward the terminal. Her heart was picking up speed.

She wasn't frightened, she was—apprehensive. This meeting with Aaden would be about seeing him again, talking about their lives. Deciding whether they could become more to each other than dreamy memories.

Deciding what she wanted. Who she wanted—if she wanted anyone.

At the Cape Air counter, she bought a round-trip ticket. The flight would leave at five-ten. She texted Sandy and then Kate to tell them that she'd be in Boston tonight, back home tomorrow. That was the magic of Nantucket. You could feel you were in a different world, but you were never far away from a city.

She texted Aaden to tell him what plane she was arriving on.

Her heart was fluttering like the hem of her silk dress.

What would she tell Nick?

She didn't have to tell Nick anything.

Would she tell Aaden about Nick? Why should she? It wasn't as if she and Nick had a serious relationship.

Her phone pinged.

It was Holly.

Blythe smiled. Her darling daughter. "Hi, sweetie, what's going on?"

"Mommy!" Holly was almost screaming.

Blythe's heart lurched. "Holly, calm down. Is something wrong?"

"Mommy, Grandmother's acting weird! She's shaking and she's rolling or something. I'm scared!"

The world shrank to this moment, her child's voice.

"Where are you, Holly?"

"In her dining room. Mommy, Grandmother fell on the floor. I don't know what to do!"

Blythe didn't think twice. "Holly, I'll be right there. Call 911. Call Aunt Kate. I'm on my way. Two minutes. I'll be there in two minutes."

As she spoke, Blythe ran out of the terminal, got in her car, and tore out of the airport, joining the endless row of cars headed into town on Old South Road. It wasn't going to be two minutes. She'd be lucky if she got there in ten.

She hit the media console to call Holly back. The line was busy. That was good, Blythe thought. Holly was calling people to help. Then her phone rang again. It was Holly, crying.

"Grandmother's trying to say something but I can't understand!"

"Stay with Grandmother," Blythe said, trying to sound calm. "See if you can hold her hand. I'm on my way."

"Mommy, she scares me."

"Did you call 911?"

"Yes."

"They'll be there soon. Is Grandmother still on the floor?"

"She's rolled up in a ball. Her face looks awful."

"It's okay. The EMTs will help her and she'll be fine. Listen, Holly, could you be brave and try to let her know you're there for her? Hold her hand or smooth her hair. Tell her she'll be all right. Tell her help is coming."

Holly whispered, "I don't know."

"Holly, when people are sick, they look scary. But try. Just pretend she's a baby who's having a tantrum. She needs to know she's not alone. I'm almost there."

Sirens blared. Blythe swerved to the side of the road. An ambulance passed her. Blythe drove behind it.

"I hear sirens!" Holly yelled a few minutes later.

"That's the ambulance. I'm here, too."

Blythe rushed out of her car and to the house. Already EMTs were bending over Celeste, evaluating her and speaking quickly to each other.

Holly ran into Blythe's arms. "Is she dying? I don't want her to die!"

Blythe hugged her daughter tight. "The doctors will know what to do."

Everything passed in a blur. Blythe and Holly watched the EMTs lift Celeste onto a stretcher, strap her in, and carry her out the door and over the lawn to the ambulance waiting at the curb.

Blythe and Holly watched as beautiful, humorous, wise Celeste lay, a tiny helpless creature with an oxygen mask over her face. The ambulance doors shut. With a shriek of the siren, it raced off.

Holly was shaking. Blythe's brain was on high alert.

"Let's find Grandmother's purse. They'll want her Medicare records."

"I know where it is!" Holly led her mother to the front hall where Celeste's book bag hung. Blythe reached inside, found the wallet, and put it in her own purse.

"Great, Holly, thank you, you've really helped. You are so brave. Let's go to the hospital."

Holly nodded. She settled in the passenger side of the car, and as Blythe fastened her own seatbelt, she realized that this simple act was calming. It was something they could do, something organized and rule-driven during this chaotic time when they couldn't control anything and didn't even know what to control.

The hospital parking lot had plenty of free spaces, and the emergency entrance was quiet. Blythe's hands were shaking as she presented Celeste's medical cards to the clerk, and when the clerk accepted them, Blythe felt a sense of accomplishment sweep through her, as if *she* was doing something to help Celeste.

Never before had Blythe realized how much she needed Celeste. For so many reasons she needed her to be okay.

"Someone will be out to talk with you soon," the clerk said.

Blythe sat on a folding chair next to her daughter. "We have to wait. Tell me, sweetie, what was Grandmother doing before this happened?"

"Nothing." Holly's eyes were wide as she spoke, but she was calmer. "We were at the dining room table, and she said she felt funny, she needed to lie down, so I said I'd come back later, and I was gathering my stuff and she grabbed her chest and groaned. She fell on the floor. She was awake, her eyes were open, but she didn't *see* me. Then I called you."

"You were a smart girl to call me, Holly. And you were so brave to stay with Grandmother. It must have been scary for you."

Holly whispered, "What's wrong with her? Is she going to die?"

"I don't know, Holly. We'll have to wait for the doctors to tell us." Blythe wrapped her arm around her daughter and pulled her close.

A woman came in with a red-faced wailing baby and was taken into the inner sanctum of the ER.

Holly whispered, "I have to pee."

"Of course. You know where the bathroom is."

Holly went off. Blythe took out her phone and called Aaden. When she got his voicemail, she tried to be concise, even though she was shaking. She was worried about Celeste, of course, but she was sad to be missing a trip to see Aaden in Boston. She really liked Aaden even if she didn't know if she loved him, even though she kind of thought she was falling in love with Nick. She needed to see Aaden to let her heart tell her the truth. How would she feel when she saw his face again? When he kissed her? For so many years, their love had been like gold buried in the deepest part of her heart.

Or had it not been gold but mica, fool's gold, its shine destined to crumble?

She said, "Aaden, I can't come to Boston. Celeste, my mother-in-law, well, my ex-mother-in-law, had a stroke or a heart attack, something bad. I'm at the hospital now. We're waiting to find out how she is. How long she'll be here."

Holly was walking down the corridor from the bathroom. Hurriedly, Blythe said, "I'm so sorry, Aaden. I love you."

As she slipped the phone into her pocket, she was glad she'd told him she loved him. Right now, life seemed so precious, and love seemed to be the only answer to any question.

She put her face in her hands and wept.

"Mommy?" Holly put her hand on Blythe's shoulder. "Grandmother will be all right, Mommy. Don't cry."

Blythe raised her head and sniffed back her tears. How crazy was she to be crying about a man she hadn't seen in years and might not ever see again?

But her tears were not only for Aaden. They were from fear for Celeste and concern for her youngest daughter and all her children, who would be confused and devastated by their grandmother's hospitalization. And what would they do, what would they *all* do, if Celeste died?

Blythe couldn't control that. Right now, it seemed she couldn't control much of anything.

Pull yourself together, she told herself.

She dug a tissue from her purse and heartily blew her nose.

"Sorry," Blythe told her daughter.

"We're all scared," Holly informed her. "It's only natural."

Blythe almost laughed. Her youngest child was so instinctively on target.

Blythe asked, "Holly, did you call Aunt Kate?"

"I didn't." Holly cringed. "Will she be mad at me?"

"No, darling. It's okay."

She called Kate. Kate's voicemail came on.

Blythe left a message. "Celeste is in the hospital. Holly and I are here."

I need to call Bob, Blythe thought, just as a nurse came out to talk to Blythe. Janet was an island woman who knew Celeste and Blythe and the entire family. She took Blythe and Holly into a small private cubicle.

"Celeste is doing well." Janet gave them a few moments for the words to sink in, like water extinguishing a flame. "She's going to stay with us in the hospital tonight so we can keep an eye on her. She's had a minor heart attack."

"Why?" Holly asked. "Is it my fault?"

"Of course not," Janet said. "Your grandmother shows every sign of returning to normal, but we need to take care of her for a few days."

"When can we see her?" Blythe asked.

Janet hesitated. "Why don't you step in for a quick hello? She's all settled, and lucid, and she's asked to see you, but she's tired. Just one person at a time, for now."

"I'll be right back," Blythe told Holly.

She hurried after the nurse, down the bright hallway, grateful that the hospital had recently been renovated. Everything was clean, bright, and cheerful.

Janet led her into Celeste's room.

"We've got a visitor for you, Celeste."

"Celeste!" Blythe forced a smile as she walked toward the older woman.

Celeste was lying in a hospital bed, clad in a hospital gown. She was pale and looked exhausted and very small.

"I'll leave you two for a moment," Janet said.

Blythe kissed Celeste on her forehead. "How are you feeling?"

Celeste grasped Blythe's hand. "Please tell Holly I'm sorry. I'm sure I frightened her."

"Oh, Celeste, don't be silly. Holly adores you. Nothing could change that. She's going to feel like a hero because she called the EMTs."

"It's so embarrassing," Celeste said. Tears welled in her eyes.

Celeste seemed *fragile,* which was actually terrifying. Everyone felt like Celeste would live forever or at least to one hundred ten. Blythe's heart surged with a tide of pity and an unexpected shiver of fear.

Blythe smiled. "Don't be embarrassed. Everyone spends time in the hospital, sooner or later." She pulled a chair up to the bed and sat close to Celeste, holding her hand.

Celeste signaled for Blythe to come closer so she could whisper. "The thing is, I feel *old* now. I feel frail! And I hate it!"

Blythe's own heart thumped hard. She shouldn't let Celeste get upset.

"Nonsense. You've been so active, and so concerned about all of us. Now it's time for you to let others take care of you."

"Dr. Margrave said I have to spend the night. Maybe two."

"I think that's smart. Plus, I've heard the food here is delicious."

Celeste relaxed back into her pillows. "You've always been optimistic."

"So do you want some food? Red or green grapes?"

"A flask of gin would be good."

Blythe saw in Celeste's smile that she was cheering up. "Would you like to see Holly, for just a moment?"

Celeste hesitated. Then, to Blythe's amazement, Celeste burst into tears.

"I hate looking like this, Blythe. In the *hospital*! What must my hair look like? I *hate* having my grandchildren see me as this wrinkled, sagging, helpless bag of flesh."

"Oh, Celeste, you're not—" Blythe held her tongue, realizing her mother-in-law needed this outburst.

Celeste continued, "*You* are young. You have no idea how the body changes. My breasts are sagging. *Everything* is sagging! My skin is *gray* and I've got freckles and moles popping up all over. I had thought, seriously, of moving away, possibly to Florida where my friends go. Or, maybe to some nice, pleasant place in Indiana where no one knows what I used to look like."

"Celeste, you're beautiful. But that's not why we all love you. You're kind and smart and funny and generous. You know so much, and we need you to help us through our lives."

Blythe awkwardly moved forward and hugged Celeste as she wept.

Voices exploded in the hall and suddenly Kate burst into the room, yelling, "She is *my* mother!"

Blythe quickly moved away from Celeste so that Kate could throw herself down on the hospital bed next to her mother.

"Mom. Are you okay?" Kate leaned over her mother, effectively blocking Blythe from Celeste's vision.

A nurse entered. "We need to keep it down to one visitor at a time."

Angrily, Kate said, "Then *Blythe* can leave! *I'm* Celeste's daughter."

"I'll go." Blythe peered around Kate's body. "Take care, Celeste."

Blythe left the hospital room and walked down the long hall. She found *her* daughter standing outside the glass doors, talking on her phone.

"She's here now." Holly handed her phone to Blythe. "I called Daddy."

As soon as Blythe said hello, Bob barked, "What's going on?"

"Celeste is in the hospital, but she'll be okay."

"What happened?"

"She had a minor heart attack."

"Good God! She could die!"

"She won't die, Bob. Calm down. I've just been with her. Your sister is with her now. Celeste's lucid. She'll be carefully watched."

Bob only shouted louder. "Holly said my mother fell on the floor. How could you let Holly see her like that? It will damage her for life."

"Holly is fine. She was calm enough to call you. She's a brave girl."

"Kate hasn't called me. She's such a tyrant about Mom."

Blythe didn't want to get into another discussion of the complications of dealing with Bob's sister. "Why don't *you* phone Kate? I've got to go." Blythe ended the call.

She turned to her daughter. "Your father is worried, Holly."

Holly peered up from beneath her long eyelashes. "I know. I'm sorry I called him."

"Oh, honey, you were right to call him. You can always call him. This is a scary situation. You were amazing, handling it as well as you did." Blythe took her daughter in her arms and held her tight. "Grandmother is going to be just fine." She was reassuring herself as much as her daughter.

Blythe had no idea what time it was, but she knew she would dearly love a glass of white wine. She wanted to take Holly away from the hospital, back to the normalcy of her home.

But should she remain here, and if so, for how long? She couldn't help Celeste. The nurses and doctor would do that. Kate wouldn't want her around.

She was at the point of telling Holly they should go when Roland came almost running toward them. His hair stood up all over.

"How is she?" he panted.

"She's okay, Roland. She's okay." Blythe put a gentle hand on the man's arm to calm him. "Don't worry. The nurses say the heart attack was minor."

"My neighbor told me. He drove me here. He didn't want me driving and having my own heart attack." Roland's laugh sounded just a little demented. "This morning when we spoke on the phone she said she just didn't feel right. I should have taken her to Urgent Care."

"Roland, she's going to be fine. Kate's with her now. Why don't you go in and see her for a moment?"

Roland winced. "Kate scares me," he whispered.

Blythe laughed. "Kate scares everyone. But I know it would give Celeste a boost just to see your face."

Roland nodded. "All right." He walked off down the corridor.

Blythe took Holly's hand as they walked out the automatic sliding doors and to the car. "Now Grandmother has her daughter and her boyfriend with her. The hospital is taking care of her. She'll be fine."

"I texted Miranda, Teddy, and Daphne and told them about Grandmother."

"Good girl. They'll probably come home as soon as they can. While we wait, I think you need to watch *Anne with an E* or *The Baby-Sitters Club*."

"I'm hungry. Can I eat some cookies?"

Blythe glanced up. The blue sky of summer made the evening bright and timeless. She checked her watch.

"Oh, Holly, what a day! Listen, eat some carrots and broccoli with hummus first, and then you can eat all the cookies you want."

"Agree." Holly fist-bumped Blythe.

Back in her house, Blythe settled Holly in the family room. She read Daphne's scrawled note on the kitchen blackboard: *Eating with Lincoln. Home later.*

Blythe stood in the kitchen, trying to gather her wits. Daphne would come home right after Holly's text. Teddy would, too. And—

She heard a cry. A wrenching, heartbreaking sob.

heartbreak

Now what?

Blythe climbed the stairs and opened the door to her bedroom.

Miranda was curled up on the bed, her hands over her face, sobbing.

"Oh, honey," Blythe said. "Grandmother will be all right."

She pulled Miranda up and gathered her oldest daughter in her arms.

"It's okay," Blythe said soothingly.

Miranda twisted around to face Blythe.

"It's not Grandmother! It's *me*! It's not okay! It will never be okay!" Miranda's face was wet and swollen from crying. Her mascara streaked down her face like black tears.

"What happened?" Blythe asked.

"Oh, Mommy! I saw Brooks kissing Serena! And they were totally kissing, slobber-kissing."

Blythe almost couldn't believe this. She'd seen Brooks a million times, always so crazy in love with Miranda. "Maybe Serena was kissing him and he went along with it?"

"I know what I saw, Mom! Brooks wasn't just *going along with it*. He had his arms around her. She had her hands in his hair!"

"Where was this?" Blythe's protective instincts began to stir.

"At Serena's. We were just swimming and hanging out and I had my period and I went into the house and up to her bathroom and I had to search around for a tampon and I couldn't find one and I stuck my head out the window to yell to Serena and I saw them. By the swimming pool. Then I knew why Serena wore her sexiest bathing suit today. And *Mom*, they were kissing." Miranda collapsed in heart-wrenching sobs.

Blythe held her daughter close, as if sheltering her from a storm. "I'm so sorry. Maybe they were just . . . playing?"

"I know what I saw! They were totally into each other."

As her daughter wept, a prehistoric maternal rage uncurled in Blythe's deepest heart. Nothing hurt as much as her children being hurt. She wanted to transform into a yeti and stomp over Serena and terrorize her with an earth-shaking growl.

But she was civilized. She had to be rational.

"Do they know you saw them?"

"I don't know. I don't think so. I didn't know what to do! I just ran home. Oh, Mommy, it was so terrible! I thought Brooks loved me."

"Maybe—" Blythe began.

Miranda interrupted, violently pulling herself from Blythe's arms. "Brooks has to *leave*! He can't stay in this house one more minute! He's a liar and a cheater and he doesn't deserve to stay here. I'm going to pack his stuff and throw it out in the yard and tell him to take the next boat home! I never want to see him again! I'm never talking to Serena again!"

"Miranda, calm down. Listen to me. Brooks can't leave. I told you both the other day that his mother asked if Brooks could stay here all summer because their housekeeper broke her leg and can't be there for him. We can't make him leave when he has no place to go."

Miranda exploded, standing up and throwing her hands in the air. "Fine! *Lovely!* You're choosing Brooks over your own daughter!"

"I'm not choosing Brooks over you. I would never do that. I wish I could throw our oldest, grungiest sleeping bag in our backyard and tell him that's his bedroom now and he can go to Visitor Services to use the bathroom and he can buy his own food because he's never eating with us again."

Blythe's anger made Miranda blink in surprise. She almost smiled as tears streaked her face. "That would be cool."

"I know. But we can't do that. I'm responsible for his safety. I can't simply tell him to get out."

Miranda paced the room. "Fine. But you don't have to talk to him. You don't have to be nice to him. You can tell him he's no longer welcome at the club to sail or play tennis or eat. Plus—" Her eyes narrowed as she had a new thought. "You really have to move him out of the family room. We all need it to watch television. He has to go sleep in that little room at the end of the hall."

Blythe had always thought of that little room at the end of the hall as a special place, a magic room. So small, with only one twin bed and one dresser and that half-moon window. It had been perfect for a little girl. But it wouldn't be magic for a big philandering male. It wouldn't even be comfortable.

"I see your point, Miranda, but Brooks is a big guy. He'll feel claustrophobic in there."

"Good! I hope he has nightmares!" With tears rolling down her flushed cheeks, Miranda laughed an insane, triumphant laugh like the wicked queen in *Snow White*. "Remember, Mom, how you said he couldn't sleep on the same floor as our bedrooms because you were so worried we'd have sex? Now he *has* to be on this floor. But my bedroom door will be *locked*. And I'll tell the sibs what he did and they'll never speak to him again." As she spoke, her lip quivered and she stood there, a beautiful young woman, shaking with grief and rage.

Blythe yearned to comfort her child, to make the bad thing go away, but she couldn't. She had no choice but to let Miranda bear it. She wished that her pain, a mother's pain, would ease Miranda's, but she knew that wasn't how it worked. Blythe remembered the brutal day she lived through after Aaden left for Ireland, and she remembered that it didn't help at all that he had left for another country instead of another woman.

"I'm so sorry, sweetheart." Blythe stood up. "I need to eat. Come downstairs with me now. I'll make grilled cheese sandwiches." Her grilled cheese sandwiches were a mouth orgy of cheddar and whole wheat fried slowly in butter that soaked into the bread as the cheese melted.

"I'm not hungry," Miranda said.

Blythe started to insist that Miranda come eat. She hadn't even told Miranda about Celeste and the hospital.

But Miranda needed her time, her space. "I'm going to my room for a while. I don't want dinner tonight."

"Just rest," Blythe said.

Miranda left to go to her own room. Blythe looked at her bed, which she had made so neatly this morning. She always liked to return to her room after a busy day to find her smooth, unruffled bed waiting for her. Now it was in a swirl of sheets, summer quilt, and discarded wet tissues.

She wished she could smooth her daughter's grief away as easily as she smoothed her quilt.

In the kitchen, Blythe fixed herself a drink, pouring vodka and tonic over piles of ice. She took a sip and held the cold glass to her neck, cooling her maternal rage.

She was shocked to see how late it was. Almost eight o'clock. She was too upset to cook dinner, and by now, the children had probably eaten at the snack bar.

She decided to make a large fruit bowl with chunks of watermelon, grapes, peaches and pears. Long ago she'd discovered that slicing food helped keep her thoughts focused on what she was doing, and good thing, too.

"That looks yummy, Mom," Holly said.

Blythe jumped a little. "I'd forgotten you were in the family room, sweetie. Are you hungry?"

"I atc some cereal."

"Let's both have some fruit," she told Holly.

While they were eating, Teddy and Daphne came home. They'd had dinner with friends but served themselves fruit and joined Blythe and Holly at the table. Everyone talked about poor Celeste, and the shock that Holly had had, seeing her beloved grandmother like that. Blythe called the hospital as she sat at the dinner table. Phones during meals were strictly verboten for all the family, but this was an extenuating circumstance. Blythe wasn't sure she could pull together the energy to stand up.

"Celeste is doing well," she told her children after talking to a nurse. "She's sleeping now. Kate has gone home and the nurses don't think we should visit Grandmother tonight. She needs to sleep."

Daphne asked, "Where's Miranda?"

"She's sleeping, I think. She's had a busy day." Blythe took a moment to decide how much of Miranda's heartbreak she should share. Not now, she thought. Not so soon, while it's an open wound.

But she remembered what Miranda had suggested.

"I've decided that it's too complicated to have Brooks sleep in the family room. We need to be able to watch television and he needs his privacy. Let's take his stuff up to the funny little bedroom."

Holly looked worried. "Is it okay if we touch his stuff?"

Blythe smiled. "Of course. He's living here and touching our stuff all the time."

"He's not touching *my* stuff," Teddy said, and for no reason at all, everyone laughed.

They went into the family room and each person chose a load of Brooks's belongings. Teddy carried his duffel bag and backpack, both bulging with clothes. Daphne and Holly took his bedclothes and pillow up to the small room and dumped them in the middle of the small twin bed.

"Should we make his bed?" Holly asked.

"He's a big boy. He can make his own," Blythe decided. She worried a little about how much pleasure she felt at moving his stuff to the little room. He would probably be glad to have the privacy.

When they were through, Blythe invited the children to join her watching a new movie being streamed on television. They'd seen it before, and it was funny, perfect for tonight.

The kids pulled the plump ottomans over and all four of them huddled together on the sofa with their feet sticking out of the light cotton blanket they always used for watching television.

Blythe wished Miranda would come join them. She thought of going up to ask her but decided not to. Miranda's sorrow wouldn't let go of her so soon.

It was almost ten o'clock when Brooks came home. He stopped in the doorway of the family room, looking confused.

Blythe hit the pause button on the remote.

"Hi, Brooks!" Holly called. "We've put your stuff in the little room upstairs."

If you don't like it, Blythe wanted to say, *go sleep at Serena's.* She should be ashamed of this petty revenge, but it wasn't as if Miranda and Brooks were eight and Blythe could call Brooks's parents.

"Yeah," Holly added, grinning. "I guess Mom's not so worried about you sneaking into Mir's room."

"Holly!" Daphne nudged her younger sister. "Don't say that."

Sitting in the middle of her huddle of children, Blythe felt a small, guilty joy at making Brooks feel left out. He was still a kid, really, and she didn't want to be cruel. Well, she did want to be cruel, but not in front of her children.

"There's fruit in the refrigerator," she told Brooks.

"I've eaten," Brooks said. "But thank you."

"We're watching *Twisters,*" Holly informed him. "It's super cool. You could have watched with us, but it's almost over."

"Thanks," Brooks said. "I think I'll go on up to bed."

"Good night!" Blythe called, and Daphne, Teddy, and Holly called good night, too, and Brooks turned away from the happy little group and went up the stairs alone.

Whose shoulder could Brooks cry on? Blythe wondered. Now sympathy for the boy washed over her. He had no siblings. And no one in this house loved him.

After the movie, the kids went up to bed. Blythe's phone pinged and her heart jumped.

Was the hospital calling about Celeste?

But it was Nick, and his voice erased the sadness of the day. She relaxed on the wicker swing on the back porch as they talked.

"How has your day been?" Nick asked.

"Well, Nick, I'd be laughing hysterically if I had any energy left."

"What's going on?"

"How much time do you have?"

"All the time in the world, for you."

"Oh, damn," Blythe said as she began to cry. The warmth in his voice undid her. So many people depended on Blythe. She was trying to remain strong . . . and she *was* strong. But how good it felt to have someone support her, simply take the time to be her friend.

She told him about her poor Holly, who had been with Celeste when she had a heart attack, and how she felt she'd spent this entire day trying to gather a flock of wild cards scattered in the storm of their fear—Celeste, Kate, Bob, Teri, Roland, and Holly—and then to come home to find Miranda brokenhearted. And Brooks, just another example of faithless men, and yet, also a boy.

Nick listened. He asked questions. How was Celeste? How was Miranda? How was Blythe?

"I've gone hoarse," Blythe croaked. "You talk. Tell me about your day."

He didn't speak, and Blythe waited while he gathered his thoughts. She assumed he would tell her about a golf game, or fishing at Great Point, or taking Sandy and Hugh to dinner.

Nick said, "I missed you. That's what happened today."

His concern made her heart open. A sob rose in her throat. She reached for a tissue and wiped her tears. "I missed you, too, Nick. It's so nice to hear your voice."

"Would you like me to come over?"

"Oh, yes, but no, it's too late. I have to go to bed. I'm exhausted and tomorrow will be crazy. But thank you."

"I hope you'll call if you need any help."

"I will. I promise."

She didn't want to end the call, but she couldn't prevent yawning so loudly and hard she thought her jaw would lock open.

"That was rude. I'm sorry."

Nick laughed. "You are forgiven for being tired after the day you've had. Sleep tight."

She held the phone close to her heart as she went up the stairs.

She quietly went down the hall, peeking in each child's room.

Holly was asleep, cradling her favorite stuffed animal, Oscar. Teddy slept with his arms and legs flung out, all his covers on the floor as if he'd fought them and won. Daphne snored what the kids called "Daphne's Signature Snore" as she lay flat on her back, her head in the center of the pillow, her covers pulled to her shoulders and everything as tidy as if she were a letter slid into an envelope.

And Miranda. Her tempestuous daughter lay on her stomach, her light sheet and cotton quilt swirled over the bed and her laptop sticking out from beneath her head.

Blythe quietly entered the room, gently eased the laptop away, and set it on the bedside table. Miranda, who slept operatically, rolled onto her back, emitting a long tremulous sigh. But she didn't wake up, and Blythe decided not to try to untangle the covers because it might disturb her sleep. She didn't need to check on Brooks. She knew he was fine.

She hoped he had nightmares.

Was she a terrible person to think that way?

Blythe returned to her room, tired, but happy. Her children were asleep. They were safe. Tomorrow was another day. She brushed her teeth and slid into bed, relaxing on her clean sheets and plump pillow. Sublime.

Someone was knocking on the front door.

Blythe's heart lurched. *No. It couldn't be about Celeste.*

But it was ten-thirty. Who would knock on their door at ten-thirty?

She pulled on her light robe and hurried down the stairs. Frightened and angry—the children might wake—she yanked the door open.

Aaden.

For a long moment, she couldn't seem to focus. Was she caught in one of those very realistic dreams?

It really was Aaden. In his suit and tie, he looked very professional and very tired. His tie was tugged down, his white dress shirt was wrinkled, and he carried his suit jacket in his hand. His jaw was bristling with a day-old beard and his eyelids drooped.

"Aaden? What— I thought you were in Boston."

"May I come in?" His voice was scratchy.

"Of course." She held the door open.

He entered. His rumpled clothes smelled of Scotch. He started to embrace her but caught himself and stepped back.

"How are you?" he asked.

"Oh, Aaden, I'm exhausted and you look exhausted, too. Come in. I'll make coffee."

She led him to the kitchen, glad she'd pulled her robe over her T-shirt and boxer shorts.

"Here," she indicated. "Sit. Are you hungry?"

"I don't know. It doesn't matter. I do need coffee. How are you? How is your friend?"

"My friend?" She found a mug and poured the water in the Keurig. How sweet of him, and how right, to call Celeste her friend. It was much simpler than ex-mother-in-law, and it was true.

"She's resting in the hospital. The prognosis is good. She's in her seventies and in general good health."

The Keurig rumbled and filled the mug. Blythe got out the milk and the sugar bowl. She didn't have to ask him how he took his coffee. She set it in front of him and sat in a chair next to him. She folded her hands together on the table, to hide the fact that they were shaking.

She watched Aaden close his eyes as he took a long drink.

"I'm sorry I couldn't come to Boston." When he didn't reply, she said, "Holly, my youngest daughter, was with Celeste when she had the heart attack and she was frightened. An ambulance came, and it was all a rush, and we were frightened for Celeste, and her daughter, Kate, took a while to get to the hospital . . ."

Aaden slipped his hand over hers. "I understand. You're very close to your family. That's one of the many things I admire about you."

Blythe looked down at their hands. It was so oddly intimate to be sitting in the kitchen at night while the others slept.

She needed to say something. He'd come all this way, but her head was filled with fog.

"How did you manage to get here?" she asked. "I thought no planes flew after ten o'clock."

"I chartered a private plane." Aaden ran his thumb over the back of her hand. "I had to see you."

She was shocked. "You flew private? That's awfully expensive." She knew she was avoiding serious conversation. "It's so late, Aaden. I'm not sure I can even think straight."

"I know, and for me it's four in the morning, Irish time. Blythe, I knew I wouldn't be able to settle until I saw you. I never expected to run into you this summer, and yes, I do know that you have a house on the island. Still, I wasn't planning to see you. I wasn't even hoping. But I did see you."

"Aaden, wait." She held up her hand.

He shook his head. "I need to say this. I came here tonight to say this. After so many years, you and I were thrown face-to-face together. That seems like fate to me. We are meant to be together."

"Aaden—"

"I need you, Blythe. I've always needed you. I don't want to live the rest of my life—and you and I have so many more years to live—I don't want to live without you."

He was so beautiful, his thick dark hair tumbled in every direction and his eyes still adorned with long dark lashes. His wrestler's body had less bulk, but he still was heavy-boned, wide-shouldered, a bear of a man. He could fold her into his arms and keep her safe. She remembered being held in his arms.

"Aaden—"

As if he read her thoughts, Aaden said, "Do you remember the night when we were all at Mike's house and we built a bonfire?"

Blythe shuddered. "I'll never forget that night. The fire got out of control. It set a dead limb on a maple tree on fire and then sent the fence into flames. Mike called the fire department. Greta found the hose and aimed it at the fire." She could remember it clearly. The speed and hiss of the fire, the sudden blaze, how they all cheered before realizing how fast the fire was spreading.

"And I picked you up and carried you out to the street, away from danger."

"Yes. You lifted me in your arms as if I were made of feathers. You were so strong."

"I'm still so strong. I still want to carry you in my arms."

Blythe released her hand from his and gently stroked his cheek. "You were like a white knight, rescuing me. A schoolgirl's fantasy come true." She allowed herself a moment of surrender. The bristles on his jaw lightly scratched the sensitive palm of her hand, as his skin had grazed her face when they kissed so fervently for so long, in the steamy car Aaden had secluded on a stranger's cul-de-sac. "My old high school friends still talk about it when we get together. They say it was the most romantic real thing they had ever seen."

Aaden turned his face slightly and his full lips brushed her palm.

Blythe pulled her hand away.

"Aaden, I'm not a schoolgirl anymore. I'm a mother and I come with four very heavy and demanding children attached." She was so overwrought that an image of Aaden carrying all five of them, three in his arms, two piggyback, with Miranda's giraffe legs sticking out, made her laugh.

Irritation flared in Aaden's eyes. Blythe remembered that look.

He quickly glanced away, and when he met her eyes again, he was smiling.

"I forgot to tell you who I met at the airport. Do you remember Jessica Langston? From high school?"

"Of course I remember Jessica." Blythe crossed her arms over her chest. She knew this movement was defensive, and she didn't care.

Jessica Langston was the beautiful girl who had shamelessly chased after Aaden in high school. She'd made it clear that she would do anything Aaden wanted to do. She was the cause of many arguments between Blythe and Aaden. Blythe had hated her.

"I was at the Dublin airport, waiting to board, and she walked by. She recognized me and stopped to say hello. She works in the travel business now. She's divorced, with one son. She told me to let her know the next time I travel. She can get me some special deals."

Blythe laughed. "I'll bet she can." She knew what he was trying to do. Once, if he'd mentioned Jessica, Blythe would have gone wild. Now, not even one small drop of jealousy stung her, and that made her sad.

"Aaden. I'm sorry, but I really need to get some sleep."

He nodded. "I do, too. I have the key to Arnie's, but I hate to wake him . . ."

Blythe stood up. "You can't sleep here. We've got a full house."

Aaden rose. He smiled down at her, his eyes teasing. "Not even the sofa?"

"Not even the sofa," Blythe told him.

For a moment, she thought he was going to kiss her, or try to, but she walked away from him, down the hall to the front door.

"I'll call you tomorrow," he said.

"Good night, Aaden." She shut the door.

bothersome bodies

It was light outside when her phone pinged. She answered without looking at the caller ID.

"Where are you?" Bob demanded.

Blythe pulled herself up to a sitting position.

"In my house, Bob," Blythe croaked. "Where are you?"

"We're at the airport. Kate said you would pick us up."

"Kate said that? All right, I can do that, but it would be quicker if you took a cab to the hospital."

Bob's voice was harsh. "You mean this is too inconvenient for you to do even if it's for Celeste?"

"Why can't Kate pick you up? I've got the kids here."

"Miranda's seventeen. I think they can survive a few minutes without you."

"Why are you being so cranky?"

"Because I'm frightened for my mother."

It all came back in a rush: Celeste was in the hospital. Why was she even arguing? "Fine. I'll be right there."

She gave herself a minute to shower and slip into a clean sundress. She wrote, in large letters, on the chalkboard: *I'M GOING TO THE HOSPITAL TO SEE GRANDMOTHER. CALL ME IF YOU NEED ANYTHING.*

She quietly left her house, stopping for one luxurious moment to breathe in the new morning air. Birds chirped and rustled in the trees. Her willowy cosmos stood tall and cheerful, with their slender stems and colorful petals. Down the street, carpenters were already working up on the roof of someone's home.

At the small island airport, Bob and Teri waited on the edge of the sidewalk. Blythe slowed the car. Bob got into the passenger seat and Teri sat in the back with their two duffel bags.

"How is she?" Bob asked.

For a moment, Blythe felt caught in a time warp as her ex-husband's familiar voice asked the question he'd asked so many times over the years.

How is she? When Miranda, at six months, had colic and cried constantly. Blythe had cried a lot, too.

When two-year-old Daphne put an eraser up her nose and Blythe had to take her to the doctor, afraid if she tried to get it out herself, she'd only push it farther in and their daughter would need an operation to extract it.

When Teddy, at a Little League baseball game, got hit in the head with a ball and developed an enormous lump on his forehead, as wounded and proud as if he'd won the baseball game single-handedly.

When Holly, eight years old, decided she was a mermaid and tried to swim from Steps Beach to a small sandbank twenty feet out, couldn't make it, and lay on her back, kicking her feet and exhausted, until Blythe swam out to help her back to safety.

Bob hadn't been there at any of those moments. Blythe had called her husband to tell him about the emergency.

"How is she?" he'd ask. Or if it was Teddy, "How is he?"

"She's okay now," Blythe would answer, feeling sick and lonely because she was the only adult there to hear baby Miranda's crying, to see the softball slam straight into Teddy's head, hitting him so hard he crumpled to the ground and Blythe had screamed. The only parent to force herself to be calm as she organized the two older children to go out with her into the blizzard to take Daphne to the doctor to extract the eraser, all the time fearing the child would suck it farther back into her complicated sinuses. The only parent—who was not that good of a swimmer—to thrash through the water out to rescue Holly, all the time cursing herself for trying to read while her children played on the beach.

Bob said, "Blythe? Hello?"

"Sorry, Bob. My brain's a little foggy right now. When I left, Celeste was doing better, they were just keeping her under observation. I'm sure Kate told you the details. Have you spoken with your sister?"

"She turned off her phone."

"Good. I hope she's getting some rest."

At the hospital, Blythe spoke with a nurse who told her Celeste could have more than one visitor at a time now. Blythe walked to Celeste's room with Bob and Teri. Kate, looking as tired as Blythe did, hugged her brother and took him into their mother's room.

Blythe was left standing with Teri.

"I wish I knew what to do to help," Teri said. She had a Hermès bag hanging off her shoulder and wore a lovely linen dress and high heels.

"Just being here is a help," Blythe said, hoping that was true.

Blythe's phone chimed. *Holly.*

"I have to take this," Blythe said, walking away from Teri.

"Mommy, how is Grandmother doing?"

"I haven't seen her yet, darling. I'll let you know when I get home."

"When will that be?"

"Soon. I want to hear what the doctor says first. Your father and

Teri are here. They flew down and I just picked them up at the airport and brought them here to the hospital. He and Aunt Kate are with Celeste now." *Listen to me,* Blythe thought, *all sweetness and light about Teri, about Celeste, about Kate.*

From the background, Daphne said, "Tell Mom I'm making pancakes for us."

"Daphne, how wonderful," Blythe said, and she burst into tears.

Holly said to Daphne, "Mom's crying."

Daphne said to Holly, "Tell Mom to drink some coffee."

Oh, her sensible daughter! Blythe laughed through her tears.

"I'll do that. And I'll be home soon," she said.

After a while, Kate and Bob came out of Celeste's room.

Teri hugged Kate. "You look like you've been hit by a truck."

Kate managed a weak smile. "I *feel* like I've been hit by a truck."

What? Blythe stood there, reality warping around her again as she realized that Teri and Kate *liked each other.*

"Have you been here all night?" Teri asked.

Kate yawned. "I have. Nothing's changed. They say she's resting peacefully."

"Let's go home, Kate," Teri said. "You can sleep for a few hours and I'll deal with the phones. Bob can stay here with Celeste."

Kate nodded. "That's a good plan, Teri. Bob, really all you have to do is sit with her. Of course, call us if there's a change."

Blythe stood a few steps away from the others, feeling left out. She *was* left out. It was as if she'd become invisible to the other three.

Childishly, she said, "I'll stay here and keep Bob company."

Why did she say that? She didn't want to spend time with Bob. She wanted to be there for Celeste, which was why she'd come in the first place.

Kate looked over her shoulder as she walked away. "You don't need to do that, Blythe. Bob will be fine by himself."

"I want to stay," Blythe called. "I've got a lot to tell him about our children."

"I'll talk to you soon," Teri assured Bob.

Blythe hoped she'd made them uncomfortable. She'd certainly made herself uncomfortable. Hadn't Kate learned by now not to ignore Blythe? And why did Blythe want to irritate Kate?

Probably she always wanted to irritate Kate.

The two women turned left and disappeared down the hall.

Bob sat on a chair, head in his hands. He glanced up and saw Blythe. "Blythe, thank you for waiting with me. I'm afraid for Mom. A heart attack . . . and she's over seventy."

"I know. But she's strong, Bob. She's healthy."

To her surprise, Bob stood up and threw himself around Blythe.

"I don't want her to die," he cried.

"She won't die," Blythe insisted.

Being this close to her ex-husband was unexpected and overwhelming. Blythe sympathized with him. She knew how much Bob loved his mother, and Bob knew how much Blythe loved Celeste. She wanted to be comforting.

But they hadn't hugged for years. Without trying, she noticed that he'd lost weight and his arms were more muscular. The children told her he'd joined a gym and was working out. It seemed she was embracing both a familiar man and a strange one. Her body swept her through a reservoir of memories she hadn't realized she'd kept, in her limbs and her skin and her deepest mind. He'd held her like this the first time she told him she was pregnant. He'd been in awe. She was going to make him a father. It had always seemed so unfair and capricious of nature to gift a woman with so many physical signs of becoming a mother while a man never had so much as a hint. She had loved being pregnant, except for the first few weeks of morning sickness.

The last time Bob had held her like this, or tried to, was the morning they stood before the judge who pronounced them divorced. Bob had pulled her to him in a brief, pro forma hug.

Now, in the Nantucket Cottage Hospital, she stepped back. "Let's check Celeste."

Celeste lay quietly in her hospital bed. She was sleeping, so very still. Her dark hair was long and streaked with silver, spiraling over the pillow like strands from a star. Blythe had known Celeste for twenty years. When Bob had brought her home to meet his parents, Celeste had been only a little older than Blythe was now.

Who could stand at someone's bedside without counting years? Years past and years to come. Celeste was only seventy. She would have years, maybe a decade or two, to enjoy life.

"She looks so small," Bob said.

"She's strong," Blythe reminded him. "She needs to rest."

"It's odd to see Celeste so still. She's always so active, so creative."

Bob pulled a chair next to the bed for Blythe, and one near her for himself.

"Yeah, and remember the Halloween she turned the house into a haunted mansion?"

Blythe laughed, remembering. "Celeste dressed up as an old witch, complete with a pointed black hat and pointed black teeth and long fingernails. When she opened the door to the trick-or-treaters, she cackled."

"Right. Holly was only three then, and she was terrified."

"Little Holly. Fortunately, she didn't connect that the witch was her grandmother."

Bob folded both hands behind his head and tipped his chair back, anchoring it with his foot on the bed. "Do you remember the Halloween party we went to that night, after Carol had come over to babysit?"

"Let me think." Blythe wasn't lying, just trying to delay the moment. They'd gone to an adult party, and she'd dressed as a lady of the night, complete with fishnet stockings and a plunging blouse, and Bob had been a cop. They'd drank too much and stumbled home and after the babysitter left, they'd made love right on the living room floor. Or tried to. Blythe was feeling nauseous from too much punch, and as her husband slowly peeled her fishnet stockings off, she'd twisted away from him and vomited.

Bob had fetched a wet washcloth, washed her face, and cleaned up her vomit. He'd helped her move to the sofa and covered her with a soft cotton throw. He'd gone up to bed, and Blythe had slept on the sofa all night.

Now she groaned. "The Halloween I drank too much and vomited."

"Yeah," Bob said. "You were really disgusting."

They both laughed, remembering.

"It was the punch," Blythe insisted. "It was always that punch."

Bob nodded. "We had some good times."

Blythe stood up. "I'm going to go buy some coffee. Would you like some?"

"Please." Bob went back to watching his mother.

It felt good to stretch her legs and roll her shoulders. When she checked her phone, she saw that two hours had passed. Her children would all be awake by now. She passed through the automatic doors and stood outside for a moment, enjoying the sun on her face.

She called Daphne to update her.

"Hi, Mom, how's Grandmother? Can I come see her?"

Love flushed Blythe at her daughter's voice. "Hi, Daphne. Grandmother's still sleeping. Her body needs a lot of sleep so it can get well. I'm going to stay here with Dad for a while—"

"Is Terri still there too?"

"Yes, she's with Kate. What are your plans for the day?"

"Well, Mom, I'm hardly going to have a normal day when Grandmother's in the hospital. I'll just hang here and wait for you to call again."

"Sounds like a good plan. Call me if you need me."

She went back inside the hospital, bought two cups of hot coffee, and carried them to Celeste's room.

"I called home. Daphne's awake and in charge."

Bob chuckled. "Daphne's always in charge."

Blythe settled in a chair. "Funny how our children are all turning out different."

"Well, look at Mom and her children. Kate's a witch and I'm charming," Bob joked.

Blythe laughed. "You can be charming when you want to."

"Do you ever think about us, Blythe?"

She studied her ex-husband for a moment. He was still handsome, and age had given him an aura of stability, even wisdom. Blythe thought age had given her a few wrinkles and some extra pounds.

"No, Bob," she said quietly. "I don't think about you and me. We've been apart for three years. You've found a new woman, and she's lovely. The kids are fine, well-adjusted."

"How do *you* feel? Are you fine?"

"I'm fine, Bob. More than fine. I'm going to start teaching again. I've agreed to teach seventh-grade English. And I'm excited about it."

"That's good, Blythe, that's good." His face changed as he had a sudden thought. "That means I'll be able to pay less child support, right?"

Oh, why did I tell him? Blythe wanted to kick herself.

"Right," she said caustically. "Because teachers are paid so well." She continued, "When I'm working, you'll need to have more responsibility for the children. Like taking them to ballet class or soccer practice."

Bob's mouth turned down. "You know I can't just leave my office in the middle of the day. I have clients who need me. I work hard. And pay the bills."

"Maybe Teri could take them."

"Blythe . . . about Teri." He took a deep breath. "Maybe I shouldn't do this, but, honestly, I think you're the only one who can help me."

Now what? Blythe waited.

"Teri wants to have a baby," Bob announced, the words rushing out of his mouth.

"And . . ." Blythe prompted.

"Jesus Christ, Blythe!" Bob ran his hands over his face. "I don't know if I can do it again. I'm too old for a baby."

"Al Pacino is eighty-three and has a toddler."

"I'm not Al Pacino!" Bob shook his head. "Honestly, Blythe, I don't think I should do it again. It's exhausting. I have enough children."

"But Teri doesn't."

"You're on her side?" Bob asked, incredulous.

"I guess I am. She's young enough. And babies are nice."

"What about our four? They'd be jealous. Angry."

"They'd be thrilled. You'd have free babysitters."

Bob stood up and paced the floor. "I'm shocked. I don't understand you at all."

Should she do this? Blythe didn't hesitate. "The very least you can do is be honest with Teri. Tell her you've had a vasectomy."

Bob fell back into his chair. "You're killing me, woman."

"Good morning, everyone!" A large, lovely nurse with a name tag telling them her name was Wanda swept into the room.

Blythe didn't think she'd ever been so glad to see anyone in her life.

Wanda said, "Could I ask you both to leave? I need some time with my darling Celeste."

Blythe almost said, "She's not *your* darling," but then she thought, maybe she was, maybe Wanda really cared about her patients and found their limp, pallid bodies endearing to her. Like some people naturally loved dogs and others loved babies but not teenagers.

"Thank you, Wanda," she said.

As they left the room, Bob suggested they go somewhere for lunch.

"Thanks, Bob, but no. I need to get home to the kids."

sometimes, doughnuts

She stopped by the Downyflake on her way home and bought a dozen doughnuts and an apple croissant for herself. She knew from experience that when a crisis arose, doughnuts were always a good idea. The house was quiet when she entered. Someone—probably Daphne—had tidied up after breakfast. Blythe took a cup of coffee and her croissant out to the back porch and sat listening to the birds. It would be hot later. A great day for swimming. If Bob was with Celeste, Blythe didn't need to be there. She could focus on the children. The first chore would be talking to Brooks. But really, should she? What could she say? When Aaden left for Ireland, Blythe had cried her heart out every day, but her parents barely tried to console her.

"You're young," they said. "You'll get over him."

And she had, hadn't she?

Her phone pinged. It was Roland, and she was delighted to emerge from the swamp of her thoughts.

"Hello, Blythe. How are you? How is our patient?"

"I'm well. I saw her briefly this morning and she was sleeping."

"If you return to the hospital at any time today, I'd be grateful for a ride. I'm on Lily Street, not far from your house."

"Of course. Want to go now?"

"Fifteen minutes?"

"See you then."

When she pulled into the driveway at Roland's house, he was standing on the front porch, waiting for her. He was a tall man, slightly hunched by age, and still handsome. He'd dressed carefully in khakis and a button-down shirt.

They greeted each other, he buckled into the car, and Blythe headed toward the hospital. Roland sat very straight, but his face was strained.

"Are you okay, Roland?"

"Oh, you know, just worried about Celeste."

"She's strong. She'll recover."

"I hope so. If I may say something, Blythe . . ."

Blythe laughed. "Now you *have* to say something!"

Roland shifted uncomfortably, straightening his seatbelt. "Celeste told me that when Bob and Kate and you and all her grandchildren were safe and settled, she wouldn't mind dying."

"Oh, my God!" Blythe wheeled the car into the emergency parking lot so fast the tires squealed. "Roland, why was Celeste talking with you about *dying*?"

Roland chuckled. "Blythe, old people are always talking about dying. Like, have you bought your plot at the cemetery yet? What do you want on your headstone?"

"Isn't that . . . I don't know . . . morbid?"

"It's being prepared," Roland said calmly.

Blythe slotted the minivan in between two other cars and killed the engine. She stared at the older man sitting next to her and forced herself to concentrate on him, on his careworn face with wrinkles and creases and hair sticking out of his ears and his nose. Age spots dotted his face and hands. She could tell by his bright blue eyes and his easy smile that he had been movie-star handsome when he was younger.

Roland reached over and took Blythe's hand. "Dear girl, Celeste and I have both had full lives. We're more worried about being a problem for our children than we are about dying." He grinned, as if telling Blythe a joke. "Celeste has written in her will that what she wants engraved on her headstone is 'I Had a Great Time.' "

Blythe burst into tears. Roland unsnapped his seatbelt and moved closer to Blythe, hugging her against him, one arm holding her close while he slowly smoothed her hair as she cried into his shoulder.

Blythe choked out a sound that was half-laugh, half-cry. "I don't want Celeste to die," Blythe blubbered. "I need her. My children need her."

"I know," Roland said quietly.

When she was all cried out, Blythe said, "Thank you, Roland."

He said, "You're welcome, Blythe."

As they left the car and walked toward the emergency entrance, she said, "If Celeste lives, I hope you marry her."

Roland laughed. "Let's go one step at a time, shall we?"

And then they were through the sliding glass doors, searching for the desk, noticing the number of chairs filled with people.

A teenage boy was vomiting into a brown paper bag.

"Oh, that takes me back to my youth," Roland said.

At that, Blythe smiled.

Blythe and Roland walked through.

Bob and Kate were in the hall, speaking with Dr. Margrave.

Blythe and Roland joined them.

"Her temperature is normal and we'll continue to give her IV fluids," the doctor was saying. "But her blood pressure is high and her heartbeat is unsteady. We've put her on beta-blockers and anticoagulants. She shows every sign of returning to normal, but we need to take care of her for a few more days."

"What can *we* do?" Roland asked.

"For now, we can only wait. Let her rest and recover." Dr. Margrave caught a nurse's eye and went off to confer with her.

A door at the end of the corridor opened. Kate's husband, Jack, came toward them.

"How is she?"

"They need to keep her another day," Kate wailed.

Blythe watched Jack fold his arms around Kate and felt a stab of jealousy but also a spark of happiness. She was glad Kate had someone to hold her at a time like this.

Blythe left the hospital and returned to her house again.

It was quiet. She headed for the kitchen. All the doughnuts had been eaten. For some odd reason, that made her happy.

She checked her messages. Aaden texted that he had to be at a meeting in Boston and he'd be in touch with her later.

Nick had called. *Hope all is well. XO*

The perfect message, not needing anything from her. Plus, the *XO* was very nice.

She went into the kitchen and read the messages on the chalkboard.

HOLLY: *going to Carolyn's*
TEDDY: *tennis*
DAPHNE: *nature walk*
BROOKS: *I'm walking to Main Street to buy some fresh fruit and veggies from the farm trucks for all of us today. Thank you for the doughnut.*

Ah, Blythe thought. *He knows he's in trouble.*

Miranda was probably in her room, talking on the phone to her best friends about Brooks's treachery.

She made herself a glass of iced tea. Was she actually here, alone, with some free time? She would call Nick.

Then Miranda drifted like a ghost into the room.

Blythe stood up and hugged her daughter.

"Hi, sweetie," Blythe said.

"Hi, Mom." She collapsed, letting the weight of her body fall on Blythe.

"How are you?"

"Okay. I cried so hard last night I vomited."

"Oh, Miranda. You need to eat. Oatmeal? Scrambled eggs?"

"I'm not hungry."

"Scrambled eggs with cheese, then." Blythe lifted her small skillet onto the stove. She melted plenty of butter, broke open two eggs, stirred them, adding sprinkles of cheddar cheese and salt and pepper. When they were done, she set them in front of her daughter. "Eat."

Miranda slumped forward. Listlessly, she lifted a forkful of eggs to her mouth. "Really good, Mom. Thank you."

Blythe put two slices of whole wheat bread into the toaster and set out the butter dish and the jar of Aunt Leah's cranberry honey. Blythe spread the two pieces with butter and honey and put them in front of her daughter.

"I'm tired, Mom. I think I'll go back to bed."

"Miranda, wait. At least finish your eggs."

Tears welled in Miranda's eyes. "I can't, Mommy. I just need to sleep."

"One more bite," Blythe coaxed, as if Miranda were four again and refusing her green beans.

Miranda took the smallest bite of eggs any human had ever eaten. She pushed herself to her feet. "Thanks, Mom." She trudged back to the hall and up the stairs.

"You're welcome," Blythe said to the empty air.

Blythe had eaten the apple croissant this morning, which seemed eons ago. She ate the eggs and both pieces of toast and put the dishes in the dishwasher, then took a glass of iced coffee out to the porch.

Amazing, she thought, how summer had taken a nosedive. Celeste in the hospital, Miranda's heart broken, Bob and Teri keeping secrets from each other.

Restless, Blythe called Kate to ask how Celeste was.

Kate's answer was brief. "No change. She's sleeping."

"Call me if you need anything," Blythe said. She felt like returning to her own bed and sleeping until everyone was well again. But household chores never stopped, and today she was glad. As she scrubbed and vacuumed and loaded clothes into the washer and dryer, she felt optimistic, as if she was doing something to organize and heal life.

That afternoon, as she stretched out on the living room sofa, her phone pinged. It was Nick, puffing slightly.

"Where are you?" she asked.

"I'm walking on the moors. I didn't realize how extensive this area is. And how varied. I can stand anywhere and see beach grass and blueberry bushes and a carpet of wildflowers extending into the distance."

"That's beautiful, Nick. All the deer and rabbits must have come out to lie at your feet."

"Why, yes, that's true, and blue butterflies are landing on my shoulders."

"Have you climbed to see Altar Rock?"

"I have. Quite a view."

"Where are you now?"

"I'm standing on a dirt road. Next to me is a kind of deer path through bushes, and I see water on the other side."

"I think I know where you are, Nick." Blythe sat up on the sofa, shoving cushions behind her. "Stoop down and go through the little tree tunnel and tell me what you see."

"Okay, then."

She heard the rustling of bushes growing next to the road, blocking out any sight of the pond on the other side.

"Wow," he said. "I'm standing on the edge of a large pond filled with water lilies!"

"Oh, that's my favorite pond. Isn't it beautiful!"

"I've been reading about this island. The Wampanoag believed that whales could swim under the island and surface in these ponds."

"I would love if that happened," Blythe said.

"Did you come out here when you were younger?"

"I came out with my grandmother. She always made a delicious lunch and she put it in a wicker basket. When we found a good spot, she would open the basket and set out real china plates and teacups and silverware and napkins."

"It sounds like lunching with Queen Elizabeth."

Blythe laughed. "It *was* like that."

Nick said, "I'd like to pick a water lily for you, but I don't know how deep this water is."

"Don't!" Blythe shrieked. "You'd be arrested by the conservation foundation."

"Okay, I've shuffled back onto the dirt road. Which way should I go now?"

Blythe relaxed against her cushions and gave her own unique directions. It felt so good to make someone happy.

She'd just said goodbye to Nick when she heard footsteps.

"Mrs. Benedict?"

Blythe turned. Brooks stood a few feet away, and he looked nervous.

As well he should, Blythe thought.

"Hi, Brooks," she replied, keeping her voice friendly. "If you haven't had lunch yet—"

"I've had lunch, thank you. I wondered if I could speak with you a minute."

"Of course. Sit."

Brooks took a chair facing her. She didn't smile.

Brooks bowed his head for a moment, then faced her full on. "I think I did something really stupid and Miranda is angry with me and I don't know how to fix it."

Blythe studied the beautiful creature sitting in front of her, a gorgeous young man with an adolescent mind. Some theorized that the male of the species never grew out of the adolescent mind. She thought there might be some truth to that.

She kept her voice level. "I don't think Miranda is as angry as she is sad." Blythe didn't want to say *heartbroken*. "Disappointed."

He flinched. "She told you."

"Yes. She was very upset."

"I'm so sorry. I'm such an idiot. I want to apologize, but she won't speak to me. I've texted and called her and she won't answer. I don't know when she leaves her room. I don't want to sit outside her door and wait for her like a stalker." His voice broke when he spoke. "I don't know what to do."

He was such a good guy, really, Blythe thought. Still, he had to figure it out himself. She didn't write self-help columns.

"I can't speak for Miranda," she said. "But I've assured your mother that you're welcome to stay here for the entire summer and that stands. You're welcome to stay here and eat with us and all that."

"That's super nice, Mrs. Benedict. I'll talk to Miranda . . . I'll *try* to talk to her. I'm so sorry and I want to make it up to her."

"That's between you and Miranda." Blythe didn't want to know any more details about their intimate relationship. She said, "I assume you have enough money to pay for tickets to movies and so on."

"Yes, absolutely." Brooks shifted in his chair. "Can I still eat lunch at the snack bar at the club?" Before Blythe could answer, he blurted, "I mean, thank you very much for letting me stay here for the summer. I'm very grateful. Maybe sometime I could treat you and the family to dinner?"

Blythe had seldom seen a guy look so miserable, and she liked him for it. And it had been only a kiss.

"It would be very nice if you treated us to dinner sometime, Brooks. Yes, you can eat at the snack bar. And I have an idea. Do you play tennis? Do you like to sail?"

His eyes lit up. "I haven't sailed but I'd like to. And I'm not very good at tennis."

"All right. Let's sign you up for some lessons at the club. Tennis and sailing. All right?"

Brooks nodded, amazed. "I can pay for the lessons."

"Nonsense. Let's go to the kitchen. My laptop is there."

She unfolded from the sofa and led the way. Sitting companionably next to Brooks, she opened her laptop. Together they organized a full schedule of lessons for him for the rest of the summer.

"You'd better get ready," she told Brooks. "First tennis lesson is in an hour. I assume you have white shorts, shirt, and tennis shoes."

"I do. I'll go change. And thank you, Mrs. Benedict. Thank you so much."

She could see that he almost hugged her but instead blushed scarlet.

"You're welcome. And this should keep you out of trouble." She gave him a look she often gave her children, a warning wrapped around affection.

Brooks nodded and went up the stairs, two at a time, to his very small room.

The next morning, Celeste was allowed to come home. Bob and Teri returned to Boston. Kate moved in with Celeste for a few days to help her, because she was supposed to rest.

Blythe stopped by that afternoon to see Celeste. She brought flowers from her backyard, already trimmed and placed in a glass vase, and a box of chocolates, and several glossy entertainment magazines.

Celeste met her at the door.

"Where's Kate?" Blythe asked.

"She's gone out to Bartlett's for food and wine. And yes, it's fine for me to be left alone. In fact, I prefer it that way. No, I don't mean you should leave. I just don't enjoy people *hovering*."

"Well, then, look what I've brought you. It seems the rogue of the royal family is in the news again."

Celeste laughed. "Just what I need."

Blythe made iced tea for them to sip while they skimmed the new gossip. For a while, Blythe didn't worry about her children, but after she kissed Celeste goodbye and walked home, the worries came flocking back, landing on her shoulders like squawking crows.

Over the next week, life returned to almost normal. Daphne spent the days with Lincoln. The other children played tennis and sailed and swam, coming home to shower and devour whatever Blythe had set out for them. Celeste returned to her normal healthy self.

One morning, it rained. Everyone slept late. It was almost nine when Blythe pulled on sweatpants and a big shirt and went to the kitchen for coffee.

She was shocked to see Brooks sitting at the table, a plate of toast in front of him, his head bent over his iPhone.

Before she could say anything, Brooks said, "I'm sorry I'm still here, Mrs. Benedict. My tennis lesson was canceled because of the rain and I think my sailing lesson will be canceled, too. I'm just trying to find where I can go . . . I'm checking on what time the library is open."

Blythe poured a cup of water and popped a recyclable pod of coffee into her Keurig. "Brooks, you don't have to stay away from here every minute. I appreciate that you've made yourself mostly scarce, but I don't want you to feel homeless."

"I'm still sleeping here. I'm just trying to stay away because I know—"

A door slammed in the upstairs hall. Footsteps padded down the stairs. Blythe and Brooks froze as they saw Miranda enter the room. She looked like a Victorian consumptive, pale and weak, with tangled hair and stained pajamas. She had dark rings under her eyes.

"Miranda." Blythe crossed the space between them, intending to hug her daughter, but Miranda lurched backward, as if seeing a monster.

"What is *he* doing here?"

"You know that Brooks is staying with us for the rest of the summer. I'm sure I told you that." Blythe kept her voice level, not harsh, not soft. Factual.

Miranda's eyes narrowed. "If he's staying here, I'm leaving. I'll go sleep at Grandmother's house." Miranda's lips trembled. "Then I'll be with people who love me."

Blythe flinched. "Come on, Miranda, don't be that way. You know I love you."

"Oh, really? You love me? Not when you let that jerk stay here even though he's a total douche and still you choose him over me!" Miranda was shaking with anger.

Desperately, Blythe said, "Miranda, please. Let's go in the living room and talk about all this."

Miranda stepped back. "You think you're such a great mom! You even think that Daphne goes to Maria Mitchell every day."

"What?"

"Mom, she's smoking pot with Lincoln. She's a total pothead. And you are so *clueless*. You make me sick." Miranda turned her back on Blythe and raced up the stairs. Her door slammed shut.

Blythe glared at Brooks. "Is Daphne really smoking pot?"

Brooks had gone white. "Maybe?"

"Maybe? What kind of answer is that!" Even as she spoke—shouted?—she knew she was taking her worry out on him, and before he could speak, Blythe said, "I'm sorry, Brooks. Please, go to the library. You can come back anytime. I just need a minute."

"Sure, yeah, of course." Brooks jumped up, put his plate and coffee cup in the dishwasher, grabbed his phone, and hurried out into the rain, as if afraid Blythe was going to detonate.

Blythe sank onto a kitchen chair and buried her face in her hands. It wasn't so much that Daphne had been smoking pot as the fact that she had lied to Blythe every single day of the summer.

Heavy footsteps sounded on the stairs.

Blythe looked up to see Miranda there, fully dressed, with her backpack bulging.

"I'm going to go live with Grandmother," she announced.

"Oh, honey." Blythe rose. "Please sit down and talk to me."

"Why? You chose Brooks over me! Teddy has Dad and Daphne has you and Holly has Grandmother. I don't have anyone. But at least I can live someplace where Brooks can't be!"

"Miranda, you can't upset your grandmother. She just had a heart attack."

Miranda skidded around to face Blythe. "I won't upset her at all. I'll be happy and fun and helpful. Because I'll be away from you."

Blythe watched her oldest child walk to the front door and leave.

Leaning against the refrigerator door, she cried quietly, overwhelmed and confused. Bob and Teri would return soon to stay with Celeste for their two-week vacation. They'd have the four children live with them then.

Blythe could leave. She could run away, fly to Ireland, or just go back to her Boston house and lie in bed eating ice cream for two weeks. Let Bob handle Daphne and her lies. Let Miranda escape from her terrible mother. Let Bob deal with everything.

But Blythe couldn't leave. She needed to talk to Daphne, to find out what in the world was going on with her. She needed to make peace with Miranda. She needed to help Miranda deal with a broken heart.

Blythe understood so well what it meant to have a broken heart.

Raindrops were pattering against the windows. Gray clouds obscured the sunlight.

Dante had said, "In the middle of the journey of my life, I came to myself within a dark wood, where the straight way was lost."

That was how Blythe felt now.

"Oh, God," she said out loud, "can I possibly be more melodramatic?"

She wiped her eyes and tied on an apron and began cutting up vegetables for the slow cooker. It was a perfect day for stew.

While the stew was simmering, Blythe made chocolate chip cookies. The aroma lured Teddy and Holly from their sleep. They decided that they wanted to stream a movie.

She took the last sheet of cookies from the oven and let them cool. At her desk, she sat in her little computer nook and tried to work on her lesson plans for her seventh-grade English class, but after a while, she gave up.

She fussed around in the kitchen, not sure what she wanted to do next. The rain had stopped, but the day was cloudy. She didn't care. She *felt* cloudy, all buffeted around by her family's needs. Brooks returned and stayed just long enough to change into his tennis whites. When he told her goodbye, she hoped she would be free for a while.

How did she get here, in the middle of all these problems? And she'd agreed to teach again, to jump right into the middle of an entire trampoline of more problems?

She walked upstairs, entered her room, and locked the door. She fell onto her bed. She knew she wouldn't sleep. She was too worried, especially about Celeste and Miranda.

Her phone pinged. *Nick.*

"Are you in Boston now?" she asked.

"I am."

"How is it?"

"Hot, congested, noisy."

"You'd better come back to Nantucket."

"I will, as soon as possible. How are you?" His voice, so silky and baritone, soothed all her ruffled nerves.

"Truthfully? I'm tired and anxious and tired of being anxious." Blythe began to cry, not harsh quaking sobs, but sweet clear tears that drifted down her cheeks. It was as if her full, crowded heart had opened and spilled out so much emotion she could breathe again. "Sorry," she snuffled.

"Take your time," Nick told her. "You have a lot going on."

His sympathy made her cry harder. "I'm not usually so weepy."

"You don't usually have days like this."

"True."

"I wish I could come over and hold you."

His voice was so warm, like a quilt wrapped around her. Like an embrace. "Oh, I wish you could, too."

"But I can talk all night if you want," Nick said.

At that, she smiled. "What would we talk about?"

"Maybe *Tear Water Tea*."

"Oh, I loved that book! We still have it at home. I read it so many times to my children." Blythe realized she was smiling. "That was *exactly* what I needed to hear. Are you *perfect*, Nick?"

"Yes, actually I am," Nick joked. "Although if I admit that I'm perfect, does that mean I'm egotistical and *not* perfect?"

"But if you say you're not perfect, and you are, does that make you a liar and therefore not perfect?"

Blythe closed her eyes as a sense of comfort spun through her while she and Nick talked nonsense with each other, which was, in a way, almost as good as if he were right there, holding her.

They talked on lazily, about favorite childhood memories, and grandparents, and vacations, good and bad. Blythe didn't know how long they talked, but when they finally said goodbye, she wanted to call him back immediately, just to hear his voice.

just when you think

The next morning as she was drinking coffee on the porch, Blythe heard someone come down the stairs. If it was Daphne, she knew she had a hard time ahead. Blythe vowed to be calm, logical, and wise when she spoke with Daphne about what Miranda had said.

It was Daphne.

"Hi, Mom," she said, as she stepped out onto the porch.

"Hi, Daphne. Want some coffee?" Now that she was face-to-face with Daphne, Blythe's fury rumbled volcanically in her chest. She couldn't stand it that *this* child of all her children had lied to her. Suddenly angry, she said, "Or would you rather have some wacky tobacky?"

Daphne burst out laughing. "Wacky tobacky? How old *are* you?"

Blythe patted the cushion on the wicker sofa. "I agree. That's a stupid way to talk about a serious subject. Sit down. Here. Daphne, have you been smoking pot?"

Daphne sat, ducked her head, and shrugged. "Yeah, a little."

"Have you really been going to nature walks every day?"

Daphne stared at her hands with their unpainted, chewed-up fingernails. "Most of the time."

"What about the times you don't go on nature walks?"

"I don't know. Nothing. I just hang with Lincoln."

"And you smoke pot."

"Not always."

"Does Lincoln's mother know?"

Daphne glared at Blythe. "What? No! Please don't call her, Mom. Lincoln has enough to deal with."

Softly, softly, Blythe thought. "How about you? Do you have enough to deal with?"

"Oh, you mean the death of the entire planet isn't sufficient?"

Blythe took a moment. "I think you're troubled by more personal matters and I wish you could talk with me about them."

"Mom, please. I'm fine."

"But are you?"

Emotions flickered across Daphne's face like light through prisms.

Blythe put her hand on her daughter's arm. Lightly. Not controlling but caring. "What's going on?"

Daphne muttered, "Nothing, Mom. Everyone my age smokes now and then."

"Have you been smoking back home? When you were at school? Like, in the bathrooms?"

Daphne shook her head. "No."

"Did you smoke last summer?"

"No."

Blythe was used to stubborn adolescent one-syllable responses. She folded her hands in her lap and waited patiently.

Daphne tilted her head down so far she almost fell over. "I love him," she whispered.

What? Blythe bit her lip to keep from barging into their moment of connection with a barrage of questions. "You love him," she repeated calmly.

Daphne lifted her face to Blythe's. Tears welled in her eyes.

"Mom, I love him. I love Lincoln and he can never love me."

"Oh, sweetheart." Blythe put her hands to her own lips to keep herself silent.

"I mean," Daphne began, and then her words spilled out, as if they'd been pressing up against her heart for days, "I mean, we all know Lincoln is gay, but he's never been *with* anyone, and he's never talked about it and this summer, we were sitting on the beach and the sun was setting and no one else was around, and Lincoln said, 'I'm glad you're here now,' and smiled at me and I felt so much love from him to me. It was real, like sunshine, it made my heart swell till I knew it would burst out of my chest, and I kissed him. I thought that was what he wanted. I kissed him. He was so warm and real. But he didn't kiss me back. I mean, I could feel that he was *tolerating* my kiss. Like he didn't want to hurt me or embarrass me because he does love me, he told me he loved me, but not like *that*."

Daphne was crying so hard, a bubble of mucus swelled out of her nose, and any other time, they would both have laughed at that. Now Blythe rose, went inside to take the box of tissues off the counter, then returned to the porch and put it in front of her daughter.

Daphne blew her nose heartily. "I was so embarrassed I wanted to die. I said, 'Sorry,' in this icky weak squeak of a voice like a dying mouse. I wanted to run away and never see him again. I'm such a dork. But he was nice. He said nice things. We talked about it, him being gay and how hard it can be even now when gay isn't supposed to be a problem."

"Loving anyone can be painful," Blythe said quietly. "Remember how sad you felt when Johnny moved away."

Daphne scoffed. "I didn't feel like *this* about Johnny."

"Okay. Lincoln is special. And you can still love him, just not in a boyfriend-girlfriend way. He's a good guy. A wonderful guy."

"I know. We talked about it. We agreed to not let it change us. But one day he said he'd had a bad night and his older brother had some skunk, that's what Gordon calls it, and we tried it. It's relaxing, Mom. It makes my heart hurt less."

Blythe sat quietly for a very long time, sorting through her thoughts, wondering how to say the right thing.

"I don't know why it works this way, Daphne, but I think sometimes we must accept the pain. Let our heart hurt. Be brave. Not hide. I mean, everyone gets hurt and sometimes it's not even by another person. It's like . . . like how we feel on a crisp October morning when we look up and see that the leaves are turning scarlet. It's so beautiful, and it stabs us in the heart. It hurts so much. Not forever, though. We get used to it, and the air grows cooler, and we have hot chocolate with marshmallows and chili and Halloween candy."

Daphne grinned. "Mom, you always go for the food."

"Okay, then, we have cozy bulky sweaters and flannel shirts and warm houses and puffy comforters to sleep under at night."

"On the moors, the sumac and poison ivy turn scarlet," Daphne mused. "You put pots of yellow or orange chrysanthemums on the front and back porches."

"Indian corn on the doors."

"But now is still summer," Daphne said, and once again, she sounded bleak.

How can I help her? Blythe wondered.

"Most people love summer." Blythe studied her forlorn daughter.

Daphne was a reader. A thinker. And she wanted to care for the planet.

Blythe put on her teacher voice. "I want you to find four books about the environment in the library. I want you to read them and summarize them. I want you to write four separate essays of at least a thousand words. And you cannot use AI."

"Mom." Daphne rolled her eyes in exasperation.

"You have to do it," Blythe said. "It's your punishment for smoking and not telling me where you really were all this summer."

"You're weird, Mom." Daphne almost smiled.

"You have no idea," Blythe shot back.

Daphne smiled. "I'm going to get dressed and go down to the library. I'll get lunch at the snack bar."

"Wear a raincoat," Blythe advised. She knew that Daphne was old enough to figure out that she should wear a raincoat in the rain, but Blythe also knew that in the language of motherhood, "wear a raincoat" meant "I love you."

"I will. And I won't smoke. At least not today." Daphne grinned and headed up the stairs.

Humidity fell over the island like a sticky net. All the children left for the beach. Blythe spent the day shopping for groceries and bread, chatting with Sandy on the phone, and making a slow cooker dinner. She was happily folding laundry when her phone pinged.

Aaden.

She checked the caller ID. She let his call go to voicemail. She leaned against the dryer and listened to his message.

"My darling, I'm flying back to Dublin. I've got piles of work to finish. Please, come to Ireland. You know there's a reason fate has brought us together again. I want to make my future with you. I know you will love Ireland. Please come soon. Please call. I love you."

Blythe stood for a long while, staring at the small rectangular piece of technology that allowed Aaden to speak to her from across the miles. She didn't understand how it worked, her magic phone that also took pictures. In a way, it was like her own mind, which now as she sat quietly brought up scenes from the past so vividly her body responded. Remembering her high school days with Aaden brought a pocket of pleasure to her days.

The front door slammed.

Her remembered world vanished.

Blythe knew who had come in from the pace of the footsteps. She knew there was something wrong.

"Teddy?"

"Yeah, Mom, it's me, I'm going upstairs."

Blythe rose and went into the hall. "Teddy. Stop. Look at me."

Heaving an enormous sigh, Teddy glared at her from the stairs.

"You've been fighting," Blythe said.

"No big deal." Teddy went up two more steps.

"It's a big deal to me if my son comes home with a bloody nose and a bruised cheek. Come down here right now and talk to me."

Teddy slumped down the stairs and into the hall. He wouldn't meet Blythe's eyes.

"What happened?" she asked.

"Nothing," Teddy growled.

At times like these, Blythe was sorry Teddy didn't have a brother. She'd watched enough football to know that for most men, if not all men, an urge to hit something or someone was woven into their DNA. Maybe she had some of that DNA pop up when she was around Kate.

"Were you at the club?" she asked.

"No. At the beach. Jack Winchester shoved Scarlett under the water."

"So?"

"So I tried to get him off her, and he hit me. But Scarlett came up for air."

"Was Azey there?" she asked.

"Yeah." Teddy grinned. "He took a video."

"He took a video?" Blythe nearly fainted. How the world had changed!

"So if Jack tells his mom I started it, we've got proof that Jack was being mean to Scarlett."

"I'm shocked."

"I'm not always the one who started the fight," Teddy said.

"I never thought you were." Blythe took a moment to think. "I'm sorry you're hurt, but you know where the first aid kit is."

Teddy didn't look at her, but she could see how his face brightened. How he got it that she trusted him to take care of himself. How she didn't see him as a baby anymore.

She heard him thud up the stairs to the children's bathroom.

He would be fine. Thank heavens Azey had been there.

Now, what had she been doing before Teddy came home? Blythe's mind had become like one of those Escher staircases that never go anywhere. She was accustomed to being spontaneous in the summer, but this summer was more complicated than usual. Celeste, Teri, Miranda, Brooks, Teddy, Nick, Aaden.

Aaden.

Oh, what a puzzle. It was exhausting.

She went to her bedroom, took a shower, put on a sundress, and called to check on Celeste. Kate told her Celeste was still sleeping. Blythe offered to take her place to give Kate a break. Kate politely refused. Teddy had gone, leaving a scribble on the blackboard: *Kayaking maybe.* Daphne was on a nature walk.

Holly had fallen asleep in front of *Loud House.*

Blythe went out to the back porch and settled on the wicker swing, curled up with a pillow behind her back and a novel in her hand. She couldn't concentrate. She worried about Teddy. She worried about Celeste. She worried about Miranda. She even worried about Teri. Bob used to criticize her for what he called "pre-worrying" about things that hadn't happened yet.

Focus, she told herself. She needed to center her mind. She should prepare for teaching in this technological age. She opened her phone and read about common changes in grammar and punctuation. When she read the example of why commas were needed, she laughed.

Let's eat Grandma.

Let's eat, Grandma.

When Nick returned to the island, he called Blythe.

—

"Let's drive out to Great Point," he suggested. "Boston is so hot and humid and the traffic is jammed and everyone's cranky. I want fresh air."

Blythe agreed and packed up a cooler of food and drink and a tote filled with beach towels and sunblock.

He picked her up in his Bronco and headed out to Wauwinet. They stopped at the Trustees of Reservations' gatehouse to let air out of the tires and trundled past the handsome Wauwinet hotel and onto the soft sandy road leading to Coskata and Coatue. The farther they went, the wilder it got, the landscape swept clean of buildings, the ground thick with beach grass growing next to beach roses twined with poison ivy. The air was sweet and as clear as crystal.

Nick gunned the engine when they arrived at the steep dune dividing ocean from harbor. They flew up the hill and suddenly they were at the end of the world. All they could see in any direction was dazzling ocean and deserted sand. A long stretch of beach extended for miles over the narrow slip of land leading to Great Point, where Nantucket Sound met the Atlantic Ocean in a great clash of waves. Gulls swooped and argued, and oystercatchers, tiny manic birds with long orange beaks, scurried back and forth at the water's edge.

Blythe said, "Welcome to heaven."

Nick grinned and focused on keeping the bucking Bronco fixed in the tracks already cut into the deep sand. The closer they came to the point of land where the tall white lighthouse stood, the more seals they saw in the water. Along the shore, fishermen were casting their lines. Finally, they followed the curve of sand to a calmer stretch of beach and Nick brought the Bronco to a stop.

"That was a crazy ride!" Blythe said. "You were really wrestling with the steering wheel. You deserve a beer and a sandwich."

Nick turned toward her. "Sounds good."

She unbuckled her seatbelt and moved closer to him. He wore a

T-shirt and board shorts and had impressive muscles everywhere, and as he undid his seatbelt, a giant wave of desire crashed over her. Her eyes met his and he reached out to pull her to him, and they kissed.

His stomach rumbled and they both laughed.

"I am so hungry," he admitted. "I've had nothing but coffee so far. I was in too much of a hurry to get here."

"I've got lots of food for you," Blythe told him. She was glad his stomach had rumbled, interrupting what was almost the best kiss she'd ever had in her life, because she wasn't ready for more than a kiss, especially not out here with bros in trucks racing past and families gathered together having cookouts on the beach nearby.

They spread the blanket near the water. Blythe handed out sandwiches, chips, and iced tea, with chocolate chip cookies in a Tupperware bowl and red grapes in another. The breeze was perfect today, just enough to cool them off and tease the edge of the blanket, but not so strong it blew sand in their food.

"We've got company." Blythe pointed to a group of seals who had stationed themselves in the water right in front of them. As they watched, the waves rolled, bobbing the animals up and down.

"What's a group of seals called?" Nick asked.

"My favorite name for that is a *bob* of seals."

Nick laughed. "It's cool that you know that."

"I've spent every summer of my life on this island, first when my grandmother lived here, and after she passed, with my children."

"Bob must have been there some of the time," Nick said. "Speaking of bobs."

Blythe hesitated. "Yes, Bob was here for almost fifteen years. He's here often, with Teri, at Celeste's house."

"Your children are lucky."

"I suppose they are. What did you and Brielle do in the summer?" As she spoke, she could sense how Nick reacted, his tense shoulders relaxing, his mouth curving in a slight smile.

"We went to France every summer," Nick told her. "Brielle's family lived outside Paris. Her friends and relatives were scattered all over France, and some lived in Switzerland or Spain."

"Wow! *Your* children are lucky!" Blythe said. "Did Brielle have brothers?"

"Only sisters. For three generations, her family had only girls. They thought it was a miracle that we had two boys." Nick's face lit up as he spoke. "They were all great skiers, and we spent some time in Paris, of course, but so often we were up in the mountains on skis."

"Somehow when I think of France, I envision only topless beauties on the beach at Saint-Tropez or drinking Pernod on the Left Bank."

Nick chuckled. "There was that, of course."

"Do you still go to France?" Blythe asked.

Nick shifted on the blanket, wrapping his arms around his knees and gazing out to the sea where the sun sent silver winks.

"I haven't. Not since Bre died. The boys are busy with their lives. I could stay with some of Brielle's cousins. We're still in touch. But . . . I haven't gone. And really, I don't want to. I'm happy hiking up Mount Washington."

They were quiet for a moment.

Blythe's heart was flipping back and forth and her mouth went dry, but she managed to say, "I'd like to try hiking with you up Mount Washington."

"Would you?" Nick sounded very pleased.

"I would. But, Nick . . . I don't mean to rush things between us—"

"Oh, you can definitely rush things between us." Nick shifted positions so that he was facing her.

"I like being with you," Blythe said.

"I like being with you," Nick answered. "I hope we can be together often when we're back on the mainland."

Blythe cleared her throat. Was this the right time to do this? She plunged ahead.

"I should tell you I have another man in my life."

"Do you mean Bob?"

"No, although, of course, Bob will always be around because of the children. But this summer, actually, the same night I met you at the yacht club, I ran into my high school boyfriend. Aaden Sullivan." Blythe kept her gaze on the sand as she spoke.

"I hadn't seen him for years. Decades. We were madly in love in high school, and I thought we'd be together forever. But his family is Irish and their business is in Ireland, and he left to go to college in Dublin. It kind of broke my heart."

"You hadn't kept in touch at all?"

"No. I was sad and angry and confused for a long time. Decided I would never ever fall in love again, and all through my college years, I never did fall in love. Secretly, I decided to be celibate."

"And yet, you have four children." Nick's voice was light.

"Yes. I met Bob and we married and had a good life. We lived in Boston and came here every summer. We wanted children, and we have really lovely kids." Blythe paused. She was trying to decide how to approach a delicate subject sideways.

"I've spent some time with Aaden here on Nantucket. He's divorced, and his daughters are grown, and he's CEO of his family's company. He's still as charming as ever."

"I'm sorry to hear that," Nick said.

Blythe laughed. "He has an office in Boston, but his home is in Dublin, and he wants me to visit."

"Ah."

"The thing is," Blythe began, and stopped speaking. "It's one thing to believe in love here in this Nantucket summer paradise. It is a quite different thing to risk *loving*."

"You're going to take a chance with Aaden?"

"No, no, that's not what I mean. I've been thinking about this, a lot. What Aaden and I had when we were in high school is different from what we could have now. And *I* have changed. What I want is not the dramatic highs and lows of high school love. I'm watching Miranda go through that right now, and it reminds me of how I felt when Aaden left. I don't want to be charmed. I don't want to be delirious and infatuated."

Nick's gaze was steady on her face. "What do you want?"

"I want . . ." Blythe lifted her chin and met Nick's eyes and said, "I want to go hiking on Mount Washington."

Nick smiled. "Good. Because I would love to take you up there and kiss you on the top of that mountain."

Blythe was breathless, but in a good way. "Well," she teased, "I've enjoyed kissing at sea level."

Nearby, a group of children ran back and forth at the edge of the sand, yelling and gesturing at the seals. The seals were not impressed. The afternoon sun blazed down on them all, and country music drifted from a truck parked a few yards away.

He placed his hand on Blythe's, enveloping her in his touch. They kissed, awkwardly at first, with the sand shifting beneath them.

"Look, Mommy, those people are kissing!" a child yelled, and the entire gang went crazy with laughter.

Blythe pulled away. "I guess this is a no-kissing zone."

Someone was cooking hot dogs on a tabletop grill and the aroma made Blythe's mouth water.

"I would really like a beer and a hot dog," Nick said.

"Would you settle for a turkey club sandwich and a bottle of iced tea?"

"I would, if I can share it with you."

It was heavenly to sit in the shade cast by the Bronco, watching the seals bob, eating lunch, drinking cold tea. The ocean was dark blue in the glare of the sun. Far out on the horizon a white sail seemed to slide evenly over the waves. High above, a plane drew a long mark white as chalk over the cloudless sky.

Blythe said, "I wonder if someone somewhere thinks that white line is a message."

Nick said, "Maybe someone in that plane thinks he's *leaving* a message."

She nudged him. "Nice."

Blythe arrived back at her house in the late afternoon, sun-stunned. Being with Nick had been better than drinking champagne, and she sang in the shower, very pleased with herself and with life.

Pulling a cool turquoise caftan over her head, she drifted down the stairs to re-enter reality.

She had a voicemail from Scarlett's mother.

"Mrs. Benedict, it's Eloise August. Scarlett's mother. I'd like to drop by your house and chat with you today if you have a free moment. Please let me know."

Blythe came back to earth with a thud.

She returned Eloise's call.

"Is this something we could discuss over the phone?" Blythe asked.

Eloise was blunt. "No. I really need to be with you in person."

"Come now, if you can," Blythe said.

Blythe scrutinized the house. It was messy, and it showed signs of lots of people living here, but it didn't look *insane*. She made a pitcher of iced peppermint tea.

The knock came on the front door. Blythe opened it. Eloise August was as crisp and controlled as her phone message. White linen pants, white linen shirt, white leather sandals, and lots of gold: watch, earrings, necklaces.

"Hello," Eloise said as she stepped into Blythe's house. "Thank you for making time for me."

"Let's sit on the back porch," Blythe suggested. "Would you like some tea?"

"No, thank you. I won't be here long." Eloise could not meet Blythe's eyes.

The two women walked through the long hall and out the back door to the porch. Blythe's hibiscus and cosmos and roses flourished their blooms from several vases, and Blythe hoped the other woman noticed.

"I've come to ask you a favor," Eloise said. She held up her hand. "I'm sorry, no, wait." She blushed, well, scarlet. "First, I must give you an apology for my rudeness the first time we spoke. I now realize it was Jack Winchester who has been teasing my daughter. And I'm imploring you to take the video down."

"Video?" *Oh, my God,* Blythe thought.

"You haven't seen it? Azey Phillips took it when Jack Winchester was holding my daughter under the water and Teddy pulled Jack off her. Probably saved her from drowning. Jack took out his frustration on Teddy . . . you must have seen it."

Blythe drew in a deep breath. "I saw that Teddy had been hit. He told me about the incident at the beach. I knew Azey had videoed it, but I never thought it would be put on, what, TikTok?"

"It's on everything. Here it is on Facebook." She held out her phone. "It's also on Snapchat and Instagram."

Blythe took the phone and watched the video. Azey had turned it into a reel, complete with the ominous *Jaws* theme. It was only twenty seconds long. In full color, Jack Winchester shoved Scarlett's head underwater and held it there. Another boy—Teddy—thrashed through the water and pulled Jack off. Scarlett surfaced, sputtering. Jack hit Teddy in the face with his fist.

The video stopped abruptly and immediately started over again. And again.

Wordlessly, Blythe handed the phone back to Eloise.

"Suzanna and I have discussed this," Eloise said. "Another mother told her to check out the video. It's always painful to believe that one of our darling angels has done anything wrong. Suzanna phoned Azey's mother and accused him of doctoring the video, or whatever it's called. Azey doesn't know how to do that, or doesn't have the equipment, and Suzanna had to apologize, and then she called me."

Blythe nodded. "I see. I'll text Teddy and ask him to get Azey to take down the video. I don't know Azey's mother well, but I'll call her, too."

"Please. I would appreciate it. I've called her, but she lets things go to voicemail."

"I'm sorry that happened." Blythe's thoughts were racing. "Do you have a son?"

"I do not. My husband always hoped for one, but we have two daughters. Our older daughter is, always has been, extremely fortunate as far as good looks go. I know Scarlett will be pretty once her braces are off. And we need to get her contact lenses."

"I'm grateful that you've come to tell me about this," Blythe said, letting her voice warm with honesty. "*Now* would you like a glass of iced tea?"

"No, thank you." Eloise rose. "I must go see Suzanna. We have a friendship to save."

two weeks in august

In Blythe's backyard, the rose of Sharon bushes put out their white, pink, and lavender flowers. They were beautiful, but they were also a definite sign of the approach of summer's end.

Bob and Teri arrived for their two-week Nantucket vacation. They settled into Celeste's house and were in charge of the children, who all moved to Celeste's house to be with their father. Brooks remained at Blythe's, but he left the house early and came home late, always talking to someone on his AirPods. Blythe often heard him laughing, so she didn't worry that he was lonely. She knew from her club bills that he was playing tennis and sailing.

One night, she invited him to share dinner with her. As they finished her special chicken curry that she'd made to please him, she asked him about his travels with his international parents.

"You've been in so many countries," Blythe said. "You're very fortunate to get to travel like you do."

Brooks smiled. “I like it better staying here all summer.”

“I’m glad. You’re very welcome, you know.”

Brooks stared down at his plate, embarrassed.

Her heart went out to him. “Brooks, I enjoy your company and I know Holly is thrilled when you talk to her about sea gerbils, and I’m sure Teddy would like to play tennis with you. He’s really good, even though he’s younger than you are.”

Blythe had intended for her words to make Brooks feel better, but she saw how his eyelashes trembled. He was biting his lips to keep them still. He was trying so hard to be stoic, she thought he would pass out right in front of her if she said anything too kind.

“Plus, Daphne doesn’t like anyone and Miranda can be”—she stalled, trying to find a word that would make Brooks feel better without betraying her daughter—“sensitive.”

Brooks managed a smile. “You have a super nice family, Mrs. Benedict.”

Reaching out, she patted his arm. “And you are a super nice guy. Now, please, go. I can deal with the dishes.”

“Thank you.” Brooks fled the room.

For days after that, when Blythe saw him in the kitchen, they exchanged a few words. One evening he spent with Holly and her sea gerbils. He was always tan and clear-eyed, and Blythe knew she didn’t have to worry about his loneliness.

At last Blythe had that most blissful of possessions—free time. She could sleep late. She could eat an entire pint of ice cream in the middle of the day, sobbing as she watched *Love Actually* for the forty-first time. She could curl up with a book and read it straight through. She could go the beach and fall asleep, waking with a lovely tan and a red nose, and she could go out to dinner with friends.

Aaden called or emailed her every day. She knew she had to make a decision. How many people had the chance to reunite with their first love? Fate was offering her something precious and she couldn’t easily dismiss it.

One night she went out to dinner with Sandy.

"I really don't know what to do. I don't want to go to Ireland, but I'm struggling to let go of what was such a delicious, passionate love."

"Well, remember that was when you were a teenager," Sandy reminded her.

"True."

"When you had no bills to pay, no stampeding herd to cook for. No children."

Blythe tapped her lip with her forefinger as she thought, before sighing and replying, "Okay. You're right. I don't want to be away from my children, even on the days when they're monsters."

"Has Aaden suggested having the children live with you?"

"No. I'm sure he doesn't include them in his vision of our future together."

"But he has a large family over in Ireland, right?"

"Yes. Siblings, aunts, and uncles, millions of cousins. Oh, Sandy, what would *you* do if you had the chance to spend the rest of your life with your first true love?"

Sandy laughed. "My first true love was my horse. But if you're thinking about being with Aaden, you probably should remember you're not the girl you were the first time you fell in love. I mean, I've seen what a good mother you are, and I've heard about what an excellent teacher you are. You're older. You've learned a lot."

"Yes, I've learned a lot, but when does a person ever learn *enough*?"

"Sweetie, you've wandered off down an existential road, and I can't follow."

"Oh, my head hurts!" Blythe wailed.

The children checked in with Blythe every day, wanting to watch television—anything but the Red Sox, which they claimed their father was addicted to and would never share the television (she was well aware of this habit of his)—or to eat some of Blythe's cookies or just hang out. They gave her the latest update of Celeste's recovery—she was fine, going out, seeing Roland. They complained because Teri's food was gross. They complained because their father arranged for them all to go on a whale watch, which meant an entire day riding in a twenty-four-foot skiff that bounced over the wind-driven waves that made Holly throw up and all of them seasick and they never saw one single whale but Miranda and Teri both came home with painful sunburns.

"Your father was trying to give you a special treat," Blythe reminded them. "Don't be so critical! I'm sure it was expensive."

"Oh, we know it was expensive. He's told us that twenty times," Teddy informed her, scowling.

"Be nice," Blythe ordered her children. "It's hard to please everyone, and your father and Teri are doing their best."

"Don't you miss us, Mom?" Miranda twined around Blythe's shoulders. She could be an aloof teenager one moment and the next, miraculously transform into a winsome child.

"Yes, I miss you all," Blythe said. "But I know you're not far away."

And sometimes, she thought, hiding a smile, *I'm having a very good time without you.*

Most of those lovely two weeks when the children were with Bob and Teri, Blythe spent with Nick.

One afternoon they biked out to Madaket on the west end of the island, where the waves were high enough to body surf and the beach seemed to stretch on forever. They dove and swam in the cold dashing water until they stumbled out, exhausted and drenched. They lay on beach towels, their backs warmed by the sun. Blythe tried to hide a hum of pleasure when Nick gently stroked sunblock on her back. They ate peaches and salty chips and drank cold clear water and were too waterlogged and sunstruck to have any kind of conversation. At the end of the day, they had dinner at Millie's, and there they talked, about everything, their favorite television show, whether there was life on other planets, their most embarrassing moments when teaching, the most famous person they'd ever met, whether or not Bob would get a reverse vasectomy for Teri, how glad they were to have biked out because they had just eaten seventy thousand calories of delicious food and needed to burn some off.

One evening, they were invited to a cocktail party in a rambling seaside mansion in 'Sconset. The guests crowded into three different rooms where platters of amazingly constructed canapés with French or Italian names were artistically displayed. A live jazz band turned the largest room into a dance hall, and while Blythe and Nick knew some of the guests, they never did find their hosts.

It was mid-August, and in spite of French windows thrown open to the lawn, the air was steamy. Everyone at the party seemed to be drinking more, laughing louder, and shouting inarticulately, like children who knew the party was almost at an end and exams started in only a few days.

After an hour or so, Nick spirited Blythe away from the crowd and out into the warm night. The quiet calm of the streets was a relief.

"How did you enjoy the party?" Nick asked.

"It was . . . exciting." She added, "But exhausting."

Nick laughed. He took her hand and they strolled away from the mansion on the cliff, toward the small village with its small antique cottages and lavish gardens. They were quiet, taking in the fragrance of roses and the shushing sigh of waves breaking on the beach below. They walked along the bluff path until they entered a leafy tunnel formed by trees. Nick settled Blythe against the trunk of a tree and stood close to her, kissing her softly. Hidden from the rest of the world, they embraced.

One day it rained. Nick came over to help Blythe assemble a jigsaw puzzle, a photo of Nantucket from the air. Sometimes as they placed pieces in their spots, their hands would touch, and Blythe's fingers sparked and she closed her eyes to enjoy the moment. Outside, the sky was dark. Thunder rumbled and lightning flashed and rain cascaded down the windows, blurring the world around them.

"I'll make more coffee," Blythe said, because it was cool in the room.

She was lifting the cream from the counter when Nick entered the kitchen, came up behind her, wrapped his arms around her waist, and kissed the back of her neck. Her heart lurched and desire flooded her body. She leaned against him and then slipped around so they were face-to-face, body to body, desire rushing through them. They kissed for so long, the coffee grew cold.

Finally, Blythe gently pushed Nick away. "We can't. Brooks might come in any moment. Actually, any of my children might arrive." She touched Nick's face tenderly.

"And I'm still Sandy and Hugh's guest," Nick murmured. He ran his hands over her shoulders and arms, as if he couldn't stop touching her. She didn't want him to stop touching her.

"We'll have to wait until we're back in Boston," Blythe said.

Nick moaned as he stepped away. "Thank God it's August."

One night they went to dinner at the yacht club, just the two of them, which was pretty much a public proclamation that they were officially a couple. Another night, Blythe invited Celeste and Roland for dinner at her house, so they could get to know Nick. Was it odd, hoping her ex-mother-in-law would like her new boyfriend? Blythe didn't think so. The world had changed, and she was glad.

Nick drove Celeste and Roland home and returned to Blythe's house. The August heat and humidity hung over the island like a damp rag, and Blythe had turned the air conditioner on.

The lights were low in the living room, which made the room feel intimate. Blythe and Nick sat in the well-loved, saggy armchairs across from each other, with their feet up on what Blythe liked to call their "heirloom" coffee table, which had been in the house for over sixty years and still stood, scarred but strong.

"I like Celeste," Nick said.

"She liked you," Blythe said. "I could tell. I hope I can be like her someday, more relaxed and wise."

"You are the mother of her grandchildren," Nick said. "That means a lot. I think you're already relaxed and wise. You seem comfortable with your ex-husband living with another woman."

Blythe laughed. "Relaxed? I'm delighted! I'm not being juvenile. I mean it. Bob is a nice man. A good father. We parted as friends, and sometimes I wonder if we were ever more than friends."

"Friendship is a good basis for marriage," Nick pointed out. "Maybe essential."

His tone deepened when he spoke. Blythe took a moment, then asked, "Were you friends with Brielle?"

"I was." Nick put his hands behind his head and settled more comfortably in his chair. "I loved her, too."

Something about the cool air-conditioned air and the shadows in the room allowed Blythe to admit, "I never loved Bob the way I loved my high school boyfriend."

Nick laughed. "I think our high school loves are like the first time we wait at the top of those crazy elevated water slides. We're already terrified and thrilled just to be there, and we can't know what the ride will be like."

Blythe shuddered. "Or like the first time on a Ferris wheel. When it stops, and you're at the top, and the bucket is rocking."

"Right. After that, everything else seems tame."

Blythe thought about that. "Or, *safe*. Everything feels safe." After a moment, she added, "But isn't it nice to have memories of . . . being enraptured?"

Nick made an odd noise in his throat, half cough, half comment. "We have memories. I'll always love Brielle. You will always love the girl you were when you loved Aaden and the boy Aaden was when he was young. It's a gift life gives you. You can keep it."

"I can keep it," Blythe echoed. She did not have to deny or forsake her memories of love with Aaden. In a teasing voice, she asked, "How old *are* you?"

Outside, a breeze set the branches of a maple tree swaying, casting shadows and light on Nick's face.

Nick said softly, "I'm old enough to know that I'm in love with you."

"Oh!" Blythe's heart was a pitcher overflowing with happiness. "How can you say that when you're way over there?"

"I'm right here with you," Nick said.

"Not close enough for me," Blythe told him. She rose from her chair and sank onto Nick's lap, wrapping her arms around his neck and folding herself close enough to whisper in his ear, "I love you, too."

One morning, Blythe gathered her children and took them to the moors to sit by the Doughnut Pond and watch the iridescent blue dragonflies skim the air. The beaches were crammed by crowds wanting one last swim before summer ended. Blythe needed quiet and she thought her children could use it, too. Really, legally, Bob should have them but she thought he and Teri could use some private time today. She ordered her children to put their phones away for ten entire minutes and simply sit by the pond, enjoying the view.

A white heron flew onto the small island in the middle of the pond and daintily picked at its feathers.

"Look!" Blythe whispered, not pointing so she wouldn't startle the bird.

"Cool," Daphne said, and maybe she meant it or maybe she was humoring her mother.

After ten minutes, the children exploded from their perches and raced off to check out the other ponds and, Blythe knew, check out their phones.

Blythe remained seated on the soft summer grass. From here she could see hills stretching toward the sky, and some of the leaves were already red. The heron flew away. The dragonflies continued to float past, and one landed for a while on her toe. She lay back in the grass and sighed with pleasure. She belonged here. She belonged here just as much as Aaden belonged in Ireland. She decided to call him that afternoon.

Later, her four children, exhausted by reality, chose to indulge in the comfort of *Jurassic World: Fallen Kingdom*. Shamelessly bribing them with popcorn and lemonade, Blythe left them in the family room and settled in the living room to talk with Aaden. It was almost midnight there, but she thought he'd be awake.

"Blythe." Aaden answered, and his deep voice could still move her.

"I can't talk long. The children are here." She was using them as an excuse to keep this conversation short. She was dreading it. "Aaden, I've decided. I can't come to Ireland. I can't see you again. I don't want to leave my children, and I'm going to be teaching, and I like my life."

"Are you saying this is final?" Aaden asked. "Do you mean that we are over?"

She heard the pain in his voice. "Not over, really. We'll always have memories—"

"I don't want you in my memory. I want you here, in bed with me, now."

Blythe paused, stunned by her own feelings. She was irritated! She wanted this to be over. With a choked voice, she managed to say, "I can't do that. I won't do that. My life is here."

"Is there someone else?"

To her surprise, a laugh bubbled up from her chest, freeing her from the chains of her own memories. "That's not for you to know. I'm sorry. I'm glad I got to see you again." She thought: *But am I?* "But we're over. I wish you well. But we're over."

"You have broken my heart, Blythe."

"I think you'll be fine," Blythe told him. "Your heart—"

Someone screamed.

"*OH NO!*" Holly cried in the family room. "Pause it! Pause it!"

Honestly, Blythe thought, how does anyone with children ever have the chance to have a conversation, let alone a love affair?

"Goodbye, Aaden," Blythe said firmly. And she ended the call.

She walked to the family room.

"You dumbhead," Teddy yelled.

"That scared me," Holly argued.

"You didn't have to toss your Skittles on the floor."

Skittles? Blythe wondered. How did her children have Skittles?

"I didn't mean to. I was scared."

"Pick them up so we can restart the movie." Teddy sounded exasperated with his younger sister, but after a moment, he relented. "I'll help you pick them up."

"Don't eat any of them. They're mine."

"I don't want your gross carpet Skittles."

A few moments later, ominous music blared from the television.

Blythe wanted to laugh and cry. Her glamorous, romantic life, filled with fighting children and carpet Skittles and Minecraft and coding and everybody always wanting something, a jigsaw puzzle life where she was always scrambling to find the piece that fit—that was the life she chose.

And she wasn't done yet.

slanting light

In late August, the sun came through the windows at a slightly different angle. The sky was blue, but huge gray clouds sped over the sun, blocking the light in a flashy, premeditated manner, as if signaling that change was coming.

Blythe pulled her ancient L.L. Bean vest on over her shirt. It wasn't cold, really, but instinctively she craved a sense of protection. Leaving for the summer on Nantucket always made her family excited, exuberant, carefree. They were headed for the beach! Sun! Ice cream!

Returning to home felt less hopeful. They were facing school, rules, schedules, and responsibilities. The children looked forward to seeing their Boston friends again, and Miranda always enjoyed buying new clothes. Once they were settled back in their routines, all would be fine, but until then, Blythe thought they were like small animals peering out from their burrows to see what was waiting for them.

Recently, without fanfare, Miranda and Brooks had reconciled.

Now they seemed like extremely good friends. They spent every possible minute together, walking around as if they were joined at the hip, inclining their heads toward each other as they whispered. Blythe waited for Miranda to explain this new relationship, but that never happened. Miranda was laughing, eating, sleeping, and that was really all Blythe needed to know. Miranda was a junior this year, and soon she'd be eager to start looking at colleges and planning her own life away from home.

Blythe was eager to start her new life, too. Teaching. Spending time with Jill and other city friends.

Spending time with Nick.

She settled on the back porch with her first cup of coffee, inhaling the fragrance of flowers, listening to the birds gossip.

Her front door slammed. She assumed it was Brooks. He'd left a message on the board that he was having breakfast in town.

To her surprise, Holly rushed in, still wearing her summer pj's, her hair frizzed into a halo.

"Mom! Mom! Mom! Something terrible—"

The front door slammed again and footsteps thudded down the hall. Daphne charged out to the porch, grabbing Holly by the elbow. Daphne was dressed, her hair was combed, and Blythe would have bet money her teeth were brushed. Daphne was her orderly, sensible child. But telltale red blotches gave away her distress. "Holly! Shut up! She worries too much and she can't fix it!"

Blythe's heart triple-timed.

"What's going on?" she asked, trying to sound rational, helpful. "Daphne, let go of Holly. Girls, sit down and tell me calmly."

Holly glared at her older sister and blurted, "Dad and Teri and Kate are yelling at each other. They've been fighting all morning. Dad's mad at Kate and Teri says she's heartbroken."

"Well, adults do yell . . ." Blythe wanted to calm her daughters, but how?

"It's *your* fault!" Holly blurted.

Daphne tried to speak quietly, but her hands were trembling. "It's because you kept a secret about Dad's . . . something."

"I kept a secret?"

"Teri wants a baby," Holly informed Blythe. "Aunt Kate said that you should have told her what is wrong with Dad!"

"Oh, sweetie." Blythe reached out and pulled Holly into her lap.

Daphne sat at the table, folded her hands, and announced in the manner of a judge handing down a sentence, "They were in the kitchen when we came down just now. We were in the hall. We heard Aunt Kate say that Grandmother told Aunt Kate something that Dad said she shouldn't know and Aunt Kate told Teri."

"Ahh." Understanding uncoiled the tight vise around Blythe's heart.

She took a deep breath. This was a complicated mess. Blythe didn't understand how it made her at fault, and it absolutely was not up to her to reveal her ex-husband's vasectomy to their children.

"*Girls* . . . " She took on her best schoolmarm's tone. "What you overheard was a private conversation. It is between your father and Teri. You need to ask them why they were fighting."

Holly cried, "But we heard Teri say she's leaving Dad! She's going to pack and go back to Boston. She's so hurt she doesn't want to be with Dad anymore."

Daphne's face went red. "I think Dad is sick. He needs something cut out of him."

The parent's trick, to be soothing and authoritative while she was quivering inside, was something Blythe had, over the years, become expert at. "Your father is not sick. He and Teri and Kate were discussing something very private and grown-up."

"If it's so private, why were they yelling?" Daphne demanded.

What should she do now? Blythe wondered. She got why it was, in some way, her fault. Blythe had told Celeste that Bob had had a vasectomy. Celeste had no doubt told Kate, who in turn had told Teri.

But this was not Blythe's problem to solve.

"Holly, stand up." She gently removed her daughter from her lap. "We're all going back to Grandmother's house. Your father can explain everything there."

She marshaled her daughters out of the house and into the minivan. She didn't even bother to take a quick glance into the mirror. She didn't care how she looked. She'd insist that Bob tell Teri the truth, and if he refused, Blythe would tell her herself. What a cad Bob was for not giving Teri this significant piece of information. How cruel! It would serve him right if Teri left him.

She screeched into the drive of Celeste's house, killed the engine, and said, "Come on, girls." She was feeling powerful, righteous—and liberated. Finally, it was clear that she was not the only parent who needed to take care of the children.

Without knocking, she threw open the door and strode into the house.

Daphne was right behind her. "They're in the kitchen."

Blythe walked to the kitchen door and stopped so suddenly that Daphne bumped into her.

Bob was sitting at the kitchen table with his head in his hands. Celeste sat at the other end of the table, pouring a shot of brandy into a cup of tea. Miranda lurked at the door into the dining room, ready to sprint away. Teddy sat on the kitchen counter, scrolling through his phone.

"Drink this," Celeste said to her son.

Blythe and her two daughters entered the kitchen and stood there dumbfounded, as if they'd been set down in some stranger's house.

"Where's Teri?" Blythe asked.

"She's gone," Celeste said, sliding the tea over to Bob.

"What?" Holly's voice had gone so high she could have joined a boys' choir.

"She's left me," Bob said. "Teri has left me."

"Kate is driving Teri to the boat," Celeste said.

"Dad!" Daphne spoke as if she were cursing.

Celeste was pale, and Blythe noticed how she tucked her hands into her pockets as soon as she had set the tea in front of Bob.

"Celeste, sit down, here." She pulled out the chair at the head of the table.

Several times in her life, Blythe had found herself in this sort of situation, where everything was a mess and there really was no easy solution. It was part of life. Inescapable. It made her heart hurt to see her family this way, and she had no magic answers.

But she loved them. She loved them all, her daughters and her son, her ex-mother-in-law, even her ex-husband, who was the cause of all this turbulence. Why hadn't he told Teri he'd had a vasectomy? Was he afraid he'd lose her? Right now, he absolutely sagged in his chair, hiding his face in his hands, his shoulders slumped. As if he thought he'd lost Teri.

Blythe pulled a chair up next to him. She put her hand on his shoulder.

"Bob. I get it. It's so hard, raising children. But you are a wonderful father. You made it through all the tears and tantrums of seventeen years—and those were only the ones *I* had." She smiled, pleased with herself for being funny.

Behind her, Miranda snorted appreciatively.

"You've been with Teri for three years. Your children have come to feel safe with her, to enjoy her, and you have been happier because of her. I know that. I can assure you of that. Maybe you haven't been perfect, like I am, but you've been pretty darn good."

As she spoke, freewheeling it, in that rare space she'd found herself in so many times over the years, speaking without knowing what she was going to say next, and talking honestly, almost helplessly, from the heart, she sensed how the mood in the room was lightening.

Bob dropped his hands. He sighed enormously. "I don't know, Blythe. Really. I don't know."

She kept her eyes on Bob, but she knew her children were watching her as if mesmerized, waiting to hear what she would say next. And what could she say? What should she say? She wasn't a priest or a psychiatrist. She was only an ordinary person.

What did she care about? What would she want her children to know?

She would want them to know about love.

First love, young love, lost love, family love.

"You say you don't know, Bob, but let me ask you this. Do you love Teri?"

Bob shot her a sideways look.

"I think you do," Blythe told him. "I think you love her and she loves you."

He nodded. With a scratchy voice, he whispered, "I do love Teri."

"Then go get her. Apologize to her. And then you two decide, because the decision belongs to both of you, about the whole vasectomy matter."

"God, Mom," Daphne said, "you should come with a soundtrack."

Bob looked around the table at his four children. "You guys like her, right?"

"We do," Miranda replied, glaring at her siblings in case they dared to disagree.

Bob stood up. "I guess I'll go see if I can catch her before she leaves."

"Yay, Dad!" Holly cheered.

Bob went to the door. Everyone followed, the children elbowing one another out of the way.

Bob opened the door. Fresh air and the fragrance of newly mown grass rushed in at them. Across the street, someone was mowing his lawn. Next door, a woman knelt to pick flowers.

A Volvo came down the street.

Holly whimpered. "Aw. There's Kate's Volvo turning into the drive. The boat must have gone."

"That's sad," Daphne pronounced, folding her arms over her chest in the way Blythe knew she did to keep her sadness inside.

"Well, Dad, why don't you take a plane?" Teddy suggested. "You'll get there before she does. You can meet her boat."

"Thanks, Teddy, I'll do that." Bob smiled at the crowd in the hallway and stepped out onto the path to the driveway.

Kate stopped her car, opened the door, and got out. "What are you doing?" she asked.

"I need you to drive me to the airport," Bob said.

"Where are you going?" Teri asked as she stepped out of the passenger side of the Volvo.

"Teri!" Daphne yelled.

"You came back!" Holly cried.

"Let's all go inside," Celeste suggested.

This time, they gathered in the living room. Celeste sat in an armchair, but the others all stood.

"I need to talk with Teri," Bob said. Holly was leaning against him possessively. "Alone," he clarified.

"Not yet," Blythe said. "There's something else."

Kate stared daggers at Blythe. "This is not about you."

"Actually, Kate, it kind of is." Blythe folded her arms over her chest, hoping this would help her stop trembling. "I don't want to keep one more secret. It's exhausting."

Celeste spoke up. "If it's about the man Teri was kissing, I told Kate."

"What?" Teri asked.

"What?" Bob had gone an unhealthy shade of purple.

Don't let him have a heart attack, Blythe thought.

Blythe said, "Before we left for Nantucket, I was lunching at the mall with Jill. We saw Teri kissing another man. Um, *really* kissing."

"Are you kidding me?" Teri almost shrieked.

"Not kidding," Blythe said. "We can phone Jill and she'll back me up."

"Wow." Teri threw her hands in the air as if she were swooshing away a flock of birds. "I can't believe this."

Turning toward Bob, she said, "It was *one* kiss. With Damon, my high school boyfriend. We ran into each other unexpectedly in the mall. I hadn't seen him or even been in touch with him for years." Sudden tears spilled from her eyes. "I was feeling hopeless about ever having children. Damon was divorced, and he said he still loved me, and we kissed. For a moment, it was like being in high school again, you know?" Teri slid her fingertips on her cheeks, wiping away the tears. "And then I told him I was living with a guy, and I loved him and I loved his children."

"Aw, Teri, that's so nice." Holly went to Teri and hugged her around her waist.

Daphne whispered, "We love you, too."

Miranda gawked. "Your *high school boyfriend*."

"But you're so old," Teddy said, looking confused. Then, seeing Teri's reaction to his words, mumbled, "Sorry."

"I wish you'd told me." Bob stood frozen.

Blythe knew that right at this moment, Bob was struggling to deal with all this information and the emotions it caused, and sympathy pinched her heart.

"It's hard to keep secrets in this family," Blythe confessed.

"I don't know about that." Teri faced Kate, her brow furrowing in sorrow. "Why didn't you tell me this, Kate? Why didn't you tell me what your mother and Blythe knew about me?"

Bob's color was fading, but his cheeks were still red. "Furthermore, Kate, why didn't you tell *me*?"

Kate shook her head. "I'm sorry. I apologize. I thought that Blythe was making it up and I didn't want to upset you."

Blythe burst out laughing. "This family should come with an instruction manual."

Daphne, the family's private detective, asked, "Have you seen him since then? This *Damon* you kissed."

Teri smiled at Daphne. "No, sweetheart, I haven't. No communication of any kind. You're welcome to check my phone."

"Damn," Teddy said. "That's invasion of privacy."

"I think I need a drink," Celeste announced.

"I think Teri and I need to go somewhere to be alone," Bob decided. "Teri, let's walk down to the lily pond."

Teri nodded, smiling up from under her lashes in a shy Di moment.

Bob and Teri held hands and walked out the front door.

Everyone else stood in the living room, as if frozen by the sudden silence.

Blythe spoke up. "Let's go out to the garden, everyone." She used her sweet but tyrannical tone of voice.

"I'll make tea," Celeste said.

"I'd prefer wine," Blythe told her. "And lemonade for the others."

"I need Scotch," Kate huffed. But she joined them at the patio table where they discussed in great detail how quickly summer was coming to an end.

A few years ago, Daphne had named this golden stretch of summer "The Days of the Lasts."

The last time they would catch a movie at Dreamland, dine at the Brotherhood, bike out to Cisco, eat Moors End's fresh corn on the cob, return books to the library, spend an afternoon sailing. For Blythe, it was the last time she and Sandy spent a day at the beach, perfecting their golden summer tans and gossiping about their own lives and everyone else's. The last time she would give her family thick beefsteak tomato slices with mayonnaise on Something Natural's Portuguese bread. For Daphne, it was the last time she'd spend with Lincoln, whose family was moving to Chicago. For the first time, Teddy would kiss Scarlett, and right in front of Holly, who would tell everyone in the family and on the entire island.

It was the last time Blythe's children would squeeze their feet into shoes they'd grown out of over the summer. The last time they would all have dinner at the yacht club with Celeste—and the first time Blythe invited Nick to join them.

One morning, all the kids headed off to the beach. Blythe picked her brightest flowers from her garden, put them in a jug of water, and took them with her to visit Celeste.

The older woman was sitting in her backyard with an embroidery hoop in her hand.

"You look well," Blythe told her, kissing her cheek.

Celeste motioned for Blythe to pull a patio chair closer. "Thank heavens you've come. I've got things to tell you."

"Really? Tell me!" Blythe leaned forward.

"I don't know why I'm whispering. They can't hear me. I mean my son and Teri. They called to tell me that Bob has an appointment with a physician at Mass General. He'll be at the hospital this morning, and then they will stay at his Boston condo for a couple of days, until—drumroll, please, he's recovered from surgery."

Blythe gasped. "He's having a vasectomy reversal?"

"He is. Apparently, the surgery will take around four hours."

"You Benedicts love visiting the hospital," Blythe joked.

"He says he'll have to lie around with ice packs and ibuprofen for a few days, and Teri will wait on him hand and foot."

"Teri must be so happy."

"She said her feet don't even touch the floor." Celeste laughed. "There's something else."

"Okay. Tell me." Blythe held her breath. *What now?*

"They're going to be married in October. Over Columbus Day weekend. They're coming here, so that I can attend the wedding, and they will want all the children with them, too."

"Wow." Blythe sat back in her chair. "Married. October isn't that far away."

"True, but the weather will still be beautiful."

"Please tell me they're not getting married on a beach," Blythe said.

"Of course not. Teri wants to wear a pretty dress. Not a gown, but a dress. And she will want to take the girls to choose matching bridesmaids dresses. Also, a suit and tie for Teddy."

"The girls will love that," Blythe said, adding, "as long as the dresses aren't magenta."

Celeste studied Blythe's face. "You don't seem sad about this."

Blythe angled her head, considering. "I'm *not* sad about it, Celeste. I'm glad I married Bob, and I'm glad we got divorced. I like Teri. I think she's been wonderful to the children. I hope she has her own child."

"You're facing a lot of changes, darling Blythe." Celeste took Blythe's hand in hers. "Your children, except for Holly, and she's almost there, are teenagers, all of them eager to leave the nest. You've loved having babies, and how will you feel when Teri has a baby and your children have a half-sibling and want to spend more time at Bob's home?"

"Well, for one thing," Blythe said thoughtfully, "I'm going to be teaching seventh grade again. That will be a challenge. I won't have much time to feel jealous or lonely."

"And . . . ?" Celeste prompted.

"And, when Bob and Teri have the children over Christmas, Nick and I are going to Saint Thomas."

Celeste laughed. "How wonderful!" Reaching over, she took Blythe's hand. "I think we should have a glass of champagne."

"Really? Why?"

"Because today, right now, everyone in our family is happy."

somebody has to

Blythe decided to hold a dinner party. Not a formal, wear-your-best-clothes meal, but a summer party, with the two most talked-about chefs in town, the beautiful Daria and Vale, cooking for the group so that Blythe didn't have to get anxious about burning a steak while talking to guests. They grilled skewers of shrimp, peppers, and pineapple for appetizers and swordfish and tuna steaks for the main meal.

Blythe, Sandy, and Teddy prepared potato salad, heirloom tomatoes with mozzarella and basil, corn on the cob, macaroni and cheese with artichoke hearts and red peppers, watermelon and feta cheese salad, and couscous with tomato and mint. They slathered butter and garlic on slices of Portuguese bread to be heated and carried out during the meal. For dessert, Daria and Vale made three pies: blueberry, strawberry, and lemon meringue.

The children were sweetly persuaded to help set up tables and chairs outdoors, covering the tables with colorful April Cornell summer tablecloths, organizing a drinks table in the shade of the porch, and lugging in several heavy bags of cubed ice.

Blythe told them, "You can sit wherever you want and bring one guest, just one, whoever you want, but you may not leave this party the moment you've finished eating. This is our big deal summer meal."

Nick was her guest. He was arriving with Sandy and Hugh. Celeste was invited, of course, and she said she would bring her friend Roland, which made the kids go silly with kissing noises. Bob's sister, Kate, and Jack came, staying close to Celeste, in case, Blythe guessed, that Blythe's cooking caused Celeste to have another heart attack. Daphne invited Lincoln and they sprawled together on the grass at the far end of the lawn to eat and make fun of everyone else. Teddy brought Scarlett, and Miranda, in a brief blip of affection for her younger brother, allowed Teddy and Scarlett to sit with her and Brooks. Holly came with her best friend Carolyn and Carolyn's parents, Carol and Russell.

The weather that evening was perfect. The sky was a cloudless blue, the humidity low, the temperature high. Brooks and Miranda helped Blythe carry out chilled bottles of white wine, ruby-colored bottles of red wine, buckets of ice, a huge bottle of Absolut vodka and several bottles of tonic, lemonade, and sparkling water to set on the drinks table. Teddy took charge of slicing limes and lemons and Holly arranged them in artistic circles on a platter.

Citronella candles were placed around the garden, and as the summer light slowly faded, their small flames glowed. Gradually, Blythe's guests left, thanking her for a perfect evening and drifting off into their own summer lives. Daphne and Holly went inside to watch television. Miranda, Brooks, Teddy, and Scarlett walked to town to buy ice cream, as if they were still hungry after the three pies they'd been tasting. Daria and Vale closed the grill and said good night.

Finally, only Blythe and Nick remained. They sat side by side on the wicker swing, holding hands.

"This was a marvelous evening you gave us all," Nick said.

"Thanks, Nick. I'm glad you were here." Blythe sighed. "It was sort of a goodbye to summer."

"I'm going back home in a few days," Nick told her. "I've got to get ready for my classes."

"Me, too. And the kids will need new clothes and shoes, and—" Blythe closed her eyes and rested her head against the back of the swing. "Oh, Nick, I don't want summer to end. I don't want to have to divide my life up into precise school days and weekends and bedtime and work time. Everything will be so crisp and organized. It's heavenly, being able to drift through the days like we have this summer."

Nick was quiet for a moment. Then he said, "Didn't you tell me you like to hike with your kids?"

"I did."

"Let's go hiking when we get home. You and me, and any child who wants to go. We can drive out to the Berkshires, climb Mount Greylock, buy apples and apple cider to bring home. If we go when Bob and Teri have the kids, you and I can make a weekend of it. We can stay at some charming B&B with a wood-burning fireplace and sleep in a four-poster bed in a room that George Washington slept in."

"George Washington? Really?"

"Or maybe Robert Frost." Nick put his arm around Blythe.

She snuggled into his warmth and put her head on his shoulder. "You know how to seduce people."

"Good to know." Nick kissed the top of her head. "Although I want to seduce only you."

Blythe smiled. "Tell me more."

"Okay . . . on Columbus Day weekend, we'll bring the kids down to the island. We'll all ride bikes out to 'Sconset and buy sandwiches at Claudette's and watch the waves crash. We'll take home a six-pack of Cisco beer for us and Aunt Leah's fudge for the kids. And when we drive back up Route 3 to Boston, we'll be amazed at how all the trees blaze with red and orange." He paused and Blythe could feel him take a deep breath. “We’ll have Thanksgiving at my house, with you and your tribe, and my two sons and whoever they bring.”

“I like that.” The evening had grown cool, and Blythe appreciated the warmth of his embrace. “I like the world you’re telling me about. You make me believe I could be happy for a long time.”

“I’d like to make you happy for a long time,” Nick said.

Blythe lifted her face to his and kissed his warm, sweet mouth. Nick pulled her closer and kissed her so thoroughly she forgot what month it was.

“We’re back, Mom!” Holly ran through the house and out onto the back porch. “Ewww,” she screamed. She ran back into the house and yelled, “Nick is *kissing* Mom!”

“Somebody has to,” Miranda said, and Blythe heard the teasing lightness in her voice.

Her daughter stepped out onto the porch. By now Blythe and Nick had stopped kissing.

“Everyone’s back and we’re going to stream *Night Swim*.”

“It’s so late,” Blythe objected. “Plus, will it make Holly afraid to swim in the ocean?”

“Mom. It’s about a swimming pool. Plus, we can all sleep late in the morning.”

Blythe shifted around on the swing, straightening her sundress that had gotten all bundled up behind her when she was kissing Nick.

“Is everyone home?” she asked.

“Everyone is home,” Miranda replied. “We’re all just watching a movie. Jeez.” She haughtily stalked away.

“I should go, too,” Nick said. “I don’t want to keep Hugh and Sandy up waiting for me.”

They both rose from the swing.

“We’ll talk tomorrow?” Blythe asked.

“We’ll talk tomorrow and for years to come,” Nick told her.

Blythe hummed to herself as she went through the house, locking the doors, double-checking that the stove was off. The cupboards were almost bare except for a couple of boxes of cereal and a can of tomato sauce. The counters were wiped clean and the refrigerator bulged with leftovers from the party. A box of pastries sat on the kitchen table with a note of thanks from Daria and Vale. She had enough coffee for tomorrow morning. She heard muted shrieks from the family room. Quietly, she went to the door and peered in. Brooks was sprawled on the beanbag chair. On the sofa, Holly was squeezing next to Miranda, who was hugging her and occasionally covering Holly's eyes. Daphne sat on the other side of Miranda. Teddy was on the other side of Daphne, his head wedged into the sofa's corner. He was sound asleep.

Blythe wished she could snap some photos, but that would alert the children to her presence and spoil this summer moment. If she could stop time, she thought she would stop it right now, while Celeste was well and happy with Roland, and all her children were home, and safe, and happy, and she was warm with love.

She left the hall light on as she went upstairs to bed.

about the author

NANCY THAYER is the *New York Times* bestselling author of more than thirty novels, including *Summer Light on Nantucket, The Summer We Started Over, All the Days of Summer, Summer Love, Family Reunion, Girls of Summer, Let It Snow, Surfside Sisters, A Nantucket Wedding, Secrets in Summer, The Island House, The Guest Cottage, An Island Christmas, Nantucket Sisters,* and *Island Girls*. Born in Kansas, Thayer has for forty years been a resident of Nantucket, where she currently lives with her husband, Charley, and a precocious rescue cat named Callie.

nancythayer.com
Facebook.com/NancyThayerBooks
Instagram: @nancythayerbooks